BRUMBACK LIBRARY
3 3045 03114 1852
P9-CFV-226

14
DAY
BOOK

OTHER TITLES BY SUZANNE BROCKMANN

Force of Nature

Into the Storm

Breaking Point

Hot Target

Flashpoint

Gone Too Far

Into the Night

Out of Control

Over the Edge

The Defiant Hero

The Unsung Hero

Bodyguard

Heartthrob

all through the NIGHT

all through the NIGHT

A TROUBLESHOOTER CHRISTMAS

SUZANNE BROCKMANN

BALLANTINE BOOKS / NEW YORK

All Through the Night is a work of fiction. Names, characters, places, and incidents are the products of the author's imagination or are used fictitiously. Any resemblance to actual events, locales, or persons, living or dead, is entirely coincidental.

Published in the United States by Ballantine Books, an imprint of The Random House Publishing Group, a division of Random House, Inc., New York.

BALLANTINE and colophon are registered trademarks of Random House, Inc.

LIBRARY OF CONGRESS CATALOGING-IN-PUBLICATION DATA
Brockmann, Suzanne.
All through the night : a troubleshooter Christmas / Suzanne Brockmann.
p. cm.
ISBN 978-0-345-50109-7 (alk. paper)
1. Christmas stories. I. Title.
PS3552.R61455A78 2007 813'.54—dc22 2007026734

Printed in the United States of America on acid-free paper

www.ballantinebooks.com

2 4 6 8 9 7 5 3 1

FIRST EDITION

Book design by Casey Hampton

To MassEquality, for helping to make the dream a reality,

To the people of Massachusetts, who've made our great state a beacon of light and hope, and a place where the words "freedom and justice for all" really do mean freedom and justice for ALL,

And to all of the friends of Jules, everywhere.
Your openness and acceptance made it possible for me to tell this story, and for that I am eternally grateful.

Find out more about MassEquality at www.MassEquality.org

And then, once again, I can dream, I've the right . . .

—Cole Porter, *All Through the Night*

all through the NIGHT

PART ONE

the proposal

FRIDAY, SEPTEMBER 14
BOSTON, MASSACHUSETTS

JULES CASSIDY WAS NERVOUS.

After years of working for the FBI, nervous didn't happen to Jules very often anymore. At least not in a situation with nary a hostile gunman, armed terrorist, angry insurgent or crazed hostage-taker in sight.

As Jules effortlessly caught a taxi at Boston's Logan Airport, as he settled back in his seat for the stunningly traffic-free ride to the downtown hotel, as the relentless, weeklong autumn drizzle that had plagued the entire east coast from Virginia to Maine finally stopped and the clouds opened in a late afternoon blast of sunlight suitable for accompaniment by a full choir of angels, he had to smile.

His entire impromptu trip north from Washington, D.C., had been a piece of cake—chocolate and practically dripping with strawberry-flavored easy.

Sign from God, anyone?

And yet, Jules was still undeniably nervous.

Some of it was from the taco Jules had grabbed in the airport. God, what a mistake. He'd thrown it away after eating only a few bites, but the portion he'd consumed had become his traveling companion—a lump of lead in his stomach.

Of course, some of what he was feeling came from the adrenaline surge of anticipation at the thought of seeing Robin after too many days apart.

Hey, babe. It's me again. God, I miss you. Call me back. And oh, may I state for the record that this phone-sex thing is no longer novel . . . ?

No kidding.

These past two weeks had been the longest the two men had gone without seeing each other since former A-list movie star Robin Chadwick had gotten out of rehab.

And no, Jules's nerves weren't from worry or fear that Robin had fallen off the wagon. Robin's commitment to his ongoing sobriety was steadfast. Same as his commitment to their still fledgling yet extremely solid romantic relationship.

Yeah, and okay, there was that shifting-of-the-taco twinge of nervousness again. What if Jules was wrong, and it was too soon for this? What if Robin *wasn't* ready?

What if Jules's last-minute, cancel-all-his-meetings-and-take-Friday-off, spur-of-the-moment, rush-up-to-Boston-uninvited trip came across as needy and possessive? *Desperately* needy and possessive.

God, he wished there was a thought-vacuum that could suck the unwanted yet still persistently loud voices of cheating ex-lovers from the caverns of one's mind. It had been years since Jules had shared both his home and his life with his ex, Adam, and yet he could still hear the son of a bitch's voice. *You don't own me, J., although you'd like to, wouldn't you? You'd like to lock me away . . .*

In truth, Jules *hadn't* wanted to own Adam or lock him anywhere. But he definitely hadn't wanted to share him, either. And if that unwillingness to share was defined as being needy and possessive, so be it.

It was the desperation that he hoped he could hide today—assuming Adam had been right and Jules was, in fact, *desperately* needy and possessive. Desperation was unattractive—so cloying, so unpleasantly pathetic. So obvious. You could smell it on a man in about a half-second of face-to-face.

Jules did a quick sniff check of his armpits. But all he could smell was that hideous taco. He definitely had a fantasy going involving a shower in his immediate future. Like, fifteen minutes after he got to the hotel. He'd change out of his FBI costume—as Robin called his collection of conservative dark suits and ties—and into jeans and a T-shirt. And there he'd be when Robin returned from the set. In bare feet and home-from-the-office hair, coated in exactly zero desperation.

It helped to remember that Robin wasn't Adam. Thank you, baby Jesus. Robin truly loved him—quite possibly as much as Jules loved Robin.

"Hey, babe, I got big news." Robin had left Jules a longer message in lieu of his standard brief morning *I'm thinking of you* voicemail. "Good news. Great news, actually." His expressive voice was laced with even more excitement than usual. Robin's mundane, day-to-day existence registered at a passion level of about fifteen on a scale from one to ten. This morning, however, he'd been up well past twenty and that had made Jules smile. "Art's writing another story arc for my character—they want me back. At least ten episodes this time, maybe even more. They totally love what I've been doing."

Yeah, like the entire world hadn't noticed that Academy Award nominee Robin Chadwick was not just acting rings around his cast mates in *Boston Marathon*, but was bringing them and the entire HBO TV show up to an entirely new level. Damn straight writer/producer Arthur Urban wanted him back for more. And yet Robin's surprise was genuine. He honestly didn't realize how amazing he was.

Robin had been bouncing back and forth between D.C., where Jules worked, and Boston, where the HBO series was in production. It had started as several intensive days of work a few months ago, when Robin was first cast in a relatively small role—a minor character for a mere two episodes. But Art Urban knew greatness when he bumped into it on his set, and he'd expanded and stretched out Robin's role over another six episodes.

It was doubly gratifying, because the character Robin was playing, Jefferson O'Reilly, was straight. It was pretty stupid, but gay actors in Hollywood rarely were cast as anything other than gay characters.

This job did, however, mean that Robin was spending more and more time in Boston. Apart from Jules.

"Don asked for way more money," Robin's voicemail had continued, "and they agreed. They didn't even fucking blink. They want to put me in the credits, which is, well . . . it's nice. I feel very Sally Field, you know?"

Jules did know. They liked him. They really liked him. And Don, Robin's agent, no doubt liked him, too. And for more than just the bigger paycheck. Robin's sister, Jane, was a Hollywood insider, and the last time Jules had spoken to her on the phone, she'd told him that Robin was garnering some early Emmy buzz.

"I haven't said yes," Robin had reported in his message. "I wanted . . . Well, I wanted to, you know, talk to you about it first, because . . . shit, it's Boston. If it was D.C., I'd've already signed, but . . ." He'd gotten quiet. "I really miss you, Jules. Call me back, okay? I need to hear your voice."

Jules *had* called him back. Repeatedly. But every time Jules had been free, Robin's phone had been turned off. And vice versa. They'd phone-tagged seven times before Jules had cancelled his lunch, his two o'clock, his four-thirty, and his six-fifteen and hopped the shuttle to Boston.

He checked his phone in the cab, only to find he'd missed three more calls from Robin. He dialed, but was bumped right to Robin's voicemail as the taxi driver took the exit from the highway.

It was then that his phone rang.

But it wasn't Robin. The call was from Alyssa Locke who, along with her former-SEAL husband Sam Starrett, were Jules's best friends.

"Are you there yet?" Alyssa asked. She knew he was heading to Boston. She also knew his evening's agenda. God help him.

"I'm at the traffic light at Arlington and St. James," Jules reported. "It's just a few more blocks to the hotel."

"You're not going to believe where I am." His former partner in the FBI was now the XO—second-in-command—of Troubleshooters Incorporated, the most prestigious personal security firm in the United States. Alyssa could well be anywhere in the entire world. Or quite possibly orbiting the moon.

"Can you give me a clue?" Jules shifted to try to find a position where the taco didn't burn at his stomach lining quite so much. "Like, which time zone?"

"Same as you," she said.

"You're in the trunk of the cab that I'm sitting in," he guessed as he popped a few more antacids from the roll he'd picked up on his way out of Logan. "Which would put Sam in the glove compartment."

Her laughter was rich and musical. "No, but you're close. We're over at the Sheraton, on Boylston Street."

No way.

"It was a last-minute courier thing," Alyssa told him. "Atlanta to Boston. Dave Malkoff was going to do it, but he had a family emergency."

"Dave Malkoff has a family?" Jules quipped. Dave was a former CIA operative who'd been working for Troubleshooters since close to its inception. He was one of those guys who never seemed to go home. The few times Jules had been to the TS Inc. office in the wee hours of the morning, Dave had been there like some kind of permanent fixture, slouched behind a desk, baggy-eyed but alert, mug of coffee steaming.

"Sam and I were relatively near Atlanta," Alyssa reported. "And since we were available . . ."

"On vacation in Florida is available?" Jules asked.

She laughed. "We're going back. It actually worked out. After three days on the beach, Sam was . . . Well, antsy isn't quite the right word . . ."

"Looking to blow shit up?" Jules suggested.

"That probably would've helped," she agreed with another laugh. "This trip north has been a good enough distraction—no C4 necessary. We're having fun in an *Oh my God, we're in Boston* way. We've already made the delivery so the work's done—and we got what I think was the last hotel room in the entire city so . . . Hang on. Sam's shouting something from the bathroom." There was a pause, then, "He wants to know if you want to get together for dinner."

"You didn't tell him." Jules didn't so much ask it as state it.

"Because you told me not to."

"Yeah, but it's Sam," Jules pointed out. "I figured you told him everything, regardless."

"Yeah, well . . ."

"What?" Jules asked, even though he already knew the answer. "You think he's not going to approve."

"I think," Alyssa said carefully, "that the last thing you need is

Sam getting up in Robin's grill, threatening to break him in two if he hurts you. At least not until after you've . . . initiated the discussion."

"I wish Sam didn't feel that way."

"He loves you," Alyssa said simply.

"Then I'd think he'd want me to be happy," Jules countered.

"He does. He'll come around," she reassured him. "Neither of us really know Robin. I'm sure when we—"

"Wait a minute," Jules said. "So are you saying that *you* have reservations, too?"

"Of course I do," she answered, with a silent but heavily implied *you lummox*. "Robin's got some pretty serious, well, *flaws*."

"And Sam-the-caveman's perfect?"

Alyssa laughed. "Touché."

"I know what I'm doing," Jules told her quietly. "I know Robin and . . . I'm not perfect either, Lys. We just . . ." He tried to find the right words. "We fit."

"Then I support you completely." All uncertainty was gone from her voice. "And Sam will, too. We should plan to get together—the four of us. That'll help."

"Not tonight," Jules said, and the taco tangoed. He dug for more of his Rolaids.

"Are you nervous?" she asked.

"No," he lied.

Amusement thickened her voice. "Are you lying?"

"Yep."

"Good," she said, in her sternest former naval officer voice. "You should be. This is no cakewalk. It's going to be hard work—and worth every ounce of sweat you put into it. I'm not talking about tonight. I'm talking big picture."

"Yeah, I got that," Jules said. "Thank you so much, oh ancient wise woman, who's been married all of, what is it? Four years?"

"I'm just trying to keep it real, my gay brothah."

"Thanks oodles, my hetero sistah, but I'm at the hotel." The taxi braked to a stop. "I gotta go, babycakes."

"Call if you want to have brunch tomorrow," Alyssa said. "And Jules?"

"Yeah?" Jules asked as he dug for his wallet to pay the driver.

"Robin's crazy about you. He's going to say yes."

Robin was in luck. There was no one in the taxi line, and a cab had just pulled up right in front of the hotel entrance.

His suitcase bumped and whirred as he wheeled it across the cobblestone sidewalk even as the doorman opened the cab's rear door for the exiting passenger. "Where ya heading today, Mr. C.?" he asked Robin in his emerald green brogue.

"Logan Airport, please, Mr. Dunn." Robin surrendered his suitcase as he dug into his pocket for his cell phone, which was wailing the theme music from *Buffy the Vampire Slayer*—which meant it was Jules on the other end. Finally. For privacy, he turned slightly away from both the doorman and the cab. "Hey, babe. Damn, it's been a freak show and a half, trying to reach you today."

"Robin, oh, my God." On the other end of the phone, Jules started laughing. "Look up. To your left."

Robin turned and . . .

Jules was standing on the sidewalk, right in front of him. He was grinning from ear to ear as he closed his cell phone and put it in the pocket of his pants.

He looked unbelievably hot. He had the whole rumpled FBI-agent thing going, jacket off and sleeves rolled up to his elbows. Of course, Robin had come to associate both that and the loosened tie with the hey-I'm-home-from-work expectation that the entire suit would soon be coming off as Jules changed into something more comfortable. Which sometimes meant no clothes at all. Which translated to very hot, indeed.

But then Jules's arms were around him, and as Robin held him just as tightly, it wasn't about sex at all. It was about . . . everything suddenly being extremely right. He had to fight the nearly overpowering urge to burst into tears at the sudden supreme rightness of the entire world. "God, I missed you," he breathed.

"I blew off the Secretary of Defense," Jules admitted. "Yashi took the meeting for me."

God bless Joe Hirabayashi. As Robin pulled back to look into Jules's face, into his incredible melting-chocolate brown eyes, he said, "My shooting schedule changed. I have the rest of today off instead of tomorrow." Tomorrow's schedule was light, but crucial, which was a crying shame. "I was going to fly down to D.C. to see you—take the booty back in the morning."

Between the pair of them, they'd racked up some significant frequent-flyer miles on the pre-dawn flight that Jules had so aptly nicknamed "the booty shuttle," for somewhat obvious reasons.

Jules laughed as he gave Robin another hug. "Wow, I'm glad you didn't catch an earlier flight. We could've passed in midair."

"That would've sucked," Robin agreed. Jules would've been in Boston, and Robin in D.C. But it hadn't happened—they were both right here, right now. He could feel himself leaking happiness from every pore.

Jules backed off to look at him. "I like the hair."

Robin self-consciously pushed it back from his face. "I don't know—they won't let me cut it, and it's getting to that obnoxious place—"

"It's hot," Jules said, and their gazes locked. And yeah. It was definitely time to go inside the hotel.

No doubt about it, even though Robin was already having the

best weekend ever, it was about to get significantly better. But then he realized that *weekend* was an assumption that he really couldn't make. Jules's work schedule was as crazy as his. "Can you stay until Sunday night?" he asked.

Jules gave Robin a sidewalk kiss—eye contact that dropped down to and lingered on Robin's mouth. But then he smiled as he looked back into Robin's eyes and gave him an even better gift. "I took Monday off, too. I'm here until Tuesday morning."

A long weekend.

It was stupid as shit, but Robin's eyes actually filled with tears at the idea of four whole days with Jules.

Jules, gallant as always, pretended not to notice. "We're going to need his suitcase back out of the cab," he announced, and then proceeded to tip both the doorman and the driver liberally. His hand was warm and wonderfully possessive against Robin's back as he ushered him into the hotel lobby, trusting Dunn to deliver their bags back to Robin's room.

"I've got to check back in," Robin said, detouring to the front desk instead of letting Jules steer him to the elevators. "I checked out—I thought I was going to be in D.C. tonight."

"Uh-oh," Jules said.

"Uh-oh?"

"Let's just . . . check back in quickly," Jules told him. "Rumor has it there's a hotel room crunch in Boston this weekend."

Words that were tragically confirmed, mere seconds later, first by Melinda of the front desk, and then by the hotel manager, Mrs. Haniford, who was a daughter of the American Revolution, related to John Adams on her mother's side, a PFLAG mom, and in possession of one of *the* most ridiculously broad Boston accents Robin had ever heard. He usually loved hanging with her, just listening to her talk, but today he didn't like what she had to say.

Not only were there no rooms in this hotel, but there was nothing available anywhere in the city, including Cambridge and various suburbs all the way out past Framingham. It was, Mrs. H. told him, parents' weekend at nearly all the colleges in the metro Boston area. During this one weekend in the fall and graduation weekend in May, there was always a hotel shortage in what was undeniably the biggest college town in the nation.

"Pretend I didn't check out." Robin gave Mrs. H. his most winsome smile. "It's been, what? Ten minutes. I wasn't supposed to check out, and I'm coming back tomorrow. The maid probably hasn't even made up the room. I'll just go back in. You don't even need to change the sheets. We can just trade towels . . ."

"But you did check out. The computer already processed it." Mrs. H. liked him. She did. She often worked the night shift, and had invited him into her office for tea on quite a few occasions. She obviously hated the fact that she was now royally fucking him. "We have a waiting list. I could put you on it . . . ?"

"Mrs. Hanniford," Robin said. "Betty." He leaned closer. Lowered his voice. "See the incredibly gorgeous guy talking on his cell phone over there?" He gestured with his chin toward Jules.

Mrs. H. looked and then nodded.

"That's Jules." He'd talked and talked and *talked* about Jules during their tea parties. Mrs. Hanniford could have been given a pop quiz on All That Was Jules, and gotten an A-plus. "I checked out of the hotel because I couldn't bear to be away from him for another minute, only he surprised me by flying up here to see me. I'm pretty sure that one of the things I'm going to do tonight is ask him to marry me. Please don't make me do that while we huddle together for warmth in the train station, breathing through our mouths to avoid the persistent and incomparable stench of urine."

"Laronda's got nothing," Jules said as he came toward them, smiling a warm greeting at Mrs. H., despite his obvious frustration, disappointment and fatigue.

Robin looked at Mrs. H. and briefly put his finger on his lips. She nodded, wide-eyed, but then shrugged apologetically, shaking her head. She still couldn't help him, regardless of how much she wanted to.

"Laronda is Jules's boss's administrative assistant," Robin explained to the hotel manager. "She's, like, the queen of his office. If there was a room in Boston, she would have gotten it for us." He knew Laronda well. Some days he spoke to her on the phone more often than he spoke to Jules.

"Sometimes the . . . organization has a hotel room on reserve, but not tonight," Jules explained, obviously not wanting to say *the Bureau* or *the FBI* in front of Mrs. H. He was clearly tired and even slightly pale. What he needed, Robin knew, was about eighteen hours in bed.

Robin needed that, too, but not because he was tired.

"Laronda also told me there's a run on rental cars," Jules continued. "Apparently a semi went off a bridge onto Amtrak's main tracks to New York. Trains are shut down. She couldn't even rent us a moped. I was thinking we could drive up to Manchester, or out to Hartford if we could get a car."

"We have sister hotels in both Manchester and Hartford," Mrs. H. said helpfully. She went tappy-tap on her computer. "There are rooms available in each."

"But no cars to get there," Robin reiterated.

More tapping and . . .

"None available from this hotel," Mrs. H. confirmed. "I'm sorry. Maybe there's a car service that could . . . ?"

"I already tried that," Jules told Robin quietly, shaking his head as Mrs. H. bustled back into her office to answer a phone call. "But everything's booked. I was trying to think outside the box. A limo. You know, at the very least take a lengthy ride around the city."

Robin had to laugh, in part at Jules's subtle yet suggestive eyebrow waggle. The first time they'd hooked up, they'd been in a limo, privacy shield up and radio blasting. But apparently *that* wasn't even an option today.

"I completely screwed us," Robin whispered. "Didn't I?" Jules had left him a voicemail saying that he was coming. If he'd taken the time to go through the twenty-something messages that had cluttered up his cell phone, and if he'd done it *before* he'd packed his bags and checked out of the hotel . . . He and Jules would've been up in his room, right now, exchanging long, slow, deep kisses . . .

"Actually," Jules pointed out *sotto voce*, laughing at the absurdity of their situation. "I'm feeling extremely unscrewed."

It was hard not to laugh, too, when Jules was laughing. Still, Robin shook his head. "Maybe we could catch the shuttle to New York, get a room down there—"

"And wake up at three thirty to get back to Boston in time for you to get to work?" Jules countered.

"I'll get up at three thirty," Robin said. "You can sleep in, catch a later flight." Jesus, Jules looked so tired.

But he was shaking his head, no. "I wanted to go with you to the studio," he said. "I mean, if that's okay with you."

Robin's heart flip-flopped. It was amazing. His relationship with Jules had lasted longer than any other relationship he'd ever had, yet the man could still make him feel like a giddy kid with a crush. "Really?"

"If it's okay," Jules said again. He touched Robin's hand, interlacing their fingers. It was a daring public show of affection for Jules—considering they were well outside of the South End, Boston's gay neighborhood. "The unscrewed thing was just a joke.

You know that, right? Sweetie, I love making love to you, but . . . right now I'm just ecstatic we're in the same city. We can go have dinner and . . . It'll be tomorrow before we know it."

And it wouldn't be the first time they'd talked through the entire night.

Mrs. H. had come back to the desk. She was hovering uncertainly, desperate but powerless to help.

"Hey, Mrs. H.," Robin said, his eyes never leaving Jules's. "My life partner's a little shy, but I'm feeling a righteous need to kiss him. Do you mind if we step into your office for, oh, two minutes?"

Mrs. H. was silent, and he finally turned to look at her. She was obviously thinking . . .

"Mind out of the gutter," he chastised her, laughing. "Two minutes? I'm good, but I'm not that good."

Jules was laughing, too, but he leaned forward and kissed Robin. Right there in the lobby. His mouth was soft and warm and so, so sweet . . .

"Come on," Jules said, with so much love in his eyes that Robin's heart nearly burst. "Let's check our bags and find someplace quiet to have dinner."

"We could get take-out," Robin suggested, his hands jammed into the pockets of his jeans as if it were cold out. With the wind sweeping in off Boston Harbor, it *was* a little nippy, but Jules was warm. Maybe too warm.

"And take it where?" Jules asked. *Find someplace quiet to have dinner*—hah. The city was overrun with students and their parents, all dining out. They'd walked all the way down to the waterfront, by the Aquarium. And now they couldn't even find an empty cab to take them . . . Where indeed? Was there really any point going back to the hotel, where they didn't even have a room?

God, he needed to sit down.

Somehow Robin knew that, and was there, helping him toward a bench.

"Let's just get in line at the Union Oyster House," Jules said. The wait there was over ninety minutes, but the food and ambiance would be worth it. Besides, it wasn't as if they were rushing to get anywhere else.

"You're sweating." Robin's tone was accusatory. He'd been asking Jules if he was okay ever since they'd left the hotel. "You've been lying to me, haven't you?"

"I'm fine," Jules lied yet again. But it wasn't just to Robin, it was to himself, too. He didn't want to be sick. He couldn't be sick. Not this weekend. He'd wanted this to be special . . .

"Jesus, Jules, you're burning up." Robin's hands felt like ice against Jules's forehead.

"I'm just a little . . . uncomfortable. Gastronomically. I had this taco as sort of a pseudo lunch," he tried to explain. "I think it was bad."

"You think you have food poisoning?" Robin's eyes were filled with such concern.

"No," Jules said. Please, God, no. "It's just indigestion."

"Maybe we should go to the hospital."

"For indigestion?"

"For food poisoning." Robin was exasperated. "Just because you don't want to call it what it is, babe, doesn't mean you get to change the facts."

The wind blew, and suddenly Jules was freezing. "Oh, shit," he said as he started to shiver violently. Just as suddenly, the taco made its play for escape. Jules barely managed to turn away from Robin as he got fiercely sick, right there on the sidewalk.

But Robin didn't recoil. In fact, he got closer, putting his arms around Jules, trying to stop his shaking. "All right," he said. "Okay." He took out his cell phone. "I'm calling an ambulance."

"No," Jules managed to say before the taco tried for an encore. "Use my phone. Call Alyssa."

Sam Starrett was a sympathy vomiter. It didn't take him much to join the Technicolor interpretive dance, so he backed way off as Robin pretty much carried Jules into the hotel room.

"Bathroom's this way." Alyssa took charge. Or at least she tried. Robin refused to relinquish control, even when, from the sound of things, Jules lunged for the toilet and started singing the age-old hymn to the porcelain god.

"Lys, you all right?" Sam called.

"I'm fine," she called back. What a difference the time of day could make.

Feeling a tad green himself, Sam stepped out onto the balcony, closing the slider tightly behind him.

This was going to be an interesting night. When Robin called, Alyssa had been in the middle of trying to get Sam naked—which was not really that difficult a task. Sam had never been much of a challenge to his incredibly gorgeous wife, particularly in the *let's delay dinner to make love* department.

It *had* been something of a mood-changer, though, when she'd suddenly turned away from him, reaching to answer her phone. Like, there was anything in the world more important than this . . . ?

But then he'd recognized the jaunty melody, too, as being Jules Cassidy's emergency ring tone. And the chances Sam was going to get some before dinner dropped to a solid "probably not."

Jules and Alyssa had been whispering together a lot recently. Alyssa didn't want to talk about it, but Sam was pretty sure it had something to do with Robin, who was a dysfunctional emotional time bomb, just waiting for the most inopportune moment to explode.

From her seat on the edge of the bed, Alyssa said, "Oh, my God," and "Of course," and "A taco? Oh, no. Poor Jules," and then? The kicker. "We've got two double beds—there's plenty of room. Definitely. Bring him here. The Sheraton. Room 842. Do you need me to come to the lobby?"

Sam let his head flop back against the pillow of one of their hotel room's beds. The place had been out of kings, which was a shame because he was tall and his feet dangled off the end of a double.

But that wasn't as big a shame as the fact that he was not only *not* getting some tonight, he was going to have to endure Jules's misery as he attempted to dry out his alcoholic fuckwad of a boyfriend, who'd no doubt gone off on another binge from hell—his first since getting out of rehab.

"Okay," Alyssa said into her cell phone. "But if you need any help . . ." And then she totally surprised Sam with her next words. "Robin, shh, sweetie, it's really okay. We're glad you called. Honestly. Just get Jules over here as quickly as you can."

Sam sat up. "*Jules* is bingeing?" It was a stupid thing to say—he knew it as soon as the words were out of his mouth. Jules wasn't a big drinker to start with, and ever since Robin had gone into rehab he'd cut himself off, too, in solidarity.

Fortunately Alyssa was accustomed to Sam's occasional idiotic verbal explosions.

"Jules has food poisoning," she informed him as she closed her cell phone. "They couldn't get a hotel room, so they have nowhere else to go. Robin just managed to get them a ride—I think he stood in the street and stopped traffic. They should be here in about ten minutes."

You better get dressed. Sam waited for the words, but they didn't come. Instead, Alyssa smiled at him, heat in her ocean green eyes.

Sam thought his wife was achingly beautiful when dressed in

bulky cammie-print BDUs. She was gorgeous in jeans and a T-shirt, too, with her long legs, perfect breasts, and athletic build, without even a hint of makeup on her mocha-colored skin, her dark hair cut short and sleek, capping her African-princess face, framing her huge, otherworldly-colored eyes.

She was beautiful, as well, when she dressed up for dinner or a party—his favorite was that red dress with the short skirt. Shee-yit.

But Alyssa, wearing only underwear that she'd clearly bought for his pleasure . . .

By all rights, Sam should have been struck blind.

But that smile was loaded, and there was no doubt about it, it was his turn to talk, and perhaps say something brilliant this time. "I can name that tune in ten minutes."

She laughed—which created a phenomenon in Sam's chest that he thought of as a pulmonary triple lutz. "Yeah, but can you do it in five?"

He reached for her, and she slipped into his arms.

Short answer? Yes.

Jules wouldn't stop apologizing.

In fact, the very last thing he mumbled before falling asleep, after the gastrointestinal explosions had stopped, after Robin had gotten him cleaned up, into a borrowed and much too large pair of Sam's sweatpants and a T-shirt, and tucked into bed, was "I'm so sorry."

Robin sat with him for a while, just stroking his hair and watching him in the light from the bathroom.

Alyssa was curled up in the other bed. Robin thought she was asleep until his stomach growled loudly.

She chuckled. "Amazing that you could actually be hungry after that," she said, speaking quietly so as not to disturb Jules. "I may never eat again."

Robin laughed softly, too. "Thank you so much for letting us come here."

"Please," Alyssa said. "If you're going to be spending time with Jules, you need to understand that there is *nothing* Sam and I would not do for him. Are we clear on that?"

"Thank you," Robin started, but she cut him off.

"No," she said. "The correct response is *yes, ma'am, I understand.*"

"Okay," he said. "Now you're scaring me a little."

She laughed, but she was still looking at him pointedly, so he said, "Yes, ma'am, I understand." But then he added, "There's nothing I wouldn't do, either. I know you probably don't believe that yet. You have reason to mistrust me—"

Alyssa interrupted him again. "Once when Jules and I were overseas, he got this really awful stomach virus. It was . . . bad. I wanted to help him, but he wouldn't let me near him. He can be so stubborn and . . . I was impressed tonight at the way you just shouted him down. You wouldn't take his shit." She laughed. "Okay. Bad choice of words."

Robin laughed, too. "Yeah, well . . ."

Just stop, Robin had told Jules at an unfortunately higher volume than he would have liked when Jules had tried to push him away. *I'm not going anywhere, so just fucking get used to it.*

Of course, maybe bellowing *Why? Because I love you, okay?* at the top of his lungs, in front of Jules's skeptical best friend, had helped lower her skepticism a little.

"Sam went out to get some sandwiches a few hours ago," Alyssa told him as his stomach rumbled again. "He thought you might be hungry after the . . . fireworks ended. He's still out on the balcony, because he's . . . well . . ."

"He's Sam," Robin finished for her. "I know." Jules had told him all about Sam's tendency to lose his lunch in response to brutal injury or death. It was kind of funny, actually—the big, tough Navy SEAL, on his knees . . . Of course, during the violence, he was always in the thick of things—kicking ass and saving the day. But after it was over? Vomit time.

He was also, Jules had said, prone to the dread chain reaction. If someone else entered the vomitron, Sam would climb right in, too. Which was why he'd scrambled outside when Robin had carried Jules in.

"If you want," Alyssa said, "I'll keep an eye on Jules while you go out there and get something to eat."

Jules was breathing slowly and steadily. He'd been tired before the fireworks—good word for it—and now he was completely wrung out. Robin leaned over and kissed him gently on the forehead before standing up.

"Thanks," he said, even though he was thinking, *A sandwich with Sam. Oh, boy.* Sam was even scarier than Alyssa. He had this way of looking at Robin as if he were fresh birdcrap on the windshield of his recently detailed sports car.

Still, Robin was going to have to sit down and have a conversation with the big former SEAL one of these days. Why not right now?

He grabbed his jacket as he crossed to the slider. But before he got there, Alyssa said, "Hey, Robin?"

He turned to look at her in the dimness.

"I understand, too," she said. "How much you love Jules. And for the record? I think it's great. He's been waiting for you, his entire life."

"That means a lot to me," Robin managed to choke out, and great. Now as he pushed past the closed drapes and stepped out into the chill of the balcony, he had fricking tears in his eyes.

Sam had the light on out there, and as Robin closed the slider behind him, the former SEAL put down the book he'd been reading.

And there it was, that birdcrap-on-the-windshield withering look.

Jesus, Robin needed a drink.

And okay. Great. Maybe this wasn't the right time for this altercation, if it meant he was going to start thinking *that* kind of bullshit.

"Alyssa said there were sandwiches?" Robin made it a question, but there was an obvious deli bag on the table next to Sam. Maybe the man would just point to it, and let Robin eat in silence, after which he'd go back inside and curl up in that bed, with his arms around Jules.

And sure enough, Sam pointed. But he also said in his Texas cowboy drawl, "Turkey and swiss, roast beef, or veggie wrap. I wasn't sure what you'd want."

"Turkey's perfect," Robin said, digging through the bag. "Thank you so much."

"There's soda, too." And there was, indeed, a second bag on the floor. "Or bottled water. Have a seat."

Robin sat, because that was an order, not a request. But he'd never been particularly good with authority, which was probably why he said, "No beer or wine coolers, huh?"

And okay. He was now disgusting purple birdcrap.

"I'm curious," Sam said when he finally spoke. "Why do you think that's funny? Because I don't find it funny at all."

"It's not funny," Robin agreed. "You scare the hell out of me, and not just because you could probably kill me with your pinky finger. I'm well aware that you don't like me—for good reasons and . . . You know, I could really use a meeting." He looked up from his sandwich and said around it, "Alcoholics Anonymous. I go. A lot."

"I know what a meeting is." Sam managed to look even more annoyed. "I've been to plenty. Both AA and Al-Anon."

Robin just looked at him.

Sam shrugged. "My mother," he said. "She's been sober for over a decade. She's still involved in the program, so yeah, I've been to my share of meetings."

"I didn't know that," Robin said.

"Jules told me," Sam said, "that *your* mom didn't make it."

This was surreal. Of all the topics to broach among relative strangers . . . Still, Robin managed to nod. "DUI and DOA when I was eleven."

"Fuck." The word was heartfelt.

"She left me long before that," Robin said. For years, he'd said those same words, but it was only recently, after going through rehab and fighting to stay sober, that he really understood what it meant.

Sam put his cowboy-booted feet up on a little side table. Clunk and clunk. "My mother pretty much checked out when I was . . . Hell, it was before third grade. I was, what? Nine?"

"I don't remember a time when she wasn't drinking," Robin confessed. "I mean, I try, but I just don't remember. She must've, you know, been okay enough to take care of me back when I was a baby. I mean, obviously she fed me—I didn't starve to death." Then again, he could remember getting his own dinner when he was in nursery school, so . . .

"I remember having corn flakes for dinner," Sam drawled. "I knew when the breakfast cereal came out, I was in for a bad week or so."

"Yeah." Robin had been there, done that. "I think I learned to read so I could use the microwave and have something hot for a change."

"Another sign that she was on a binge," Sam said, "was the empty lunchbox. It'd be out on the kitchen counter, and I'd grab it and go and then . . . I still remember the feeling in my stomach when I opened it in the school cafeteria and realized it was empty . . . That sucked—that sense of unavoidable doom."

Robin nodded. He could relate. "She hit you?" he asked.

"Nah," Sam said. "That was my father's job. He traveled a lot, though." He looked at Robin, and his blue eyes were actually warm. Sympathetic, but without pity, which was pretty remarkable.

Jesus, they had way more in common than Robin had ever dreamed.

"Did your mom hit you?" Sam asked him quietly.

Robin looked down at his sandwich, lying there on a piece of white deli paper.

"Mine used to just go upstairs into her bedroom and close the door," Sam continued, "while my father was kicking the shit out of me. She never stood up to him. Parents are supposed to protect their kids—not the other way around." He sighed. "Then, when I got a little older, I used to beat *myself* up for not being able to get her sober. It took me a long time to learn that not only was I a kid—what could I do?—but that *she* was the only one who could make herself stop drinking."

Robin nodded. "That was one of the bonuses of rehab for me," he told Sam. "I let go of a lot of guilt I was carrying about my mother. I should have been able to save her. Stuff like that." He met Sam's gaze. "And yes, sometimes she hit me."

His mother hadn't hit him often—just enough. And more damaging than the actual blows had been her inconsistency. Robin had never known when she might scream at him and knock him across the room. And then cradle him in her arms afterward, weeping and apologetic.

"I haven't, um, told anyone that before," Robin continued. "Not outside of therapy."

"Not even Jules?" Sam asked.

"No," Robin admitted. He looked down at his sandwich again. His appetite was definitely gone, so he wrapped it back up. This was beyond strange.

"You should tell him."

"Yeah," Robin said. "It's just . . . That part of my life is over, you know?"

"I hear you, but . . ." Sam didn't sound convinced that it could be that easy. "It's still part of who you are."

"It's just that Jules . . . He's so . . ." Robin struggled to find the right words. "Unbroken."

"So . . . what? You don't want him to know how broken *you* are?" Sam was starting to look less friendly again.

"I don't want to ruin his day," Robin corrected him. "He knows I'm crazy-glued together. He knows exactly who I am and . . . If you want to know the truth, I'm too busy being happy to dredge up old crap like that, okay?" He forced himself to meet the SEAL's gaze. "For the record, I like making Jules happy. And I do. I make him very, *very* happy."

And now it was Sam who looked away. "I bet you do."

Robin had to laugh. "I'm not talking about sex."

Sam met Robin's gaze. "Maybe we should. Talk about sex. I mean, sure, we could sit here and ignore the fact that you and Jules have . . . that kind of relationship. We could go that way, if you really want, but I'd prefer to throw it out on the table, look each other in the eye, man to man, and acknowledge the fact that you're getting it on with one of my best friends, which, yes, freaks me out a little bit, but I'm a grown-up—I can deal."

"Well, good," Robin managed. "I hope things are going equally well for you and Alyssa."

It was definitely time to stand up and go back into the hotel room, but Sam wasn't done.

"What I can't deal with," the SEAL continued, and his eyes were arctic again, "is you stepping out, or messing around, or doing some backroom hustle with someone who isn't Jules. It's not just a matter of breaking his heart, it's an issue of health. You put him at risk, I *will* rip out your lungs."

Son of a bitch.

"With your pinky finger," Robin said, as his outrage came to a boil. "Right? It's a little detail, I know, but it helps build the right amount of terror in me. I mean, because without that paralyzing fear holding me back, I just might go out and fuck random strangers."

Sam was clearly a little taken aback at his vehemence.

But this time *Robin* wasn't done. He let Sam have it, death by pinky finger be damned. "Don't you have the tiniest clue, you fucking homophobic Neanderthal, how completely you just insulted me? I'm gay—I must be promiscuous, right? Oh, and you can *deal* with the idea of Jules and me making love—aren't you courageous to have to face that, you poor thing?"

"That's not what I meant," Sam protested.

Robin pushed the deli bag toward him. "Here you go—just in case you need to *throw up* at the thought of—"

"Jules and I have been friends a long time," Sam was getting mad now, too. "Way longer than you've known him."

"I was unaware this was a contest," Robin threw back in his face. "You've known him longer, but I've known him more intimately. Hmmm, I wonder who wins. I'm feeling pretty certain it's me, because *damn*, your good friend Jules? He's freaking great in bed."

"If that's all he is to you—"

"Fuck. You," Robin said, fumbling in his jacket pocket for the jewelers box he'd been carrying around for the past three days, since he'd gotten the crazy idea to . . . No. It wasn't crazy at all. It was the most sane idea he'd ever had. He put the fuzzy little box somewhat forcefully on the table in front of Sam. "And fuck your holier-than-thou bullshit, too. I'm the one who said I make him happy. You're the one who made it be about sex."

Sam looked from Robin to the jewelers box and back. He picked it up and opened it and . . .

Sam looked at him. Jules was always saying that Sam was extra smart for someone who wore cowboy boots, and Robin could see from his expression that he knew exactly what he was holding.

Wedding rings.

"You can threaten to rip my lungs out if you want," Robin told him more quietly now. "It's not going to change a thing. I want Jules. Only Jules. And I want him forever. I love him—I don't give a damn if you don't believe me. The only one who needs to believe me is Jules."

Sam snapped the ring box closed. "I don't think you're promiscuous because you're gay," he said just as quietly. "I think you're promiscuous because you're a drunk."

Robin felt sick, because he knew that there wasn't much he could say in response to that. There was a seven-minute-long digital video, showing Robin on his final and most famous drunken binge, that was still enjoying a record number of weekly hits on YouTube and proving Sam's point.

"I also think," Sam said, holding out the ring box for Robin, "that you really want to stay sober."

"And we both know," Robin couldn't keep himself from saying as he put it back in his pocket, "how well your threats will help me do just that." He stopped himself. Took a deep breath and exhaled hard. "I know I've earned your mistrust. I understand that. I accept it. What I don't accept is your disrespect of Jules—as if you think he's unable to take care of himself, so you're going to do it for him."

To Robin's surprise, Sam actually nodded. "You're right, I definitely crossed the line. I apologize."

"That makes it all better." Robin stood up, brushing the crumbs from the sandwich off of his jeans. "Excuse me. I'm going to go check on my lover."

"I love him, too," Sam said. "If that's worth anything."

"Sorry," Robin said. "You're hot, but I'm not into three-ways."

"That's not what I meant, and you know it."

"Yeah, well, I just thought I'd get that out on the table," Robin retorted.

Sam actually laughed. "You're okay."

And that was the final straw. "Oh, good," Robin said. "I was worried that maybe you thought I wasn't okay. I'm so glad I passed your test. But guess what, asshole? You've got a long way to go before you pass mine."

So Sam had really fucked *that* up.

The last thing he'd wanted was a serious rift between himself and Jules's significant other. And yet he *had* doused himself in some serious holier-than-thou during their little talk. Robin had gotten that right.

But Sam had lived through the final few months of Jules's relationship with Adam. He'd watched his friend get destroyed again and again as he'd discovered Adam's countless infidelities.

Jules had assured Sam that, despite living together, he and Adam had never reached a point of trust sufficient to go bareback—which was gayspeak for having sex without the protection of condoms.

Yup. That had been one hell of a conversation. Still, Sam had brought it up because he needed to make sure Jules was being smart and safe.

But that was then, and this was now, and Sam suspected that things would be different between Robin and Jules in terms of trust, and yeah, that scared him.

Less so now, though, after Robin's outburst.

Still, a drunk was a drunk, and if Robin slipped and relapsed, God only knew what he'd do.

But Robin *was* right. The decision to trust Robin—or not—was going to have to be Jules's. Not Sam's.

With a sigh, Sam turned off the light and went inside.

It was freaking dark in there, and he felt his way to the bathroom, where he relieved himself, washed up and peeled down to his shorts.

Then it was another fumble back through the pitch darkness to the bed where Alyssa was fast asleep.

Sam quietly slid in beside her, aware as hell that he could hear Alyssa breathing, and he could also hear Jules. The fact that he couldn't hear Robin meant the movie star was probably still awake.

And probably still pissed from their little heart to heart.

Maybe if Sam just said, *Look, I meant well, but I'm scared that you're going to hurt my friend, so I fucked it up but good, and I'm sorry about that. Can we maybe start over?*

Alyssa shifted in the bed, spooning against him, which was nice, but would have been nicer without the other slumber-party guests in the room. And of course, since the option of having sex with his wife was completely off the table, Sam now found himself unable to think of anything else. He'd had similar trouble sitting across the conference table from Alyssa during Troubleshooters briefings, or riding in the elevator with her at the headquarters of one of their corporate clients. He had to work very hard to concentrate on anything besides how sweet it would feel to slide into her tight heat.

He'd told her about it once, and she'd laughed, thinking he was kidding. He'd managed to convince her that he wasn't.

"Robin?"

Sam froze as, in the darkness, from over in the other bed, Jules stirred.

"Shhh," Robin's voice was gentle. "I'm right here, babe. What do you need? What can I get you?"

"Oh, God," Jules said. "My mouth tastes like . . . pigshit."

Sheets and blankets rustled, Jules said, "Oh, ew, don't—" and then there was something that sounded like . . . Yup, it was definitely kissing. If Sam could've squinted with his ears, he would have.

But then it stopped and Robin whispered, "I don't know about pig. Dog, maybe."

Jules laughed. "Shut up."

The bedcovers rustled some more. "Here, take a sip of ginger ale. Just a little one—we don't want to get the fireworks started again."

That got another weak laugh from Jules. "God, I'm so sorry. This was supposed to be—"

"Shhh," Robin said again. "We've got a long weekend, remember?" There was a clunk as he put the glass of ginger ale down and then . . . "Mmmm. Now you taste like dog crap with a zesty ginger sauce."

"Fuck you," Jules laughed again, but then he stopped and drew in a hard breath. When he spoke again, his voice sounded different. It was breathless and low, with an undercurrent of urgency that Sam had never heard coming from his friend before. "Better yet—"

"Whoa," Robin spoke over him. "Jules—"

Oh, shit.

"I'm feeling much better," Jules said.

"I can see that." Robin's voice sounded choked. "But, alas, babe, we are so not alone."

In the other bed, about four feet away from where Sam was lying next to his wife in the pitch darkness, Jules got extremely still. For several long moments, the only discernable sound in the room was Alyssa's slow and steady breathing.

"I have no idea where we are," Jules admitted. "Are we . . ." He sucked in his breath, and when he spoke again, there was wonder in his voice. "Do I remember seeing Alyssa?"

"Yes, you do," Robin said. "We're sharing a hotel room with her and Sam."

Jules started to laugh. "Oh, crap," he said.

"Yup," Robin said.

"Hi, Sam," Jules said.

"Yeah," Sam said. "Saying hi at this point seems . . . woefully inadequate."

That got the pair of them laughing, but it was the way a couple of kids might've laughed at a sleepover. They were trying to be quiet so as not to wake Alyssa.

These days she could, however, sleep through a storm.

"I really didn't know you were here," Jules apologized.

"Yeah, that's kind of clear," Sam said. "I'm, uh, glad you're feeling better."

They were laughing again, and now it reminded him of the way he and Alyssa laughed when they were giddy just from being together, particularly after spending weeks apart.

"Thank you for rescuing me, SpongeBob," Jules said, when he caught his breath.

"I didn't do anything, Squidward," Sam said quietly. "It was all Robin. He's, um . . . He takes good care of you."

"Yes, he does," Jules agreed.

"He really loves you," Sam said.

"Thank you, Cyrano," Robin said. "But it's going to take way more than that to pass my test."

"What test?" Jules asked.

"I'm just keeping it real," Sam said. "Telling it like I see it."

"We were, um, kidding around before," Robin told Jules.

"I insulted Robin," Sam corrected him, "and he's now being gracious, trying to fool you into thinking it was just a joke, when I was really pretty damn rude."

"Oh, good," Jules said. "Thanks so much, Starrett."

"It's what I do best."

"I apologize for bringing logistics into this conversation," Robin said, "but it looks like it's almost dawn. Are you and Alyssa checking out today or . . . ?"

"No, we've got the room until Sunday," Sam told him. There was definitely light leaking beneath the heavy drapes. "We'll be getting up and out at around nine—we're visiting Lainey and the kids. My sister, Elaine, and her husband live out in western Mass," he explained to Robin.

"Crap," Robin said, but then added, "Okay. That's okay. I was hoping you guys could stay with Jules, but . . . I'll just call Art. They'll reschedule the shot."

"I'm really feeling much better," Jules said. "Now that the Death Taco's gone."

"I'm not leaving you alone."

"Don't be silly—"

"This is not open to discussion." Robin was serious.

Jules apparently didn't know the meaning of *not open to discussion*. He began to discuss. "You said it was a really important shot, but that it wouldn't take long," he pointed out. "I think it's probably smart if I don't do much of anything today, but I'm certainly feeling well enough for you to—"

"They'll have to reschedule." Robin was adamant.

Jules tried reason with a little admonishment this time. "This can't be the best time for you to diva up," he told Robin. "You're in the middle of negotiations—"

"No," Robin said. "I'm not."

"What?" Jules shifted in the bed, no doubt so that he could see Robin in the growing but still dim light. "You made the deal? I thought you were waiting to, well, talk to me."

Oopsie, as Jules sometimes said.

"No," Robin said. "I mean, yeah, I *was* waiting, but what's to talk about? What's the point? I hate this—me in Boston and you in D.C.

It sucks. It was fine for the short shoots. A day or two, maybe three? That was working. But this . . ." He shook his head. "So I'm just going to tell them no. No deal. No more. I'll finish out my contract, but then I'm coming home."

Jules sounded bewildered. "But you love this job. You said you loved playing Jeff O'Reilly."

"It's a great role," Robin agreed. "And maybe in a year or two . . . But right now . . . I just want to be with you."

"I want to be with you, too," Jules said quietly. "Which is why, I, um, well, I got the ball rolling to, uh, get transferred up to Boston."

"No fucking way." Whoops. Sam hadn't intended to say that aloud.

"Yes, fucking way," Jules retorted tartly. "And since it's not your fucking business, Mr. Insult-My-Partner— "

"Max is never going to let you go, Cassidy." All right, so this was really dumb. Shutting the fuck up was what he should be doing, not arguing with Jules, who was already pissed enough at him to use the word *fucking* twice in one statement.

"Max thinks it a good idea," Jules defended himself.

"Yeah, because it means that you're out of the running as his replacement. He doesn't have to come up with some other excuse for why you're not going to be promoted."

And yes, that was indeed a very cold silence that was suddenly nipping at Sam's nose, considering that the real reason why Jules wasn't going to get that promotion was lying beside Jules right that very moment, and everyone in the room knew it, too.

"Sorry," Sam added.

"You don't really want to be transferred out of D.C.," Robin said quietly. "Do you?"

"It's a temporary position," Jules said just as quietly. "It'd be for a year—maybe two at the most. And I'd still be part of Max's team.

Yashi and Deb and even George would come with me. I'd still have to travel every now and then—that wouldn't change. Plus I'd be making a lot of day trips to D.C. But when I was home, I'd . . . be home. With you. We could actually have a home. You know, something that belongs to both of us, instead of you moving into my apartment—which is fine, if we end up doing that, but . . ."

Sam was silent. Robin was, too.

"What, no comments or criticisms from the peanut gallery?" Jules was clearly asking Sam.

"I'm just wondering what the hell Robin is waiting for," Sam finally said. "An engraved invitation? You going to speak up there, Boy Wonder? Jules just asked you to make a home with him. You need something more than that?"

"God, I love you," Robin breathed.

"Aw shucks, I love you, too, pumpkin," Sam said.

"He was talking to me," Jules said.

"Yeah, I was just practicing being an asshole. It takes hard work and constant dedication to my craft to excel the way I do. But FYI, Robin has something else to ask you."

"Are you sure you want to do this?" Robin asked Jules.

"That wasn't it," Sam said.

"I'm very sure," Jules said. "Zip it, Starrett."

There was silence then, and Sam closed his eyes, because he knew that Robin was kissing Jules again.

It was then that Robin finally asked for what he really wanted. Well, after Jules gave him another honking good segue.

"Life partner." Jules was a little out of breath. In fact, he sounded a lot like he'd sounded when he'd said *I'm feeling much better . . .*

And that was making Sam a little nervous. He glanced over at Alyssa, who was still sleeping like a baby, just as she'd been when this conversation, as it were, had started.

"When we were talking to the hotel manager," Jules continued, "you called me your life partner. Did you mean it?"

"Yeah," Robin said. "I did. I do. I want to spend my life with you." It was then, finally, that he took a deep breath and said it. "Marry me, Jules."

Jules laughed, but not because he thought Robin was funny. It sounded to Sam as if he were completely surprised. "Wow."

"Seriously," Robin said. "If we're moving to Boston, we can really get married."

"Yeah," Jules said. "I know and . . . Wow."

"I want to marry you," Robin said. "I want to make a home with you, and grow old with you and— "

"Yes," Jules said. "Absolutely, positively, yes. God, Robin, I want to marry you, too."

And there was that silence again. Which, oddly enough, seemed kind of sweet this time. But still, enough was enough.

Sam leaned over and kissed Alyssa. "Wake up, sleepyhead," he said, and her eyes opened.

"Hey." She smiled at him, the way she always did, even when he woke her up at oh-what-the-fuck-hundred.

"Throw on some clothes," he told her. "I got this crazy urge to take an hour-long walk along the Charles River. We'll be back in an hour," he repeated just in case he hadn't been clear enough.

Alyssa was an experienced operator. She could go from sound sleep to completely alert in a flash. True to form, she didn't disappoint. She didn't need another word of explanation. She just moved. She pulled on her jeans, jammed her feet into her boots, slapped a hat on her head and grabbed her jacket, even as Sam threw on the clothes he'd left in the bathroom.

They were out in the hall, door closing tightly behind them in a matter of seconds.

It was only then that she questioned Sam. "He did it, didn't he? He asked Robin to marry him?"

Sam nodded. But then he realized what she'd said. "You mean Robin asked Jules." And besides, how did she know?

"Robin asked Jules?" she repeated, breaking into a wide smile. "Jules was planning to ask Robin. Tonight, as a matter of fact."

So that was what they'd been whispering about over the past few days. Sam pulled her toward the elevators. "Robin was planning it, too," he told her as he pushed the down button. "He showed me these rings he got. They were . . . nice. Kind of gay, but that works, because *they're* gay, so . . ."

"You're okay with this?" Alyssa asked. "I know you had your doubts about Robin being good enough for our boy."

"He's pretty young," Sam pointed out as the elevator door opened and they got in. "My mother was what? In her fifties, when she stopped drinking. He's not even thirty."

"Everyone follows their own path." She pushed the button for the lobby. "He really loves Jules—I don't doubt that. And Jules . . ." She laughed. "He was miserable tonight, Sam. I've never seen him that sick. And yet . . . Everything was okay, because Robin was with him."

Sam pulled her tight and she nestled close, her head against his heart. "I know the feeling," he whispered.

"Robin was so patient and . . . tender," Alyssa said. "And he made Jules laugh, even as sick as he was." She shook her head. "Everyone comes with some kind of baggage." She looked up at Sam, amusement in her eyes. "You yourself aren't exactly low maintenance. But you always make me laugh."

He kissed her. "That's nice to know."

"They really love each other," Alyssa told him, and he realized she was still trying to convince him.

"I'm good with it," Sam said. "I am. Yeah, I'd feel better if Robin had five years of sobriety under his belt, but . . . As Boy Wonder himself told me tonight—he makes Jules very, *very* happy. I don't doubt that at all."

Alyssa smiled at him. "I'm glad."

Speaking of making Jules very, *very* happy . . . Sam was pretty sure, that back in the hotel room, the happiness index was currently off the scale for both of his friends.

And he also knew that, despite their rocky start, all was forgiven. Yeah, no doubt about it. Sam had just passed Robin's test.

PART TWO

the surprise wedding shower crasher

NOVEMBER 10
BOSTON, MASSACHUSETTS

OVER FIFTY PEOPLE WERE STANDING, SILENTLY, BEHIND the tightly closed door of the wedding-theme-decorated living room, as Jules and Robin burst through their front door, soaked from the pouring rain.

Dolphina Patel still hadn't gotten used to their high energy entrances, and if she hadn't been watching through the front window, half-heartedly flipping through the day's mail while waiting for them, she probably would've jumped clear out of her seat in what had once been the front parlor of the pre-Victorian-era townhouse. And this despite the fact that it was the one-month anniversary of her employment as their personal assistant.

She put down the mail—mostly replies to invitations for their mid-December wedding—and went out into the foyer, unable to conceal her dismay. "Didn't you take an umbrella?" she asked. It had been her job not just to get them out of the house while the guests were arriving, but also to see that they were appropriately casually dressed. Now they were both completely drenched.

"Yikes," Jules said, stepping back onto the carpet runner just inside the front door. They'd just had the beautiful bird's eye maple floors refinished. "Sweetie, your shoes."

"It wasn't raining when we left." Robin stepped out of the shoes in question and started pulling his sodden sweater over his head. "Jesus, my jeans are soaked."

"By all means," Jules said, laughing, "strip right in the foyer, in front of Dolphina."

"Dolphina doesn't mind," Robin pointed out, shedding his pants as Jules looked at her and rolled his eyes in mock despair.

The two men were like a living, breathing advertisement for the joy that came with finding true love. They brought a sense of togetherness and lighthearted fun to everything they did. Even when the sewer line in their new home had backed up into the first floor bathtubs, there had been an excessive amount of laughter echoing through the then-furniture-free rooms. Dolphina had gone home early that day, not wanting to bring her two bosses down with her teeth-clenchingly negative reaction to what Jules had insisted was "no biggie."

Only slightly less funny had been the bat colony that had come with the house. Yes, *colony.* As in forty bats—give or take a few dozen—living beneath the roof and in the walls of the 150-year-old dwelling.

Occasionally, before Eddie the Bat Guy, bless his soul, had come and saved the day by putting one-way bat doors on every entrance and egress along the roofline, a flying rodent would wander out and wing its way through the humans-only part of the house, creating no small amount of hysteria—mostly from Dolphina—and a great deal of laughter.

And the comedy show that was the master bathroom renovation? Starting with the hysterically funny broken pipe and the laugh-riot of a waterfall that went *through* the kitchen ceiling, and continuing to what was now day twenty-eight in what had been estimated as a four-day project—four days, at *most* . . .

"We're looking at it as an opportunity," Jules had told Dolphina around day eighteen—when they'd given up on all hope of a quick repair. "We're just going to tear everything out and create the master bath of our dreams. It'll be done by the end of October—Thanksgiving at the very latest."

Although she supposed that, compared to getting shot at—and occasionally wounded as Jules had been while working for the FBI—sewage in the bathtub, thirty to forty bats in the attic, and a waterfall through the kitchen ceiling *was* no big deal.

Robin, too, had followed Jules's example and rolled with it all quite easily.

Dolphina had worked for the actor back during the dark time she thought of as "Before Jules." She adored Robin, truly she did, but back then his method of coping with the slightest amount of stress had included consuming copious amounts of alcohol. But he was clean and sober now, and working hard to stay that way.

And she had never seen him so thoroughly, joyfully happy as he'd been these past few weeks, despite bats and bathroom crap and even bat crap.

Robin was working here in Boston, acting in a high quality cable TV series that was critically acclaimed, living in this gorgeous, sunlit antique of a home, and planning his impending Christmas-season wedding with the man of his dreams.

A man who probably wouldn't mind a whit if Robin walked around in only his boxer shorts, 24/7. Jules was looking at Robin right now as if he could not believe his good luck.

"Dolph, grab a laundry basket, will you?" Robin asked.

Um . . .

The laundry room was off the kitchen, which was on the other side of the living room. If she opened that door . . . "Why don't you run upstairs and get some clothes on?" she suggested. "I'll take care of this."

But Jules had finally sat down on the rug in order to undo the laces of his boots. "Dagnabit, my fingers are frozen."

"It's starting to slush out there," Robin told Dolphina as he crouched to help Jules with the knot. "It's not quite snow yet, but it's definitely not rain either. It's amazing."

"Amazing?" Jules laughed as he peeled off his sweater. His T-shirt beneath it came off, too, but it was wet as well, so he just left it off. "Wait until March. By then you'll be calling it something else entirely."

Robin was the movie star, but Jules was quite possibly even better looking. He was dark-haired in contrast to Robin's bottle blond, brown-eyed to Robin's neon blue, and seemingly slight compared to Robin's lean, muscular height. But his vertically challenged stature was deceiving—he was, in truth, extremely buff. When both men had their shirts off, as they did right now, it was like living in an Abercrombie & Fitch ad—a six-pack celebration, complete with triceps and biceps galore.

No doubt about it, Dolphina loved her new job.

"You've got ice in your hair," Jules pointed out.

"You do, too, babe." Robin ran his fingers through Jules's closely cropped waves. "That's so wild. Ice is actually falling from the sky."

"It does that now and then," Jules said. "We call it *winter,* here in the real world outside of the Los Angeles area code."

"Your Win-Ter is strange to me, earthling," Robin countered, then switched back to his regular voice. "You know, I've seen it in movies, but up close and personal, I'm finding the ice in the hair thing *really hot.*"

Oh, dear. Although in truth, Robin found most things *really hot,* especially when Jules was in the room.

Why Robin had hired her to work for them, Dolphina couldn't quite figure out. Too often, especially when they were laughing together like this, she felt like Eeyore—a damp blanket of doom and gloom, willing to accept that love existed—Robin and Jules were proof of that—but convinced it would always remain well out of her lonely, depressing grasp.

"California Boy wants it to snow for the wedding," Jules told her, his eyes never leaving Robin's.

"Don't you think that would be romantic?" Robin was talking to Dolphina, too, but smiling back at Jules. "Snowflakes falling in the silence of the night?" He started to sing. "I'm dreaming of a . . . white wedding!" It was a perfect mix of both Bing and Billy Idol, and it earned him more laughter and even a kiss from Jules.

A kiss that Robin repeated, and deepened.

"Um, guys," she said, and Jules, who usually erred on the side of overly polite, at least when she was around, pulled back.

"Sorry," he said, clearly embarrassed, which was silly. Surely he should feel comfortable kissing his fiancé in the privacy of his own home. She'd told him that about four hundred times, but he remained overly self-conscious.

He liked his privacy, and was something of a Yankee when it came to public displays of affection. Dolphina kept telling him that she was not the public and, truth be told, he *was* loosening up a little. But progress was slow.

Robin, on the other hand, had no qualms about soul-kissing his soulmate in front of other people—even out on the street. "I'm not," he said now.

"There's something you need to know." Dolphina took a deep breath, ready to spill all, because clearly there were times when a surprise party should not be a surprise, and this was rapidly turning into one of them.

But it was already too late. Robin was not paying attention as he pulled Jules to his feet with that glint in his eye that meant any second he was going to say . . .

"Take the rest of the day off, Dolph." But then he looked at her and blinked. "What are you doing here on a Saturday, anyway?"

"That's what I'm trying to tell you," she started.

But now it was Jules who was distracted by their wet clothes. He still had his jeans on, although the top button was unfastened, making him look more like a high fashion model than a high ranking FBI official. He'd gathered up their wet things and was heading for the living room door.

"Jules, wait," Dolphina said.

"Yeah, babe, you're dripping on the floor," Robin pointed out.

"I'll get a towel and wipe it up," Jules said, as Dolphina said, "Guys, really, you need to listen—"

"Dolph has worked with plenty of actors," Robin spoke over them both. "She doesn't care if you take off your jeans."

"Yeah, well, I kind of think she *would* care today, because I happen to be going commando," Jules said—to fifty close friends and co-workers as he opened the living room door. "Hi . . . everyone. Wow. Jeez. TMI."

Too much information, indeed. Jules's good friend Sam, who was standing near the front of the crowd, started to laugh.

Dolphina met Robin's eyes and smiled weakly. "Surprise?"

Will Schroeder tried to blend into the background of Robin Chadwick's living room, wishing he could find the bar in the crush of people and laughter.

He finally gave up and asked one of the men standing near him—tall, with military short hair—where they were hiding the beer. The guy gave him the strangest look. Or maybe he didn't. Maybe the strangeness was all in Will's head. GI Joe did, after all, have almost freakishly pale gray eyes. It was definitely disconcerting to be the focus of his full attention.

"Soda's in the fridge," he said, holding out his hand. "I'm Cosmo. Robin's brother-in-law."

"Will." He'd learned, the hard way, that it was always better to use his real name. Making one up would surely come back and chomp him on the butt. "I'm a friend of Art Urban's." Not entirely a lie, although the word *friend* was stretching it into the realm of fiction.

And as an award-winning, old-fashioned journalist, a reporter of the facts-and-truth-delivery-vehicle school, writing fiction was something he swore he'd never fall back on.

Of course, lying to get a story was vastly different from lying while writing one.

Or so Will told himself—especially at times like these.

Although right now, he was feeling both enormously guilty and humongously brass-balled. He'd just walked in, joined this party. No one had challenged him. Not yet, anyway. Everyone he'd met so far had been incredibly friendly, but the guilt didn't keep him from asking questions of—Cha-ching!—Robin Chadwick's brother-in-law.

"You were in the . . . Marines, right?" Will had done way too little research for this gig, assuming he could fill in the blanks later, when he was writing the piece for *The Boston Globe*. But he did remember hearing that Chadwick's sister—Hollywood producer Jane Mercedes Chadwick—was married to some kind of former bodyguard type.

"Navy SEAL," Cosmo corrected him. "Active duty."

Whoa. Okay. "Must be kind of weird," Will said. "You're a SEAL, but your wife's brother is . . . you know."

"An actor?" Cosmo was either dumb as a stone or playing with him.

Will had met some SEALs and former SEALs during his world-traveling, investigative journalism days, and dumb as a stone didn't line up. So he went point-blank, just to gauge the man's reaction. "Gay," he said.

"Why would that be weird?" The SEAL crossed his massive arms, as if resisting the urge to snap Will's neck.

So Will pushed it further. "You're completely cool with this," he countered, half question, half statement. "Robin gives up a lucrative movie career, announces he's gay, and that he's getting married to another man . . . ?"

Cosmo gazed at him expressionlessly for several long moments. "Who are you again?" he finally asked.

Definitely not dumb as a stone. It was time to run away. Fast. "Friend of Art's," Will said, pulling his cell phone out of his pocket. "Excuse me, I've got to take this call."

Phone to his ear, even though no one was really on the other end, he made his way across the crowded room.

He almost regretted the fact that Cosmo didn't follow him, grab him, and toss him out of the party into the still-steadily-falling icy rain.

What was he doing here? It felt surreal.

He'd crawled through jungles to interview guerilla leaders. He'd investigated and dug until he'd uncovered the location of an al Qaeda training camp, which had helped the U.S. apprehend dozens of terrorists. He'd stood on the ruins of an earthquake-ravaged city and written articles that had moved people and convinced them to send desperately needed aid.

He was a journalist, not a fluff-piece reporter.

So some gay movie star was getting married. Who on earth cared, besides Paul, his editor? And Will suspected that his editor cared more about watching Will fail, then about getting this feature.

But failure was not an option. He *was* willing to take whatever assignments he was given, because he could no longer simply pack up and go walkabout, searching for the next big story. Thanks to his sister, Arlene, he actually had an apartment now, and rent to pay.

He needed this job, so he was going to deliver the impossible—an interview with publicity-shy Robin Chadwick.

It was then, almost as if he'd willed him there, that Robin himself appeared right in front of Will. He wasn't in the middle of a conversation. He wasn't heading somewhere else. He was just standing there, as if looking for someone.

Will pocketed his cell phone. "Hi. Robin."

"Hey, have you seen Gina?" The actor was taller than he looked on screen, and even better looking, which was kind of backward to the way it was supposed to be. He was younger than Will had expected, too, but that was possibly an illusion due to the obvious pleasure radiating off the man. He'd clearly recovered from being surprised while wearing only a pair of boxer shorts, and was now both fully clad and enjoying this party to the utmost.

Will shook his head. "I . . . I haven't." He didn't know who Gina was. "Great party."

"Yeah," Robin agreed. "Not *quite* the way I was intending to spend my Saturday afternoon, but this is very nice. Have we met?"

"No," he said. "I'm Will." And Robin shook his hand. He had a warm, solid grip.

"Do you work with Jules?" Robin asked.

Moment of truth. Sort of. "No," Will said, aware of Cosmo's eyes still on him, from across the room. "I'm new in the office. There was an e-mail going around about this shower, so . . . I hope it's okay that I came. I wanted to introduce myself."

He resisted the urge to touch his nose, see if it had gotten any longer, even though technically it wasn't a lie. He hadn't said *which* office, and if Robin assumed that he meant Art Urban's, so be it.

"Of course it's okay." Robin's legendary generosity was obviously not just a legend. His charisma was also unbelievable. When he talked to someone, he was talking only to them. It was impressive. Will had met his share of celebrities whose eyes constantly swept the room, looking for someone more important to talk to. "Welcome. Although I gotta be honest, it's a no-cell-phone day—for me and Jules, anyway. That means no calls, no *business*—just fun, Will, all right?"

"You got it."

"Good."

"But I was hoping to set up a time we could sit down and talk." Will watched as Robin's smile faded. He felt like an asshole, which was exactly what he was. "It can be outside the office—in fact, I'd prefer it. More casual—relaxed. Maybe we could meet for coffee—or drinks?"

Robin was too polite to simply turn and walk away. "Will, can I be honest? You're kind of pushing the no-business boundary here. Why don't you call my personal assistant on Monday and set something up? Her name's Dolphina—she's around here somewhere. Get her card, and call her, okay?" He shook Will's hand again, giving him a farewell pat on his shoulder with his other hand.

"I'm sorry," Will said quickly, before Robin could turn away. "I just . . . I'm new and I wanted to jump right in to fight the bad news—you know, the most recent ratings lag."

"Crap," Robin said, taking the bait. "Are we really down again?"

They were. Will had done *that* research at least. And wasn't *he* a total turd for giving the man that grim news during a party. Still, he made himself nod. "It's the time-slot thing." He didn't know why the critically acclaimed show was struggling to keep its audience, but surely that wasn't helping. "They keep moving you. My own TiVo can't even find you."

Robin's smile was rueful now. "Terrific."

Will pushed it. "I know you've said no interviews, especially in regard to your upcoming wedding, but . . . It's a good story, Robin. People are curious about you. They're curious about your fiancé. We can stay away from invasive questions, you know, who's top, who's bottom—that kind of thing."

Robin was shaking his head in disgust. "But those are the questions that would be asked—you and I both know that."

"Maybe the solution lies in anticipating it," Will said. "We could come up with a response that—"

"Not even close," Robin cut him off. "I say anything at all about sex, even if it's obviously a joke, you know—even if I'm mocking them, like, *What I really love is doing it in a pig mask, while swinging from a chandelier*, and suddenly it's a sound bite all over TM-fucking-Z dot-com."

And wasn't that the truth. Will fought the urge to say, *Stop right there. Don't say another word to me. My iPod is recording you.*

"You know what the problem is?" Robin lowered his voice to confide in him. "There's no story here. Everyone thinks there is, you said it yourself, but there's not. I fell in love with a terrific man and . . . I made some choices about what I wanted my life to be like—sunlight instead of shadows. I'm convinced I made the right choices—I don't regret a thing. I enjoy my work—I hope the show stays afloat, but if it doesn't, so be it. What's important to me is that I'm in an amazing relationship, and hallelujah, Jules loves me, too. We're getting married for the same reason that everyone else gets married—because we want our commitment to each other to be both publicly known and legal. We're incredibly happy—and really boring. There's no conflict, no story. So the media tries to create one, because sex sells, and because gay sex still scares some people. Although you know what's really scary? It's why so many alleged conservatives want to know the details about what goes on in the privacy of *my* bedroom. No offense, Will, I like you, but I really don't want to know what floats your boat when you're naked with your significant other. You do your thing, and I'll do mine, and as long as we're all consenting adults, what's the problem?"

Will shook his head, but Robin, God help him, was just getting warmed up.

"The way I see it, sex is an important part of every loving, romantic relationship. And yeah, it's definitely part of my relationship with Jules. But it's beautiful. It's not scary. It's me loving him and him loving me. It's *making love*. And being with him makes me happier than I've ever been, and it makes me feel complete, and all those other fucking hokey things that people always say about falling in love, but the bottom line is it's not a news story unless I say something stupid like *yeah, we take turns being top or bottom*."

Damn.

"The story," Robin continued, "is that there are people out there who want to tell me who I can and cannot love. Like, if they just make some law, I'm going to walk away from Jules. Three pictures, fifteen million, Will. That's what I'd be earning right now if I'd stayed in the closet. Instead, I chose happiness. I chose self-respect. I chose *love*. You find me a reporter who understands that? I'll talk to him. But it's not going to happen."

"Reporters are just . . ." Will felt an idiotic urge to try to explain. "They're just like everyone else—trying to pay their bills."

"But they're doing it at my expense," Robin said.

"You didn't have to be an actor," Will pointed out. "When you were making those choices, you also chose to step into the spotlight. You can't complain when—"

"Into the spotlight," Robin said. "Not under a microscope."

"Well, like you said," Will told him. "Sex sells."

"Tabloids," Robin pointed out. "Not real newspapers. No legitimate, self-respecting news reporter would waste his or her time on a story like this."

Ouch.

"Talk to Dolphina," Robin said again. "If you still want to sit down with me, fine. Set something up. But I'm telling you right now that I won't be talking to any reporters about my wedding *or* about my relationship with Jules."

"Dolphina." Will repeated the somewhat odd name, thinking, *Too late, brother.*

"Hey, here she is now," Robin said, pulling a dark-haired young woman out of the crowd. "Dolph, this is Will. Do me a favor, and set up a coffee meeting with him for early next week. I gotta run, I promised Gina a tour of the new house."

And with that, he was gone, leaving in his place . . .

The world tilted. It actually shifted and moved, and Will had to widen his stance to keep from falling over onto his ear.

Truly, Robin's personal assistant was the most beautiful woman Will had ever seen in his entire life. But he'd traveled the world and seen his share of beautiful women, and her pretty face and slender figure wasn't what had nearly knocked him off his feet.

It was her eyes—those incredible dark eyes. She was looking at him as if she could see clear inside of his head, or maybe as if she recognized him as someone she'd known in some distant past life—

And wasn't *that* the biggest load of bullshit his addled mind had ever come up with—probably because it had been way too long since he'd last gotten laid.

But then she smiled at him, pushing her long, dark hair over one shoulder, and somewhere, very nearby, angels sang and fireworks went off, because she was looking at him as if she, too, could not believe the connection they had, just from gazing at one another.

"Will, right?" She held out her hand. "I'm Dolphina Patel. What can I do for you?"

Her voice was like music and touching her hand was like coming home, and Will knew that he was so screwed, because this wasn't just about sex. No, he, the big cynic, Mr. I-Can-Walk-Away-From-Anyone, had just fallen head over heels in love at first sight.

"Dolphina," the tall, chisel-faced, red-haired man Robin had told her was named Will repeated. "Like the fish?"

Okay. So much for that point-zero-four-second fantasy that Dolphina had finally found her soul mate. It must've been a trick of the dim afternoon light, creating what had felt like a genuine spark.

It was almost funny—this man was the exact opposite of what she would have thought of as her type. Assuming that someone who'd had exactly three and a half boyfriends in her entire life had a type. Especially considering that one and a half of those boyfriends had been back when she was in seventh grade, when boyfriends were procured by hastily scribbled notes and conversations held at a distance, through third party negotiators.

Redheaded Will had a scruff factor of around eight, which was *so* not her thing. Even though he was wearing a jacket and tie, she got the sense that they were borrowed. He smelled good, though, and he was close-shaven, his cheeks and chin smooth. But there was something about him—in the hard planes and angles of his lean face and in the gleam in his hazel eyes—that made her think he'd done some hard living somewhere down the line.

He was also older than she'd first thought, probably closer to forty than her own almost-thirty.

She took her hand back. "Dolphina, like the sea mammal. If it's too much for you, feel free to call me Ms. Patel."

"I'm sorry," he said. He really did have a very nice smile for someone who was either genuinely stupid or stupidly trying to be funny. "A dolphin's not a fish—of course. I must've been stupified by your beauty."

Funny he should use that word . . . But okay. "That's been known to happen," she told him, as flippantly as she could manage. "That's why I work for gay men. My powers of stupification don't seem to affect them."

He laughed. "She's funny, too. Well, well."

"And she hates being referred to in the third person." Dolphina led him out of the living room and toward the front parlor. "My calendar's in here. What am I setting up again?"

"Something post-work," he said. "Maybe drinks?"

She looked at him. "Robin said coffee in the morning."

"Or drinks," Will said. "Either was fine with him."

"He's a recovering alcoholic," she said flatly. She narrowed her eyes at him. "How could you be at this party and not know that?"

As she watched, he was clearly trying to think up a good excuse. But he ended up just shaking his head. "I'm obviously factually challenged. I have to confess that I really don't know very much about Robin. I promise I'll do more research before our meeting."

"Hmph," she said as she flipped through her calendar. "How's Tuesday at ten thirty?"

"Ooh," he said, making a face as he wandered around the office, taking in the books on the shelves and the colorful painting that hung above the fireplace mantel. "No chance to make it Monday?"

Monday, Robin would be on set all day. "You really don't want to talk to him when he's in character."

"Well, actually, that might be—" Will started.

"I'm sorry," Dolphina said. "I was trying to be tactful. Robin's been trying to get me to work on that. But the truth is, Robin doesn't talk to anyone while he's filming. Except for his fellow actors and the director, and maybe the A.D. And Jules, of course. And me. Sometimes. But not you. No offense."

He was smiling at her again, and if she hadn't known enough to keep her distance from handsome, scruffy, silver-tongued men who could twinkle their eyes on command, her heart might've skipped a beat. But no. If she were looking to get plastered against the windshield of tragic romantic reality, there were about a half a dozen perfectly good Navy SEALs waiting for her in the living room.

"Tuesday at ten thirty is fine," he told her as he wandered toward her desk and picked up the envelope that was atop the unopened mail sitting next to her computer. "Thank you."

She took it out of his hands. "No touching."

He looked down at her and once again their gazes seemed to lock. And there it was again, that electric spark. "Do you often get mail from 1600 Pennsylvania Avenue?" he asked.

Dolphina looked at the return address. Huh.

"That's a response to their wedding invitation," Will realized. "Did Robin really invite President Bryant to his wedding?"

Jules and Robin had indeed done just that. It was, Jules had reassured Robin, merely an inclusive gesture. Bryant was, after all, his boss's boss, which made him Jules's boss, too. But, bottom line, there was no way the U.S. President was actually going to attend.

Which was a good thing—because both Jules and Robin wanted a small wedding. A quiet, private ceremony with family and friends—really just a few dozen more people than were at today's party.

The President's attendance would turn the affair into a three-ring circus, both in terms of security and media coverage. If they thought they had to fight off hoards of reporters now . . . God forbid the President showed up—there'd be no way they could keep the press from attending.

"Hot damn." Will, meanwhile, had jumped to conclusions. "The President is coming to Robin and Jules's wedding."

"His secretary probably just sent his regrets," Dolphina said.

"Open it and see," he urged.

She looked at him. "I won't be able to tell you what it says. It's not your business."

"Yeah, but don't you want to know?"

She put the envelope down. "I'll find out later." On second thought, she took the entire pile of mail and put it into her desk drawer, locking it shut.

She picked up her calendar book again. "Kuhlman or Hartz?"

"Excuse me?" he said.

"Your last name." Dolphina again looked up at him. There were two different Williams on the party's guest list. Well, three, including little Billy Richter, Robin's pint-sized nephew. William Kuhlman was the real estate agent who'd helped Robin and Jules find this amazing house. William Hartz worked for the FBI.

Her Will was hesitating, and she could see from his eyes that he was weighing the pros and cons of . . . lying to her?

She flipped to her guest list and quickly checked and . . . Of course. William Kuhlman was attending the shower with his wife, Jodie.

Nice.

Apparently he *was* her type—already married.

She waited.

He gazed at her.

She lifted an eyebrow.

"What the hell," he finally said. "It's Schroeder." He spelled it for her as she continued to stare at him. "It's German," he added, as if that would somehow make it more believable.

"Really?" she said. "Because Kuhlman sounds German, too."

"Kuhlman?" he asked. "Yeah, it probably is. Who's Kuhlman?"

"You are," she said. "William Kuhlman."

He laughed. "Wait a sec—you mean Bill, Robin's real estate agent? I just met him in the kitchen. Nice guy. Glasses. Goatee?" She must've continued to exude skepticism, because he took out his wallet. "You want to see my driver's license?" He held it out to her.

She took it. Looked at it. *William T. Schroeder, six feet one inches tall, born May 22, 1967, 214 Massachusetts Avenue . . .* She turned, flipping on the office copy machine, slipping the license onto the glass and closing the lid.

"Hey," he said.

"You don't mind, do you?" Dolphina asked him as she pushed the button to copy his driver's license.

"I, uh, kind of do," he said as the machine whirred.

She turned it off again, then handed him back his license and put the copy she'd made in with her notes.

"You can have my phone number, too, if you really want it." He put his wallet back into his pocket.

"Considering Jules works for the FBI," Dolphina said sweetly, "I'm sure we'll be able to find you. If we have a reason to."

"Great," he said, although he didn't sound as if he meant it.

Because William Schroeder was not on today's guest list. A fact that he clearly knew, since party-crashers tended to know that they were crashing a party.

Despite the fact that this wedding shower was being held here in Jules and Robin's home, the official hosts were both Robin's sister

Jane and her husband, Cosmo, and Jules's best friends, Sam Starrett and Alyssa Locke. Dolphina had helped them by being in charge of the guest list and all the RSVPs that had come in.

She'd done significantly better with *that* task than she had with her job of getting the grooms to the surprise party in something other than their underwear.

"So, do *you* drink?" Will asked her now.

Dolphina found herself blinking at him. Surely he knew that *she* now knew he'd crashed this party . . .

"Because if you do, maybe we could, you know, go out for drinks some time," he finished.

"You're asking me out," she clarified.

"Yes, I am." He was definite. "The stupification's wearing off. I find I'm regaining my usual working vocabulary, and I would like very much to go out with you. I don't suppose you want to copy your driver's license for *me*?"

That was so not going to happen. "Thank you, but no, Mr. Schroeder," she told him. "Both to the copying and the drink. I'm very much unavailable. For the entire rest of my life."

"So . . ." he said, actually settling in to talk, perching on the arm of the leather sofa that was under the bay windows that looked out onto the busy street. "You're seeing someone and it's serious?"

"No," she said. "I'm not. But thanks for offering that as an option for a tactful excuse. Thing is, I'm just not feeling the need for tact right now."

He laughed. "Then you're just . . . not interested?" he asked. "Because maybe I'm wrong, but I'm picking up what feels like at least a little bit of interest."

"Absolutely," she admitted truthfully. "I think you're very interesting. Too interesting."

"Too interesting," he repeated. "Is that really possible?"

"You tell me," she countered, sitting down behind her computer and turning it on. "Or should I just Google you?"

He was so busted—there was no way now that he was going to just sit there and pretend that he wasn't.

"Look," he started to say, but whatever he was going to tell her, he didn't get a chance to finish.

"Hey, Dolph." That was Jules shouting down the hall. "Is Robin with you?"

"No, he's not," she shouted back. They really had to get an intercom. "He said something about giving someone a tour of the house?"

"Will you do me a favor?" Jules came down the hall to ask at lower decibel levels. He was carrying Robin's little nephew on his hip. "Oh, hey, hi, how are you?" he greeted Will. "I'm sorry, Dolph, but would you mind running to the third floor, see if he's maybe locked in the library again?" He rolled his eyes at Will. "We have a slight issue with the locking mechanisms on the doors. They're all really old—the wood's mahogany. They're beautiful, but you never know when a knob's going to just . . . come off in your hand. You pull and . . . If it happens when the door's closed . . . you're screwed."

"Don't go anywhere," Dolphina ordered Will. "Don't talk to him," she likewise ordered Jules.

"What? Why?" she heard Jules ask, clearly bemused, as she took the stairs up, two at a time.

Terrific. Wonderful. Freaking great.

Robin could not believe this.

He was locked in the basement.

He'd been giving a tour of the house to a group of Jules's friends from the FBI, including Gina Bhagat. Gina was an old friend of Jules's who was now married to his boss, Max. Robin had met Max a number of times in work situations, and it was funny. He'd nearly tripped over the man in the kitchen today, and he hadn't recognized him without his dark suit and tie. Wearing jeans and a sweater, smiling, with his arm around his beautiful wife, Max Bhagat seemed like a completely different person.

Gina had been fascinated by the history of Jules and Robin's home—particularly the rumor that the place had been a stop on the underground railroad. Slaves escaping north to Canada had been hidden here, probably in this very basement.

So Gina had wanted to see it.

While they were down here, Robin had noticed that one of the narrow ceiling-level windows had blown open, and a puddle of icy water was collecting on the cellar floor. Since this was the last stop on the house tour, he'd sent his little group back upstairs where it was warm, and went about finding a stepladder so he could push the window shut.

It wouldn't latch, though. He was handy enough when it came to fixing things, and he quickly saw that part of the metal lock had rusted through and snapped off. He ended up jamming a piece of wood against the window, which did the trick of keeping it closed.

He'd put away the ladder and gone up the stairs and . . .

The fricking doorknob came off in his fricking hand.

Jesus, if he didn't love this old house so much, he would hate it. Just last week he'd gotten locked in, up in the third floor library.

And okay. Just because the knob was in his hand didn't mean that he couldn't manipulate the mechanism and open the door and . . .

Thud.

The metal rod and other knob fell out on the other side of the door, leaving nothing for him to grasp and turn. The hole where it had once been was too small for him to fit more than one finger in—his pinky at that—and he couldn't disengage the lock. The hinges, of course, were on the other side.

Robin banged on the door for a while, but the basement entrance was out of the way, in the back of the kitchen mudroom. If the additional door between the mudroom and the kitchen was closed, that, combined with the noise from the party, meant that no one was going to hear him no matter how loudly he banged and shouted.

There was a basement door leading out into the tiny back garden, but it was dead-bolted shut, and there was no key in sight.

And, of course, his cell phone was up in the bedroom that he shared with Jules—plugged into its charger and set on silence. *Let's have a no-cell-phone day, babe.* That had been Robin's brilliant idea, conceived as they hurriedly changed into dry clothes after getting the bejeezus surprised out of them by fifty of their friends and coworkers.

He still had to smile at that expression on Jules's face when he'd realized he'd just told nearly everyone that he knew—including his boss—that he wasn't wearing any underwear.

It was usually Robin who stuck his foot in his mouth that way.

"Welcome to my world," Robin had murmured to Jules, who had laughed as they'd dashed upstairs to get dried off and changed.

But now, after too many minutes of sitting on the chilly basement stairs, just waiting for Jules to notice he was missing, Robin got the ladder out again and went back to the window with the broken latch.

He saw that he could, with just a little effort, knock away the wood frame, and take the entire window out of the wall. The screen came out with the assembly, leaving an open hole that was slightly larger than the window itself.

Larger was good, but larger than tiny was still pretty freaking small.

There was a half-circular stone well outside of that opening. A strip of flower garden—with what looked like bunches of freeze-dried marigold plants, blackened and skeletal—was actually several feet above both that leaf-filled well and the window. If Robin was going to crawl out there—if he really could fit his head and shoulders through the narrow slot—the only way to do it would be backward, with his face to the top of the window, so he could haul himself up, into a sitting position, with his back to the wall of the well.

Good thing he'd been doing his ab work religiously.

The rain was coming down harder now, blowing in onto him, thick and cold.

Robin went up the stairs and hammered on the door. "Hey! I'm locked in down here! Anyone?"

But no one answered.

He went back to the window and rolled up his sleeves.

"We haven't met," Jules said to the man who'd managed to pull Dolphina away from the party—no small feat, that. "I'm Jules, and this is Billy, my soon-to-be nephew-in-law."

"Will," he said, coming over to shake Jules's hand. He had a solid grip and a nice smile. He ruffled Billy's hair. "Hey, I was a Billy when I was little, too."

"No," Billy said.

"Yeah," Jules told the little boy, laughing. "Billy and Will are both nicknames for William. And you met Uncle Robin's friend Bill in the kitchen, remember? He's a William, too. And William's your dad's middle name, right?"

"No," Billy said, but he nodded his head yes.

"Yeah, you're just being silly now," Jules said.

"You silly, too, Unca Jules," Billy told him.

"I am very good at being silly. You got that right," Jules agreed as the little boy hugged him hard around the neck. Yeah, he could get used to this. "So why doesn't Dolphina want me to talk to you?" Jules asked the larger William.

"I asked her out," Will admitted. "Maybe she's afraid I'm going to talk you into pledging my troth for me. Assuming that . . . troths still get pledged."

Jules laughed. "And I would do that for you because . . . ?"

"You're a romantic," Will told him. "You're getting married in a month to a guy who's over the moon about you. I'm not gay, but even I'm a little jealous after talking to him. He loves you very much, you know."

Jules nodded. "I *do* know, but thanks. It's always nice to hear."

Will was looking at him in the weirdest way, like he was about to confess to being the real Boston Strangler or something equally awful. But then he said, "You've got something really good going, and . . . it's human nature to try to infect all your single friends with your couple-itis. And here I am—new to the scene, but smitten with your inimitable Ms. Patel. She, in turn, finds me interesting. Her word choice. Unfortunately, she's going to have a vastly different word for me after she comes back downstairs. One that Billy probably shouldn't hear."

"Because . . . you're a writer," Jules realized, and Will nodded.

"I am," he admitted.

Oh, this was not going to be good.

Jules looked at Billy. "Go and find your daddy, okay?"

"No," Billy said, but again he nodded yes, and Jules put him down, watching as the little boy ran into the living room. It was only then that he turned back to Will.

"What paper are you with?" Jules asked, as he heard the sound of Dolphina's footsteps, coming lightly down the stairs.

"Robin's not up there," she called down, as Will reached into his inside jacket pocket and pulled out a business card.

It was bent and slightly battered around the edges, kind of like the man himself. *William Schroeder*, Jules read. The Boston Globe.

Oh, good. The *Globe*.

"Who invited you?" he asked the man, working to keep his voice even.

"No one," Will said. "I just . . . heard about the party and thought I'd show up. See if I couldn't get in. See who I could talk to."

Robin. Damnit, he'd said he'd talked to Robin.

"So what do you want?" Jules asked. "Money? Because *that's* not going to happen."

"What? No. God." It was possible that Will really was offended. Or, he was simply a good bullshit artist. "I just, I don't know, wanted to give you a chance to comment. On the record. It doesn't have to be right now, we could set something up for later in the week. Do it right. Sit down, the three of us, and do a real interview."

Jules was already shaking his head. "I think you better leave."

Dolphina was back, and she was looking from Will to Jules and back. "Interview?" she said, horror in her voice.

Jules handed her Will's card. To her credit, she didn't start to scream. But she was a good outside-of-the-box thinker, and she immediately started brainstorming. "Can we have him arrested?" she asked. "He crashed the party. He didn't break and enter, but you don't need to do that to make it a crime, do you? Home invasion. Isn't that what it's called?"

"I'm betting someone invited him in," Jules said.

"Yeah, but it's not like he's a vampire," she countered hotly. "He knew he wasn't really invited, yet he came in anyway." She turned to Will. "You should be ashamed of yourself."

"I guess hooking up for drinks is off the table," Will said.

"You think?" Dolphina said. "Can we sue him?" she asked Jules. "Or how about if we just kill him and bury him in the basement?"

"Now, that *is* a crime," Jules pointed out. "Mr. Schroeder was just leaving."

"I'd love to get a comment from you," Will said, "at least about the news that the President's going to be attending your wedding."

Jules looked sharply at Dolphina.

But she was shaking her head. "We received his reply today," she told him. "But it hasn't been opened."

That was the last thing they needed right now. Not just the President attending—which would be bad enough—but news of it leaking out before they organized their game plan.

"Time to go," Jules told Will. "Do me a favor please, Dolph, and just . . . go find Robin?"

It was then that the doorbell rang and kept ringing as if someone insane were out on the front porch.

The locked door handle rattled, too.

Jules pushed aside the curtains on the door's window and . . .

It was indeed someone insane out there—someone insane enough to be in the cold without his jacket on. Robin stood there shivering, and . . . Oh, God. The parts of him that weren't soaking wet were covered in . . . mud? He had leaves matted in hair that was plastered to his head.

But he was grinning at Jules and pointing to the sky, where the rain had finally changed from sleet to big, white, fluffy snowflakes.

Jules yanked open the door. "What happened? Are you all right?"

"I got locked in the basement—had to crawl out the window." Robin shrugged it off. "Look, babe, it's *snowing*!"

His delight was contagious as he pulled Jules outside with him, then jumped down the steps to spin around on the sidewalk in front of their house, snow falling on his face, in his open mouth, in his muddy hair.

"Hey, Will." Robin greeted the reporter with a wide smile, as Will buttoned up his tired-looking overcoat and tucked a scarf in around his neck, preparing to brave the elements. "Leaving so soon?"

"Yeah," Will said. "I gotta go." But he paused, stepping closer to Jules and lowering his voice. "I thought he wasn't drinking anymore," he said.

"He's not," Jules said, his outrage making his voice clipped and tight. "And if you write that he is . . . Let's just put it this way—no one will find your body."

Will looked at him and Jules looked steadily back. *Be afraid. Be very afraid, motherfucker.*

The reporter finally made something that might've been a nod. "I'm going to give you a free pass and pretend I didn't hear that," Will said. "But as far as this goes . . ." He gestured to Robin. "I gotta write what I see."

"He got locked in the basement," Jules told him. He raised his voice. "Robin, what window did you climb out of?"

"The one by the driveway," Robin pointed around the side of the house. "It was smaller than I thought. I kind of got stuck." He grinned at Will then looked down at himself. "What a mess. Don't try this at home, kids." He came over to them. "I grew up in Southern California. This is my first snow, ever, can you believe it?" He gazed out at the street. "Jesus, it's beautiful . . ."

Ah, damn. "Robin," Jules said quietly. "Let Will smell your breath."

Robin looked at him, surprised, and even a little bit hurt.

"I know you're clean," Jules told him. "I know. I trust you. But . . . he's a reporter. And he just asked me if you were drinking."

"What?" Robin said. He turned to Will. "You lying *fuck*." He exhaled, hard, right in Will's face, but then he said, "That's not going to be enough. I mean, I could have had vodka, right?"

"It's enough," Will confirmed, clearly unhappy about all of this. "I believe you."

"No." Robin was adamant. "I'll take a complete drug test and have the results faxed to you." He looked at Jules. He was really upset. "I want to."

"Okay," Jules said quietly.

"Sorry," Will said, turning to look back at the house where Dolphina was standing in the doorway, her arms wrapped around herself. "I'm just . . . doing my job."

"Your job sucks," Dolphina said, and Will nodded.

"Yeah," he said, "sometimes it does." And he walked away.

"Please tell me he's not from the *National Voice*." Robin looked sick, and Jules put his arms around him, to hell with the mud. All of his joy over the still-falling snow had evaporated.

"*Boston Globe*," Jules said. "He said . . . you talked to him?"

Robin nodded. "Oh, yeah. Oh, Jules, oh my God . . ."

"It's all right," Jules tried to reassure him.

But Robin shook his head. "No, it's not. He's going to sound-bite me saying that we like doing it in pig masks."

Jules laughed. "What?"

"It's not funny."

"It kind of is." On a certain level, it was extremely funny. "We should order a case—see how long we can keep this story alive."

Robin sat down heavily on the steps. "Aw, Jesus."

"Just out of curiosity," Jules said, sitting beside him. "*Pig* masks . . . ?"

Robin rolled his eyes. "It's from this movie I saw on pay-per-view back around, I don't know, ten years ago? I was maybe sixteen and it, like, scarred me for life." He laughed his disbelief. "This couple was in their underwear, getting ready to get it on, right? They were wearing these masks and grunting like pigs—don't ask me why. It wasn't erotic—it was horrific, I think intentionally. The man said something, I don't even know what he said, but the woman gets all snitty and goes, *It ruins it for me when you talk.*"

Jules laughed. "Wow."

"Yeah." Robin was finally smiling, too, but it was still rueful. "Ever since then, the idea of having sex in pig masks has been, like, the biggest soft-on I can think of. It just came out of my mouth when I was *talking to the reporter from The Boston Globe.*" He was instantly back in agony-land. "God, I fucked up. He told me he was new in Art's office, and I believed him."

"Why wouldn't you?" Jules put his arms around him again. "He came into our home, and he lied to you . . . Sweetie, really, it's going to be okay. Come on. Let's get you inside and cleaned up. What's done is done." He pulled Robin to his feet.

Dolphina was hovering, right by the front door. She opened it as she saw them coming. "I'm so sorry," she said. "I should have—"

"Not your fault," Jules cut her off. "We—all of us—should have been ready for this kind of thing. It's not going to happen again—let's just focus on that."

"I kind of liked him," Robin said. "Will."

The stupid thing was, Jules had kind of liked him, too.

Dolphina surprised them both. "I hate his freaking guts." She looked at Jules. "I photocopied his driver's license in case you really do want to kill him."

"You threatened to *kill* him?" Robin asked.

"Kill who?" Sam had wandered out of the living room, clearly in search of them. "Dang, who'd you mud wrestle, Boy Wonder?"

"Robin got locked in the basement," Dolphina told Sam. "Right after he unwittingly talked to a reporter who crashed the party."

Sam looked at Jules. Thankfully he didn't say anything to make Robin feel any worse than he obviously already felt. But the look in his eye was pure *here we go . . .*

"Well, go and de-mud, the both of you," he said. "Alyssa says it's time to open your presents, and you don't want to get her mad. Although she'd be a good team member for the murder you're planning."

"No one's going to kill anyone," Jules announced.

"I have to take a drug test so I can send the results to *The Boston Globe*," Robin reminded them. "Who wants to come watch me pee into a cup? It needs to be someone besides Jules, because that's just not *quite* humiliating enough."

And now the look that Sam flashed Jules was sympathetic. "I'll be your witness."

"Thanks," Jules told his friend.

"Before you go upstairs, I think you need to know," Dolphina said, and they all stopped and looked at her. She took a deep breath. "The President and Mrs. Bryant are planning to attend your wedding."

Jules started to laugh. Of course they were.

Sam said it all, in one heartfelt word that he Texified into two syllables. "Shee-yit."

"You said they wouldn't come," Robin said, looking at Jules.

"Oops," Jules said.

"It's a huge honor." Dolphina tried to bright side it.

"But you didn't want a big wedding." Robin was worried, not about himself, but about Jules. "It's going to have to be big now. There'll be Secret Service and—"

"I don't care." Jules interrupted him. "I just want to marry you. I just want to stand up in a church, and tell everyone that I'm going to love you forever. I don't give a shit how many dozen whirling ninjas with fiery batons are spinning in circles around us."

"Well, that's good," Sam pointed out. "Because the ninjas—they're working up their routine, starting right about now."

PART THREE

thanksgiving

TUESDAY, NOVEMBER 20
BOSTON, MASSACHUSETTS

BAD THINGS CAME IN THREES.

Robin couldn't remember where he'd heard that or who it was who'd repeated it so often during his childhood that it should now take up so much real estate inside of his head.

But here he was, waiting for the third bad shoe to drop.

The first bad thing—the grim news from Art Urban—had been quickly eclipsed by the day's second bad thing: Will Schroeder's so-called "news" article.

It had finally come out today—two fricking days before Thanksgiving. Only it wasn't in *The Boston Globe*. It was in Satan's Weekly, that mother of all trashy tabloids, the *National Voice*. And it was *so* much worse than Robin had even dreamed possible, because along with including fictionalized information, Schroeder had also sold the recording of their conversation to TMZ dot-com. And there it was—confirmation of nearly everything Robin was quoted as saying in that nasty-ass article. It made it seem as if the rest of the crap Schroeder had written was also true.

Robin hadn't had a chance to talk to Jules about it yet, but his fiancé would probably try to put a positive spin on it, or at least turn it into a joke. Maybe he'd put a pig mask on later tonight when they were getting ready for bed. And then, when Robin was laughing in horror, Jules would say something like, *Look, it happened. You said some things to someone that you shouldn't have trusted, but anyone who listens to that recording is also going to get it all in context. And frankly, Robin, I thought what you said was beautiful. You love me—no one who listens to the tape is going to doubt that.*

Yeah, but what about all the people who read the article but didn't have Internet access? Or the so-called TV news stations that broadcast sound bites without any context?

If Robin ever so much as *saw* Will Schroeder again, he was going to rip his lungs out, a la Sam Starrett.

Of course, that wasn't likely to happen, since today's third bad thing was probably going to be Robin getting hit by a bus.

The lights from all of the trendy shops on Newbury Street sparkled through the lightly misting rain. Robin picked up his pace as he circumnavigated a stalled group of Berklee students. He had to use fancy footwork to dodge some early Christmas shoppers who were moving with the determination of heat-seeking missiles.

It wasn't the cold temperatures that made winter seem so different here in Boston, but rather the fact that the sun went down so damn early in the afternoon. It was only going to get worse, or so Jules had told Robin. By the winter solstice, the days were going to be ridiculously short.

The nights decadently long.

Which made it pretty perfect timing to have a wedding night.

At the corner of Dartmouth, Robin crossed Newbury Street carefully, heading toward his and Jules's favorite spot to meet for dinner. And he found Jules standing outside under the streetlight, talking on his cell phone, wearing his FBI agent face.

Crap, that wasn't just his regular FBI agent face. Something bad had happened.

What a surprise. *Clunk* went that third extremely fugly shoe.

Robin clearly saw the words Jules was about to tell him. They were there in his eyes, as he shut his phone and turned to Robin. "I have to go."

"Where?" Robin asked, because that was not a *I have to skip dinner and go back to the office, I'll be home around midnight* face. No, this was the big one, the *I have to catch a plane* face. And yes, that *was* Jules's overnight bag on his shoulder.

"Afghanistan," Jules told him.

Oh, God. "When?" Another stupid question because it was clear the answer was *now.*

"My flight leaves as soon as I can get to the airport," Jules confirmed. "They're holding it for me."

Robin nodded. *But it's our first Thanksgiving* . . . Things not to say, particularly since Jules's obvious regret was already dripping off of him. "I'll ride with you to Logan." He turned to the street, to hail a taxi.

"I'll be on the phone the entire time," Jules told him, as, yes, his cell phone began to ring, as if the sound effects crew had heard his cue. "It's probably better if you don't."

"Better for who?" Robin turned to ask as a cab swerved to the curb. Try as he might, he was unable to keep his temper from flaring. "You? Because it's sure as hell not better for me." He faltered. "Unless you really don't want me to go with you . . ."

Jules's entire heart went into his eyes. "I'd love it if you rode with me," he admitted quietly as he silenced his phone without answering it. "But I know you have to get back to work. This time of night, traffic's going to suck. I didn't want you to have to—"

"Just get in the cab," Robin told him, climbing in first.

WEDNESDAY, NOVEMBER 21

Dolphina was stunned. She couldn't believe this. "What did Jules say?" she asked.

Robin was sitting on the sofa in the front parlor office, dressed in sweatpants and a T-shirt, his feet bare and his hair a mess.

She'd been surprised to find him still at home when she'd popped in to supervise the morning's grocery delivery.

"You should tell me when the shooting schedule changes," she'd admonished him when he'd staggered into the kitchen for coffee, clearly right out of bed. She'd obviously woken him up, and was afraid she'd interrupted a lazy, sleep-late morning with Jules. God knows with their combined work schedules and the ongoing construction of their bathroom, they didn't get enough of those.

But Jules was out of town—way out of town. And the shooting schedule had been more than merely changed.

Robin now was staring at the framed picture that hung over the fireplace mantel, the one he and Jules had bought early in their relationship, during a weekend trip to Mexico. He finally shifted his gaze to Dolphina, who was sitting at her desk. "I didn't tell Jules."

"Why not?" Now she was doubly stunned.

"Because he was on his way to Af-fucking-ghanistan." Robin's tone implied that she was mentally challenged, and maybe she was, because this didn't make any sense. None of it, including Robin's keeping a secret from Jules. "I didn't want to distract him," he added miserably. "I mean, God . . ."

"How could they cancel your show?" she asked. Okay, sure, the ratings were low, but *Boston Marathon* was critically acclaimed. *TV Guide* was doing a feature next week, calling it the "Best Little Show No One's Watching."

"Apparently it was easy. They called up Art and they said, *it's cancelled*," Robin told her morosely. "We'll finish up this episode after Thanksgiving, put it on the DVD. These last three we've done won't get aired." He shook his head in disgust.

Robin had told her weeks ago that some of his best work was in those recent episodes.

"What are you going to do?" she asked him now.

"Pray to a higher power that Jules comes safely home," he said. "Tonight, if possible."

Dolphina sneaked a look at her watch. According to Jules's flight schedule, he'd only just arrived in Kandahar a few hours ago. Even if he turned right around, which was unlikely, he wouldn't make it home tonight.

"I meant what are you going to do about the fact that you're suddenly available for other jobs," she rephrased her question. Robin had had a recent slew of movie offers, all secondary roles, some of them enticing. But all were being filmed either in Hollywood or on location somewhere far from Boston.

He stood up. "My partner's in harm's way. You really think I'm thinking about anything else?"

The situation in Afghanistan was bad. According to the twenty-four-hour news networks, al Qaeda had captured five doctors and nurses from an Army field hospital—the modern equivalent of a MASH unit. They were holding them hostage, threatening beheadings, if a team of Rangers didn't back off from where they had a group of terrorists pinned down in a mountain cave.

Jules had gone with his boss, Max Bhagat, to aid in the negotiations—even though the U.S. held tightly to its policy of never negotiating with terrorists. Dolphina knew that Jules's job in a case like this was to help stall. Give the Spec Op teams time to create and facilitate a rescue plan.

Jules was probably going to stay safely in Kandahar. Although, these days, with the resurgence of the Taliban, not even Kandahar was really all that safe.

"I'm sorry." Dolphina shook her head. "I just thought maybe a distraction would help."

"Thank you." Robin somehow managed to smile. "I know. It just . . . Doesn't."

"Robin, this is what Jules does," she said as gently as she could. "You're going to have to get used to it."

To his credit, he nodded. "I know. Let's just find a distraction that doesn't involve me planning to spend a solid month away from home, okay?"

I could schedule a spa day, she was about to suggest. Or they could do a twenty-four-hour *Buffy the Vampire Slayer* marathon. And, oh hell. They were going to have to discuss what to do about tomorrow's Thanksgiving dinner. Robin and Jules had invited their friends Sam and Alyssa, but they'd already been called away to Afghanistan, too. Jules's co-worker Yashi—Joe Hirabayashi—had been planning to attend the meal with his widowed father. And Dolphina was on the guest list, too.

Dolphina suspected Robin and Jules were trying to set her up with Yashi, no doubt because they'd noticed the funk she'd fallen into after the debacle with that anti-Christ of reporters, Will Schroeder.

It wasn't the lack of a man in her life that had made her depressed, but rather her ongoing relentless attraction to men who turned out to be world-class liars. She should offer her services to Jules and the FBI.

Just put her in a room with a bunch of men, and she would naturally gravitate toward the ones with the biggest, ugliest secrets.

Before she could figure out the best way to bring up the subject of Thanksgiving dinner without rubbing Robin's face in the fact that Jules wouldn't be there to share it with them, the doorbell rang.

The look on Robin's face was one Dolphina would remember for the rest of her life. She knew exactly what he was thinking—that if something were ever to happen to Jules, Robin would be notified in person, not through a phone call. And now someone had come, unannounced, to the door.

"Don't answer that," he said, as if that would keep any bad news away.

"It's probably just . . ." But she couldn't think of who it might be. The mail carrier had already come, and they weren't expecting any packages from FedEx.

Flowers. It was entirely possible that Jules, an incredible romantic, would do something thoughtful like send Robin a huge bouquet of tulips, his favorite spring flowers, to provide at least a dash of color over these next few bound-to-be-dreary days.

The bell rang again.

Dolphina went into the foyer, pulled back the curtain that covered the window on the old-fashioned door, and . . .

"Oh, Jesus," Robin said.

It was Joe Hirabayashi, standing out there—Yashi—who worked with Jules. As he met Dolphina's eyes through the glass, her heart fell. Whatever he was here for, it wasn't going to be good.

Robin sat down heavily on the stairs leading up to the second floor. "Oh, fuck, please, no . . ."

Dolphina opened the door, and Yashi, bless him, didn't waste time with small talk. He just looked past her, directly at Robin. "I spoke to Jules twenty minutes ago," the FBI agent reported, and Dolphina's heart started beating again. She could only imagine the relief Robin was feeling at that news. But then Yashi went on. "And he was uninjured. He's with Max and Deb Erlanger. The hotel where they were staying as well as Spec Op HQ have both been bombed, but they're okay," he repeated. "But more shit's going down—the entire city's under attack, and as of about fifteen minutes ago we lost both cell and satellite communications. The story of the bombing is about to hit the news. I didn't want you to hear it there first."

Robin nodded, his face pale. "How bad is it?" he asked.

Yashi didn't lie. "It's bad," he admitted.

Dear God. "Please come in," Dolphina said.

"I can't," Yashi told her. She'd met him a number of times, and he'd always been rather deadpan, as if his average pulse rate was around twenty beats per minute. But now he clearly had some adrenaline going. "I'm on my way to Logan. I gotta get to D.C. I really shouldn't have stopped here, but . . . It was on my way, and I wanted you to know. He's okay, you got that, Robin? We're going to do everything we can to get him out."

"Yeah," Robin said. "Thank you."

"And in the meantime," Yashi was trying to reassure him, but there was definitely worry in the man's eyes, "he's with Max and Deb, and the three of them are the best field agents I've ever worked with."

"Right," Robin said. "That's good."

"Do yourselves a favor," Yashi told them both. "Don't watch the news. All they do is speculate, and you don't need that. I'll call you when I hear something."

Dolphina closed the door behind him, and turned to look at Robin.

But he'd already gone into the living room.

And turned on CNN.

Will knew that there was never going to be a good time to do this.

So he might as well do it now, while he had a sitter with Maggie. He'd do this, and then he'd stop at the grocery store and get the fixings for a real Thanksgiving dinner. Not that he'd ever cooked a turkey before.

But there was a first time for everything, and God knows the past few days—hell, this entire year—had been chock full of firsts.

Will rolled his neck and shoulders as he stood on Robin Chadwick's front porch, trying to relieve some of his tension. But that wasn't going to happen, so he finally just did it. He reached out his finger and rang the bell.

He didn't have to wait long before the curtain was pulled back and . . . The door opened to reveal Dolphina Patel, who was no doubt working extremely late.

Damn. Another of his reasons for doing this now had to do with his reasoning that at least Dolphina wouldn't be around to witness his groveling. At least he wouldn't have to bear the sting of seeing scorn and disgust in her eyes.

Yeah, so much for that hope.

She was even more beautiful than he'd remembered, which was saying something. Just looking at her made his chest hurt.

"You scared me." She was furious, which was pretty much the way he'd left her, the last time he'd been here. "It's all right," she called back into the house. "It's no one."

Ouch.

"I'm sorry to bother you," he said. "Are Robin and Jules at home?"

"Not for you, scumbag." She closed the door in his face.

Will sighed and rang the bell again.

The door opened almost immediately. "Stop that," Dolphina whispered. "Go away. He doesn't need this right now. Shoo." She waved at him, like he was some kind of scumbag of the stray dog variety.

He stood his ground. "This is important."

She laughed. "Oh, really?"

"It is."

"If you don't leave, I'll call the police."

"Who is it, Dolph?" That was Robin's voice, coming into the foyer behind her.

"Prepare to die, asshole," Dolphina whispered to Will, and with a flourish, she opened the door wider.

Robin actually laughed when he saw him standing there. "Wow," he said. "You've got some balls."

Will held out the file he was clutching in his nearly frozen fingers. One of these days, preferably before winter ended, but probably not without the help of a support group, he was going to accept the fact that he was no longer living in tropical Indonesia, and get himself a pair of gloves.

"I didn't write the story that was in the *Voice*," he talked fast, because he knew he was probably not going to get another chance to say this.

"It had your by-line," Dolphina pointed out.

"Yeah, but I didn't write it," he said. "I wanted you to see the story I *did* write, the one for the *Globe*. They didn't run it, because of the fucking *National Voice*. Excuse me," he said to Dolphina. "But there's no other word that describes it quite as accurately. My computer was hacked and my notes were stolen. I wrote a second story, today, about how it happened and who from the *Voice* was involved. It's in here, too. It was supposed to run tomorrow, but it's getting pushed off the page by a friend's story about, well, more volatile world events. He's in the thick of things, so . . ."

Robin actually reached out and took the file. "Afghanistan," he said.

Damn, but the actor was exuding grim. Will hadn't expected Robin to be friendly, but this was intense. He nodded. "In a nutshell."

"Your friend is actually over there?" Robin asked him.

"He's more like a frenemy," Will admitted, "but yeah. Jack Lloyd. He's in Kandahar, where the fighting's going down. He's been sending out e-mail updates to everyone at the *Globe*. It's crazy, what's happening."

"I've been watching the news," Robin said.

"They're hours behind," Will told him. "They're good at breaking big events, but not so good on the details."

"No shit," Robin said. "How's he getting e-mail out? Jack."

"I have no idea," Will said.

Robin nodded. He tapped the file. "You want me to read this?"

"That *is* why I brought it over here." Will wasn't looking for forgiveness as much as understanding. Of course there was also the little matter of the digital recording that he'd sold to TMZ, as an attempt to let the world see what Robin had actually said, in context. A check for the full amount of the sale—ten thousand dollars, in Robin's name—was in the file, too. There was no way Will was going to keep that. He hadn't sold the tape for profit, but rather in the name of truth.

"Why don't you come in," Robin surprised him by saying.

"Robin." Dolphina's voice held a warning. Will made the mistake of glancing at her. Her eyes were filled with concern, but then she turned to gaze at him. And he'd thought it was cold out here on the porch. After that look, it was possible that he was going to crumble into little shards of ice. "Don't."

It wasn't quite clear whether Dolphina was speaking to Robin, or warning Will against coming inside.

But Will did it. With one foot and then the other. And then Robin closed the door behind him and he was back inside Chadwick's beautiful old house, standing in the very same foyer as Dolphina Patel—which was something of a shock to his system, even with the icicles dripping from her palpable hatred.

But the surprise hits just kept on coming. "If you show me Jack's e-mails," Robin told Will, "if you hang out here tonight, and tell me when news comes in from him, I'll read your file in the morning."

What was going on? Will looked at Dolphina, but she was shaking her head. "Robin, you're not going to find out anything more than you already know." She looked at Will. "Please just leave."

But Robin had hold of his arm. The man had one hell of a grip. "Do we have a deal?" he asked.

"Yeah," Will said, and not just because he was suddenly aware that Robin's muscles were not merely for show. "I just have to call my babysitter, make sure she can stay. If not, well . . . I don't live that far away. It'll only take me about thirty minutes to go pick up Maggie and get back here. I mean, if that's okay. She could just crash on the sofa."

"That's fine with me." Robin was already leading the way into the front room where Dolphina kept her desk. "Here. You can use Dolph's computer. If you e-mail him, do you think he'll respond?"

He was talking about Jack again. "If he's online," Will said. "Sure." Jack would certainly be up for some heavy-duty gloating over the fact that he was in the right place at the right time for the story of the year.

"*You* have a *daughter*?" Dolphina followed them. She asked her question in the same tone that she might've used to inquire about a roach population explosion in his apartment.

"She's my sister's kid," Will explained. "She's twelve." He wasn't sure why he'd told her that. What difference did it make if Mags was twelve versus any other age?

"You live with a twelve-year-old." Dolphina snickered. Her tone had probably been snarky disbelief, but Will preferred thinking she was bemused.

Because it *was* a bemusing concept—his sharing an apartment with a twelve-year-old girl.

And with that thought, he knew why he'd told Dolphina that Mags was twelve. Because Maggie was the reason he'd crashed that wedding shower. Maggie was the reason he did everything these days. He wanted Dolphina Patel to know that, and to fully understand what happened with those fuckers from the *National Voice*, and even to forgive him.

And okay, honestly? He wanted her to fall into his arms and, yes, into his bed, which ironically was not going to happen even if a multitude of miracles occurred—because as of two months ago, Will had a twelve-year-old living with him.

Truth be told, he'd come here tonight not just because he wanted to set things right between himself and Robin and Jules. He'd come because a significant chunk of him hoped that Robin, or probably more likely Jules, would do more than understand—and somehow, some way talk Dolphina into giving Will a chance.

Damn, he was a fool.

He was still hoping that Jules Cassidy would help him pledge his freaking troth.

"Where *is* Jules tonight?" he asked as he used Dolphina's laptop to sign online.

Neither of them answered right away, and he glanced up over his shoulder at Robin.

"He's in Kandahar," Robin finally told him.

And suddenly, with a chill that came from neither the north wind nor Dolphina's eyes, Will understood exactly what was happening here.

Max's wife, Gina, called at nine o'clock—about an hour after Will had arrived. "Unlock your front door," she told Robin. "We're in your driveway. I didn't want to ring the bell."

"We" was not just Gina and her toddler daughter, Emma, but also a woman Robin had never met before, who introduced herself as Joan DaCosta.

"We're the East Coast contingent," Joan told Robin breezily as she enveloped him in a hug. She was tall and big-boned, and it wasn't until he hugged her back that he realized she wasn't queen-sized, she was pregnant. "We're on point, as the froggish types like to say. The West Coasties'll take a bit longer to arrive—and you are totally confused, aren't you?"

She had a pretty face, with lively dark eyes and a warm smile. Robin liked her already, but he still had no clue who she was.

"I'm Mike Muldoon's wife," she explained, although it didn't help that much. "Lieutenant Muldoon?" She tried again. "He's the officer who's leading the SEAL team that's going in there to get Jules out. Not *try* to get him out—*get* him out. Next time that Yashi guy uses the word *try*, you have my permission to smack him upside the head. Mike doesn't *try*, he gets the job done. He'll bring Jules home."

"And Max and Deb. Let's bring them home, too, please," Gina said, coming down the stairs after she'd tucked her daughter into one of the guest-room beds on the second floor. She looked exhausted, her beautiful face drawn with her own worry, but still she managed to smile at Robin. "You hanging in, Boy Wonder?"

Robin nodded, managing a smile, too. Sam Starrett's nickname for him had clearly made the rounds.

"Robin's already got some friends over," Joan told Gina, giving Robin another squeeze. "It doesn't surprise me that Jules would find himself a smart one."

"You know Jules?" he asked.

"Honey," Joan said. "*Everyone* knows Jules. And usually he's the one saving everyone else's butts."

"I'm going to make some tea," Gina announced. "Do you mind if I . . . ?"

"Make yourself at home." Robin was still trying to make sense of his sudden houseguests. "So, you flew all the way up from D.C.?" He followed Gina into the kitchen, leaving Joan with Dolphina. Will was still in the front parlor, glued to the computer. There'd been no word yet from Jack.

"We wanted to be with you," Gina said simply as she rummaged through his cabinets, looking for tea bags.

"Mugs are to the right of the microwave," he told her as she came up with a box of vanilla chai—Jules's favorite. His heart clenched. *Please God, keep him safe . . .*

"Thanks," Gina said.

"Joan doesn't even know me," he pointed out.

She crossed the kitchen and filled the tea kettle with water from the bubbler. "Yeah, but she knows what it's like to be in our shoes. She's married to a SEAL. She's white-knuckled it through reports of downed helicopters and . . . She knows that it's easier with a hand to hold."

"Easier," Robin repeated.

Gina forced a smile. "Marginally." She paused, and then said, "Jules asked me to do this, you know. Especially for your first time. He was concerned and . . . He understands how excruciating the waiting can be—for news, for results. He asked me to organize a support group if something like this ever happened—if he was out there and communications went down. He asked me to remind you that he's very good at taking care of himself. He also wanted you to remember how much he loves you. And if there's ever a time that he *doesn't* come home . . ." Her voice faltered. She had to be thinking about her Max, who was out there, too, but she still managed to finish, "it's not because he didn't desperately want to."

And fuck, Robin had been keeping it together—just barely—right up to now. He'd always been mortified by crying in front of other people, but Gina apparently didn't have that problem because she burst into tears. She just suddenly lost it, right there in his kitchen, which in contrast made *him* look as if he weren't crying at all.

Which, come to think of it, was probably why she'd let go.

Robin grabbed her and hugged her—to comfort her, yeah right. And there they stood, clinging to each other. And it was weird, but on some level, he *did* take comfort in knowing that Jules was with Max right now.

And Deb, too. FBI Agent Deb Erlanger was one tough operator.

Gina murmured a reassurance that Robin knew was as much for herself as for him. "They're going to be all right." Her voice was muffled because he was holding her so tightly.

"Yeah," he said. *Please God, let Gina be right . . .*

"Yashi's been updating you, right?" Gina asked from his armpit, where he'd smooshed her.

"They've narrowed down the sector of the city where they think Jules, Max and Deb are, but they still haven't pinpointed their location," Robin repeated the info Yashi had last given him, releasing her slightly.

She pulled back even farther to look at him, the little makeup she wore smudging her face. Her nose was red, too. She was not one of those women who cried beautifully, but she clearly didn't give a crap about that, and he liked her even more for it. "They'll find them," she said.

"Here's something you might not know," Robin told her. "There's a reporter somewhere in Kandahar who managed to send out e-mail communications as recently as six o'clock, our time. Yashi thinks this guy—Jack Lloyd—has access to some kind of landline that still works. Or at least it was working a few hours ago. No one's been able to contact him since. Will—he's here, in the front office, with Dolphina—did you meet him?"

She shook her head, no.

"He's a reporter, so watch what you say in front of him," Robin warned her. "But he's frenemies—his word—with this Jack guy, so . . . Hopefully Jack will e-mail him back."

"That's great," Gina said. "It is. But . . . you need to know that the people they've got looking for Jules and Max? They're very good at what they do. We don't need to help find them. Really, Robin. We just need to wait, which sometimes seems like it's the hardest job of all."

No kidding.

"My mother once asked me, didn't I wish Max was just, like, a postal worker," Gina told him. "And you know what I told her?"

Robin nodded. Like her, he was laughing and still crying a little, too. What a mess.

"Same answer you would give," Gina said. "Right?"

Robin nodded again. Like Gina, he'd fallen in love with a man who ran toward, instead of away from, danger. Although he had to admit, at times like this, the postal worker thing sounded freaking tempting.

At one a.m., Will stood up from Dolphina's desk and went to find Robin.

The house had slowly been filling with women ever since he'd first arrived, and he'd tried to remain as invisible as possible. Thanks to Dolphina, they all knew who he was—the spawn of Satan—and what he'd done. Conversations had stopped the one time he'd gotten up to use the facilities.

It was a miracle that he hadn't been lynched.

Dolphina didn't bother to introduce anyone to him, but he'd recognized Robin's sister, Jane, the Hollywood producer, as she'd arrived. She was with another woman—her mother-in-law. Will deduced that from the fact that everyone greeted the older lady as "Cosmo's mom."

He'd overheard all the others' names—Kelly, Meg, Teri, Van. They were wives of SEALs or former SEALs. There were plenty of children, too, most of them small and asleep in the beds upstairs. There was one teenager—Amy—who reminded him of his own niece, Maggie. Amy had poked her head into the office earlier, no doubt to get a closer look at the evil reporter.

He headed now toward the kitchen, but Dolphina materialized out of nowhere before he even reached the living room.

"Any word, Mr. Schroeder?" she asked, her voice as frosty as her eyes.

"Nothing from Jack yet, Ms. Patel," he answered. "Is Robin . . . ?" He pointed toward the kitchen.

She crossed her arms and blocked his path. "It's better if you just talk to me."

It was not what he wanted, but as was often the case these days, he didn't seem to have a choice. "I have to leave," Will told her. "It's not because I don't want to stay and help, I mean, as much as I *can* help. But my babysitter is about to turn into a pumpkin, so . . ."

She blinked at him. "You said you would go pick up your niece if your sitter couldn't stay."

"Yeah," Will said, scratching his chin. "I did. But that was before I . . ." He shook his head. "Turns out I can't do that. I'm sorry." The temperature dropped about twenty degrees there in the hallway, and it had started out sub-zero.

"But you *said*—"

"I know what I said." His patience snapped. "And I know you

think I'm a scumbag, but you know what? I *would* be one if I brought Maggie back here. My sister Arlene—her mother—is Army Reserve. She's in Iraq. Maggie and I both work overtime to keep the fear at bay, and frankly, coming here and seeing this—" he gestured around them "—would scare her. And God forbid Robin actually gets the news that Jules is—"

"Don't say it." Dolphina cut him off.

"Sorry." He understood more than she knew.

But then there they stood, just staring at each other.

"Please don't get me wrong," Will finally spoke, more quietly now. "I think this is great, I do. Robin is a very lucky man to have this kind of support from his friends. But . . . I'm Maggie's support group. I'm it. And as much as I want to help you, I can't bring her here."

Apparently, he'd rendered Dolphina speechless. For once, she didn't have much to say.

"I'm sorry," she finally managed. And from her sudden inability to bore an icy hole through him with her eyes, it appeared she actually meant it.

"Me, too," Will said quietly. Maggie spent every single day waiting for a precious e-mail from her mom.

"I could babysit," Dolphina said hesitantly. "For you. If that's okay? That way you could stay here. I don't know how realistic it is, but Robin's got this idea that as long as there's a chance you can get in touch with Jack Lloyd . . . Maybe he can somehow help Jules." She shook her head. "At the very least, it gives him hope."

"Hope is good," Will said. "Hope is . . . important."

She met his eyes very briefly. "If this works for you, I'll just . . . get my cell phone and a book. Maybe you could call your sitter and tell her I'm coming over? I'm happy to show her my driver's license when I get there. You know, so she doesn't have to worry about leaving Maggie with some stranger."

Will nodded. "I'll tell her not to copy it though."

Dolphina actually laughed at that, and she even glanced into his eyes again. But then she frowned. "I still hate you," she said. "I want to make that perfectly clear. I'm doing this for Robin."

He nodded. "I remain hated," he reiterated. "Okay. I mean, it's not *really* okay, but it is what it is."

"Write a note for Maggie, too," Dolphina ordered him. "I don't want her waking up and wondering who I am and where you are. I don't want her to be scared."

"Good plan." Will went back into the office, where he'd seen some legal pads on Dolphina's desk.

She followed him. "I won't give her details about what you're doing here," she promised. "Just . . . do me a favor, and if . . . Robin gets bad news . . ." She had to choke the words out. "Don't call me. Just come home so I can leave right away."

"All right," he said, as he scribbled a quick note. He tore the page off the pad and folded it in thirds. "Do you have an envelope?"

She gave him a disbelieving look. "What, do you think I'm going to read it?"

"I know you will," he countered. "That's why I asked for an envelope. It's a note to Maggie. I'd like an envelope. Please."

Dolphina rolled her eyes at him. "MapQuest me directions," she commanded as she opened a cabinet and got out an envelope.

"I can just write them down," he said, doing just that on another sheet of the legal pad. The route from here out to his place in Newton was pretty direct. Over to Comm Ave., and then west . . .

"You want an envelope," she said, holding it up out of his reach. "I want my directions MapQuested."

"Fair enough." He sat behind the computer.

And his e-mail alert started to wail.

Dolphina leaned over his shoulder to look at the monitor. Damn, she smelled good. "What is that?" she asked.

"Jack Lloyd," Will told her, quickly scanning the e-mail Jack had just sent in response to Will's.

Immediate assistance needed, Jack wrote. *Trying to reach the FBI, the Marines—ANY U.S. authority, but not getting through. If you get this, SOS!!! 10 Americans, including FBI agents you asked about, are pinned down in an apartment building. 7 are reporters, all injured in initial bombing. Mobility and speed limited by those injuries—amazing they got as far as they did. But now need help . . .*

Sweet Mary, Mother of God.

Jack and an FBI agent named Deb had managed to escape, the e-mail continued, in an attempt to access Jack's e-mail communications.

The remaining Americans—including Jules and Max—were under direct attack from the insurgents. With limited weapons and ammunition, time was running out.

"Go get Robin," Will ordered Dolphina as he quickly zapped an e-mail back to Jack. *Your e-mail received,* he wrote. *Let me know if you just got mine.*

But Dolphina hadn't moved. She was staring at the computer screen. So Will said it louder as his e-mail alert went off again, as Jack sent him a four-word reply. *E-mail received. Situation dire.* Shit. "Get Robin. We need Yashi on the phone, *right now.* Apparently Jack can't get through to the authorities, but he *can* get through to me. We have to set up a communications relay. Dolphina, *run.*"

She ran.

THURSDAY, NOVEMBER 22
KANDAHAR, AFGHANISTAN

During a lull in the fighting, Howard was the first to say it. "Maybe it's time to surrender."

Jules didn't look up from his position at the cellar window, the weapon he'd taken from the body of a dead Marine—God rest his soul—held at ready. They'd retreated as far as they possibly could. Their current position was strong—outside the window was a small courtyard, surrounded by a high stone wall with barbed wire atop it. There was one gap in the wall where a wooden door had once hung. It was the only way into the part of the building they now occupied.

He and Max had held off the attack for over an hour since Deb had left to get help.

But it wouldn't be long before the insurgents brought in some heavy artillery. As soon as that wall came down, they would be in much deeper shit.

Jules didn't need to turn around to know that Max was shaking his head to the suggestion of surrender. He knew, too, exactly what Max was going to tell Howard and the other reporters.

"Surrender's not an option."

The insurgents who had them pinned were ultimately as surrounded as Jules and Max were. Although the bad guys had superior firepower right now, the U.S. Marines would be coming, and in a matter of days, they would take them down and out. The insurgents were dead men fighting—martyrs for their cause. And dead men didn't take prisoners.

"Go check on the wounded," Max ordered Howard, and the reporter eventually faded back, out of earshot.

Max moved up to the window, shifting closer to Jules. And here it came. The conversation he'd been dreading. If Deb had made it through, help surely would have been here by now.

Max was going to say it—that it was looking more and more likely that Deb hadn't made it out alive.

So Jules spoke first. "Deb's the best. She'll come through."

Of course, even if Deb *had* survived, there was a chance that news reporter Jack Lloyd's miracle phone line was now out. But Max didn't bring that up.

Instead he said, "You should go. Take Howard. Two of you, moving quickly—you could probably make it out. Get help."

"Great," Jules said, his heart sinking, because he knew that what Max was really telling him to do was to rescue himself. "I get to wander the streets of Kandahar with Mr. Whiney, while you get a chopper ride home? I don't *think* so."

Max laughed. "Yeah, I didn't think you'd go for that."

"Damn straight," Jules said.

Max was silent then, and Jules knew he was thinking about his wife, Gina, and their little girl, Emma.

Jules looked at his watch. It was nearly one a.m. in Boston. Robin would have gotten the news that Jules was missing by now. He'd be sitting in their living room, in front of their TV.

Waiting.

They'd planned to get up early on Thanksgiving, get the turkey stuffed and into the oven, before crawling back into bed. God, Jules loved those long, lazy mornings, just sleeping late with his arms around Robin.

Right before the first bomb had gone off, close to twenty hours ago, Max had asked him what he and Robin were planning for their honeymoon.

"You know, we thought we'd stay home for the first part," Jules told Max now. "Of our honeymoon. It seemed kind of dumb to get married and then immediately leave the one state where we're legal. Besides, the construction on our bathroom will finally be done by then." He laughed. "It better be. We were promised Thanksgiving, like it would definitely be finished by now, but it's not. Anyway, second part, a few days after Christmas, we're going to Spain. There's a resort on the coast that's both gay friendly and alcohol free. It got a great review in *Out Traveler.*"

"That sounds nice," Max said. "It sounds . . . really perfect."

"Yes, it does," Jules agreed. It also sounded suspiciously like wishful-thinking speak. Like, we both know we're going to die, so let's pretend we're not by talking about next month's plans.

"Gina's pregnant again," Max told him.

"Wow," Jules said, smiling even though his stomach twisted. Max really did think that they were going to die here today. God, Jules so didn't want to do that to Robin . . . "Congratulations. I guess you're moving up into an expert rating in terms of that baby-making thing. Well done."

Max smiled. "It's still . . . a little too early to talk about with everyone, but . . . I wanted to tell you."

Jules looked at this man who was both his boss and his friend. And he did what he swore he'd never do in a situation like this. He accepted the fact that a possible outcome was that this could be the end for the both of them. Or maybe not both—maybe just one of them. "You should take Howard," Jules said quietly. "*You* should go for help."

"Leave you here."

It wasn't a question, but Jules answered it as if it were. "I can hold the insurgents off." He embraced the lie. "Until you, you know, get help."

But probably more likely until his ammo ran out.

At which point his life, and the lives of all the injured reporters, would end.

Somewhere in Boston, Robin's hair was surely standing up on the back of his neck as Jules acknowledged that option.

And there it came. The next wave of the attack—the unmistakable sound of machine-gun fire. It was as if someone, somewhere—maybe Robin's higher power—had realized that Jules's faith had been shaken.

And holy shit, the wall out front dissolved in a massive explosion that made Jules and Max both pull back from the window. The very foundation of their building shook, and dust and debris filled the air, choking them.

Jules yanked the crewneck of his T-shirt up over his mouth and nose.

Beside him, Max pulled the last of their ammo clips closer, preparing to rock and roll.

And in that instant, Jules could practically hear Alyssa Locke's rich voice, as if his best friend were whispering into his ear. *Rule one: You gotta believe you'll make it out alive.*

Beside him, Max squinted through the settling dust, bracing himself for the attack—for their last stand.

Last stand?

Screw that.

Jules *was* going to see Robin again. He was going to marry the man in less than a month. And Max was going to meet his new baby, and even get plenty of chances to go for child number three. Enthusiastically, if the way Jules had often seen Max smiling at Gina meant anything at all.

"Deb's the best," Jules said again, shouting over the ringing in his ears. "She'll come through. You got a name picked out yet for the baby?"

"Here they come," Max said. And sure enough, there were darker shadows in the dust as the insurgents moved in.

"Not yet, huh?" Jules said, his finger tightening on his trigger, waiting for them to move closer . . . "It's still early. I mean, when's Gina due? May? June? Don't sweat it. You've got plenty of time to find the perfect name."

"Here they come," Max said again.

But they weren't coming closer. They were fading back. And then nothing moved out there, except the dust and the dirt. But it wasn't settling. It was . . . swirling? And that thrumming sound wasn't his blast-punctured eardrum going haywire. It was a helicopter.

No, calling that thing a helicopter was like calling a Tyrannosaurus Rex a lizard. It was a gunship, its weapons suddenly blazing, forcing the insurgents even farther back. There were two other helos, right behind it, doing the helicopter equivalent of riding shotgun.

One of the birds hovered above their recently obliterated courtyard, and a team of BDU-clad men fast-roped down to the ground. They were SEALs—thank you, thank you, sweet baby Jesus. Yeah, and they weren't just any old SEALs—it was Team Sixteen. That was Muldoon, with Cosmo Richter right behind him. Gillman, Jenkins, Zanella—Jules knew them all. Lopez was there, too, carrying a medical kit—he was their hospital corpsman.

Jules *was* going to see Robin again. And Deb truly was the best.

Jules and Max unbolted the basement door, letting the reinforcements in.

The SEAL officer introduced himself for the benefit of Howard and the other reporters, who still weren't quite sure what was happening. "I'm Lieutenant Mike Muldoon," he announced as Lopez headed for the wounded. "We're U.S. Navy SEALs. We're here to get you out."

Jules turned to Max. "Michael," he pointed out. "Michael is a *very* nice name."

THURSDAY, NOVEMBER 22
NEWTON, MASSACHUSETTS

"So how did you and Uncle Will meet?" Maggie asked.

Dolphina focused her attention on the pancakes she was making them for a post-midnight snack. Will's niece had still been awake when Dolphina arrived at his apartment. Apparently, the reporter gene may have been connected to the one for red hair, because the freckle-faced girl with the wild mop of red curls had been grilling her for the past half hour.

What's your favorite color?

Red.

Who's your favorite band?

The Dixie Chicks.

Do you use an iron to straighten your hair?

No, it's naturally straight.

Don't you think it's stupid and unfair for a twelve-year-old to have to have a babysitter?

Not when your uncle wasn't sure exactly when he'd be home.

Will says this isn't a very good neighborhood. Do you think this is a bad neighborhood?

I've never been here before, so . . .

Did you need a babysitter when you were twelve?

No, but I had two brothers, both older, so . . .

Are your parents divorced?

Nope, still married. They live in California. Near Los Angeles.

The constant barrage of questions was actually good. It kept Dolphina from worrying about Jules, worrying about the e-mail Will had received from Jack Lloyd. *Situation dire.* Dolphina had left amidst the uproar, as Robin had gotten Yashi on the phone and relayed the information Jack had given them.

Will had tossed her his house keys and the note for Maggie—sans envelope—which she *hadn't* read, thank you very much.

It took only fifteen minutes to get out here to Newton, and to get the obviously long-suffering sitter on her way home. Dolphina had her cell phone in her pocket, and she kept touching it like some kind of talisman, praying that it would ring and she'd get the news that Jules was safe.

But it didn't ring. And Maggie kept up her constant questioning.

Are you married?

Nope.

Have you ever been married? Uncle Will was married once, but his wife slept with someone else. A bunch of someone else's.

No, and that might be information that good old Uncle Will might consider extremely private.

Will? No way. He's cool—except for the babysitting thing. Besides, he'd never tell you that himself, and frankly, it's helpful to know when dealing with his bad moods. Have you ever been in love?

That one had given Dolphina pause, but she'd answered honestly. *Yes.*

What was his name? *Was* it a him?

Simon, and yes, he was a him.

Why didn't you marry him? Did you *want* to marry him?

Well, I thought for a while that I did, but it turned out that he'd neglected to tell me that he was already married.

So he was kind of like the male equivalent of Will's ex-wife. She used to sleep with guys and not tell them that she was married to Will.

Will told you that? Dolphina had managed to get a question of her own in as she mixed the pancake batter and heated up the frying pan.

"Yeah, right," Maggie had scoffed as she perched on one of the kitchen stools, all long gangly arms and legs. "Like he'd talk about that with anyone? I heard my mom telling one of her friends." Which brought them to "So how did you and Uncle Will meet?"

"He, um, interviewed one of the men I work for."

"You work for Robin Chadwick? Sweet. He's, like, the best actor. And you *work* for him." Maggie was amazed.

She wasn't the only one. "Will actually *told* you . . . ?"

"Are you kidding?" Maggie said as Dolphina used the spatula to slide four rather damaged-looking pancakes onto the girl's plate. "He was crapping monkeys when he found out what happened with the *National Voice*." She motioned Dolphina closer, lowered her voice. "I thought, at one point, he was actually going to cry. Instead he said a whole bunch of words that he told me he'd lock me in my room if I ever said, especially in front of my mom." She snorted. "As if I didn't already know them." But then she paused. "My mom's in Iraq."

Dolphina nodded, pouring more pancake batter into the frying pan, trying to wrap her brain around the concept of Will Schroeder nearly in tears. "Will told me that."

"He worries about her," Maggie said. "It's hard for him. She was always his little sister, you know? Kind of like you and your brothers. He worries about her a lot."

Dolphina's heart was her in throat. Maggie was trying to be so casual about it. "It must be hard for him," she agreed. "And for her, too. Being so far away from both of you."

"Yeah." The girl reached for the plastic bottle of maple syrup, squeezing almost an entire cup of it onto her plate. "So how long have you been seeing him?"

"Excuse me?" Dolphina said.

"Uncle Will," Maggie said through a mouthful of pancakes. "He said in his note that I should be extra nice because you're his new girlfriend."

"Oh really?" Dolphina said.

"Yeah, you want to see it?" She pulled it out of her pocket and handed it to Dolphina.

Mags. Meet my new girlfriend, Dolphina Patel. (Cool name, huh? By the way, a dolphin is a mammal, not a fish. Don't piss her off by making fish jokes. She's heard them all, anyway. Probably too many times.) She's going to stay with you until I get home tonight. I'm help-

ing with an important project, but I promise to be home in time to make Thanksgiving dinner. BTW, you better be ready to help, or that turkey's going to suck.

Be nice to Dolphina. Seriously, try to win some points for me. She's music, Mags.

He'd signed it, *Your favorite uncle.*

Will had to have known Dolphina was going to end up reading this. She shook her head as she handed the note back to Maggie. "He was kidding," she said. "I'm not his girlfriend."

"He called you music," Maggie pointed out. "He wouldn't kid about that. Look, maybe you started off on the wrong foot—"

"Because he crashed a party and lied to get a story—"

"Did you read what he wrote for the *Globe*?" Maggie asked as she took her plate to the sink and quickly washed and rinsed it, setting it into the drying rack. "Because it was really good."

"I read the article in the *Voice.*"

"He didn't write that." Maggie was scornful. "Some loser named Marcus Grant wrote *that* piece of crap. Come here and look at this."

She went into the living room, and Dolphina followed her. A laptop computer was set up amidst a pile of papers and books on a corner desk. Nudging the mouse, Maggie woke up the computer and opened the word processing program. There was a file called Chadwick, and, as Dolphina watched, she opened it, clicking on a document named *Globe article.* It appeared on the monitor, with the title "There's No Story Here."

"Sit," Maggie ordered. "Read."

On December 15th of this year, television star Robin Chadwick is getting married here in Boston. Like most people who are eager to take this step, to make this kind of momentous lifelong commitment . . .

"I'm going to bed," Maggie announced. "Thanks for the pancakes."

"You're welcome," Dolphina said, dragging her gaze away from Will's article.

"It was nice meeting you," Maggie told Dolphina. "I hope whoever you're waiting for to call calls you soon."

Dolphina took her hand out of her pocket, where again she'd unconsciously reached to touch her cell phone. "I hope so, too," she said.

"He's a good person, my uncle Will," Maggie turned back to say. "He's kinda cute, too, for an old guy."

Dolphina gave her a look. "Good night, Maggie."

Maggie was undaunted. "I'm just saying. Good night."

Dolphina turned back to the computer.

Like most people who are eager to take this step, to make this kind of momentous lifelong commitment, Chadwick is in love.

This reporter wishes that that were the sole reason he had been assigned to write this story—that the good news of a man who is so enamored of his beloved that his every movement, every word, every breath resonates with his deep feelings would be considered worthy of all these inches of column. But in this age of fear and destruction, of corruption and war profiteering, of government run by rich men getting richer while wounded veterans are housed in rodent-infested barracks, that kind of good news can't compete with the bad.

So there's just no story here . . .

It was after six a.m. when Will got home, unlocking the dead bolt of his door with a quiet click. Damn, he was tired. He hadn't slept since the *National Voice* article came out, first while getting to the bottom of how his notes had gotten into Marcus's grubby hands, and then while writing his story about the theft for *The Boston Globe*.

And then there was last night . . .

He closed the door quietly behind him, sure Dolphina was asleep and—

Damn! She'd startled him.

She was standing in the middle of his living room, as if she'd jumped to her feet when she'd heard him at the door. She was looking at him as if he'd just run down her favorite puppy in the street.

"Oh, no," she said, and she started to cry, and for several extremely confusing moments, Will didn't know what the hell was happening, until he realized.

No one had called Dolphina to give her the good news.

She'd told him not to call if the news was bad—just to show up and tell her face-to-face—so she could leave without frightening Maggie with her tears.

And sure enough, Dolphina swiftly gathered up her jacket and her book and her keys. But Will intercepted her as she ran for the door, catching her by the arm.

"Jules is safe," he told her. "He's all right."

She wasn't able to understand him—she was that upset, tears just running down her face—so he said it again, trying a different combination of words. "Jules is alive, Dolph. We helped get him out—and all the others, too. They're fine. *He's* fine. He's got a couple small burns and a punctured eardrum, and he's a little dehydrated—they all are. They didn't have water and . . . I am *so* sorry. I was sure Robin had called you."

"He's alive," Dolphina repeated, and now she was crying for an entirely different reason. "Oh, God, thank God . . ."

Will knew how she felt. Relief had even made him tear up a time or two tonight. He pulled her into his arms, and she clung to him. "It's all right," he told her. His voice sounded breathless and strange to his own ears. She was a perfect fit, as if she'd been built to spec, specifically for him. "Everything's all right now."

He kissed the top of her head—he couldn't help himself—as she sogged up his shirt. She felt cold, as if she'd been sitting here, hardly daring to breathe, just freezing for all this time. He rubbed her arms and her back. "You should have turned up the heat or found a blanket or . . ."

She said something, but it was muffled and he didn't hear it.

"I'm sorry, what?" Will bent closer just as she lifted her head to look up at him, and there they were, their faces—their mouths—a whisper apart.

He could have kissed her. She was looking at him as if she maybe wouldn't mind if he kissed her, but he knew if he did, she would give him hell for it, probably for the rest of his life.

So he didn't move. He just lost himself in the bottomless darkness of her beautiful eyes, and settled for wishing he was kissing her.

And apparently that old adage about good things coming to those who wait was true. Because a very good thing *did* come to him.

Dolphina lifted her mouth that necessary extra one-thirty-second of an inch and . . .

She kissed *him.*

She tasted as sweet, as delicious as he'd always thought she smelled, and her mouth was much, much warmer than the rest of her. And Lord, she was soft—her lips, her tongue . . .

It took everything he had in him not to jam his own tongue down her throat, to press her hard against him, his hands cupping her exquisite posterior. He didn't scoop her into his arms, either, or carry her into his bedroom and throw her onto his bed.

Instead, he stood there, absolutely still, his eyes closed as he let himself get kissed.

It was lovely—there was no other word for it. A lovely, lovely end to two completely hellish, horrible days.

He knew when it was over, though. She kind of froze, and that was it—reality had reared its ugly head. She stopped kissing him as abruptly as she'd started. Apparently, she'd suddenly remembered that she detested him.

He didn't try to hold onto her. He just let her step back. And he opened his eyes.

Her own eyes were wide. She looked as if she were about to go into shock—part horrified, part terrified, part mortified. And yes, way more than part attracted.

She'd liked kissing him. She didn't want to, but she did.

His heart pounded and his blood sang through his veins. He wanted to laugh or dance or do a cartwheel.

Instead, he threw himself on the grenade, and took the blame for what she no doubt would see as a dreadful mistake.

"I'm sorry," he said quickly. "I, um, shouldn't have done that. Taken advantage. Of you. I apologize. Please forgive me. It was . . . just such an emotional moment. I'm still really shaken from . . . God, it *was* amazing tonight, Dolph." He wasn't bullshitting her now. "I helped save them. I actually helped. It was incredible—Jack couldn't reach Yashi, but he could reach me. I got Yashi the information the FBI needed to locate Jules and Max, and a SEAL team went in and got them out. All of them. Even Jack and Deb."

He'd nearly talked her down from whatever ledge she was on—maybe the ledge of forbidden fruit? But she was still a little freaked out. "Just . . . don't do it again, okay?" she said.

"Save Jules?" Will purposely misunderstood.

Dolphina looked at him in exasperation, as if she thought he was a jerk—which was far more solid and familiar ground for her. "Don't kiss me," she clarified.

"For the record," he said, "it was a very nice kiss. As far as kisses go, it's right up there in the hall of fame. Top three—no. I'm going to go big and say that it's definitely my all-time favorite."

She went into the kitchen, got a paper towel and used it to blow her nose. "Don't be an ass."

"*But, masters, remember,*" he said, "*that I am an ass, though it not be written down . . .*"

She ducked down to look at him through the pass-through into the living room.

"Yes," Will verified. "I'm straight and I'm quoting Shakespeare. There aren't many of me out there. You sure you don't want me to kiss you again?"

She laughed. "I'm quite sure."

Liar, liar, pants on fire.

She came back out of his kitchen. "I made pancakes for Maggie. She's great, by the way."

"Unfortunately, I had nothing to do with her greatness," he admitted.

"She told me you take a digital picture of her every day and e-mail it to her mom," Dolphina said.

"It's one of our projects," Will said. "I try to catch her when she's rolling her eyes at me, or giving me the *whatever* look because I won't let her do something dangerous like juggle knives or walk through the Fenway with a group of friends at midnight. I don't want Arlene—my sister—to feel as if she's missing out on anything. That was a joke," he added when Dolphina didn't laugh. She didn't even smile. She just stood there, looking at him.

And okay. It was starting to make him self-conscious now. He could have handled it, if it had been a *what an ass* look. But this still had a hint of *I want to jump your bones,* which was disconcerting.

"Maggie said you were going to cook her a traditional Thanksgiving dinner," Dolphina finally pointed out. "I couldn't help but notice the lack of a turkey—or anything else to eat in your kitchen. Besides the pancake mix."

"Ah," Will said. "Yes. It was my plan to stop at the grocery store last night after I dropped off that file with Robin and Jules." His plan had been thwarted.

"Maybe," Dolphina said, but she stopped herself. "I should probably ask Robin first— "

"He invited Maggie and me for dinner," Will said. "I told him no because I knew you were going to be there, and I didn't want to ruin your day. You know, on account of your intense hatred for all things Schroeder."

"I didn't hate the article you wrote," she admitted.

"You read it." He was surprised.

"Both of them," Dolphina said. "You're a good writer. But you obviously suck at computer security." She headed for the door. "Dinner's at two o'clock. Arrive any time after noon."

"I'd be fine with Chinese food," Will confessed. "But it matters to Maggie, so . . . Thank you."

She turned to look back at him with those eyes that made his heart sing. "It's Thanksgiving," she told him. "And I'm actually thankful you crashed the wedding shower." She laughed her disbelief. "Who would have *ever* thought I'd say that? But I am. I'm thankful we're . . . frenemies."

Will laughed as she closed his door behind her.

Frenemies. He couldn't remember ever kissing a frenemy before, but he'd let her get away with calling it that.

For now.

Good things also came in threes, and today was no exception to the rule.

Robin had been awakened with an early morning phone call—which usually would've been not quite a *bad* thing, but certainly a vaguely unhappy thing. But it had been producer Art Urban on the other end, which had made Robin sit up and try to clear the sleep from his voice.

Art had spent the entire night, he'd told Robin, brainstorming an idea he'd had for his next pay-cable TV series, and he was wondering if Robin was interested in sitting down after the holiday and talking about taking the starring role in the project.

You *think?*

Art didn't want to get into a whole lot of detail here and now, but Robin would play a closeted gay A-list movie star who spent most of his time and energy trying to fool the world, including his posse of best friends, into thinking he was straight. "Think of it as *Entourage* meets *Queer as Folk,*" Art had told him, "only even edgier."

The character had grown up in blue-collar Boston, and the majority of the filming would be done here in town, at Urban's studios. There'd be some location work in both Hollywood and New York City—but not a whole lot.

Art had started writing the pilot, most of which he hoped to crash-cast and film before Robin's wedding. If Robin was interested, he'd fax over the script as soon as it was finished—probably sometime before Sunday.

If Robin was interested?

Okay, so that had been good thing number two.

Number one being, of course, Jules and Max's successful rescue—and the fact that they were both safely in Germany. They'd be back in D.C. tomorrow noon. Robin was going to fly down with Gina and Joan in the morning, so that he'd be there to meet their plane.

He spoke to Jules on the phone shortly after dinner.

"I heard you have a full house," Jules said, his voice wistfully warm in Robin's ear. "I wish I could be there."

"Me, too," Robin told him. "Babe, your friends are great. I don't know what I would've done without Gina. Although . . . is she okay? She's not, like, bulimic, is she? I heard the most godawful sounds coming from the bathroom this morning—speaking of which, I just want to state for the record that it's Thanksgiving and our master bath still isn't even close to finished, but I don't give a flying fuck. I got my priorities in order, and I am thankful today. Bathroom, what bathroom?"

Jules laughed. "Let's put Dolphina into ass-kicking mode on Monday."

"Ooh," Robin said, excited. "We're going to sic Dolph on the contractor again?" That was always so much fun to watch.

"On Monday," Jules reminded him, still laughing.

Jeez, he loved the sound of Jules's laughter so much. His throat tightened. "Monday," he repeated, thickly. He still got a rush of emotion when he thought about how close he'd come to never having another Monday with Jules.

Jules was quiet, too, clearly thinking the same thing. "I'm sorry about—" he started.

Robin cut him off. "I know. So stop. You didn't bomb Kandahar. You went to try to help save some lives—"

"We didn't save them."

Robin had heard from Yashi that the five missing medical personnel had been executed by their terrorist captors at just about the same time that Jules and Max's plane had touched down in Afghanistan.

"But you went there to try," Robin pointed out. "It's what you do—it's one of the reasons why I'm crazy in love with you."

Jules was silent for a while. "I have astounding luck," he finally said.

"You have good karma, babe," Robin told him. "I got a house full of people who think you're the man. Everyone's got a Jules story for me, and it usually involves you cleaning up someone else's clusterfuck. Gina alone could write a book."

"She's not bulimic, by the way," Jules told him. "She's pregnant."

"Ah," Robin said. "That explains a lot."

"Don't tell anyone," Jules cautioned him. "Max told me in confidence. They're not ready to make it public yet."

"Did you know Joan Muldoon's having a baby, too?"

"I didn't. Wow. Mikey Muldoon's going to be a father. He's, like, your age," Jules told him. "And, hey, you know who else is pregnant? You're going to love this. She was actually part of the task force who came to pull us out. She stayed on the helo with the other non-SEALs, but you better believe she would've been boots on the ground if we'd needed her."

"No way," Robin said, starting to laugh. "Alyssa?"

"Yeah. Sam doesn't know whether to shit or go blind," Jules said, laughing, too. "He alternates between being beside himself with excitement, and stricken with terror. He was dying to tell us back in September—you know, when we shared the hotel room?"

Yeah, Robin definitely remembered that.

"Alyssa took one of those home tests later that week," Jules told him. "Her little sister had severe complications—she actually died as a result of a pregnancy, so they wanted to wait for the end of the first trimester before telling anyone. They were planning to announce it at our house—during Thanksgiving dinner."

"I had no idea," Robin said. "Either about her sister or the fact that she was pregnant."

"Yeah, apparently Lys has been wanting to go for it for a while. Sam made them wait until he studied up on her sister's condition and convinced himself that it wasn't hereditary. He's trying hard not to drive her crazy," Jules told him. "It's funny to watch them. And there she was, in the field, so apparently he's managing to control his anxiety."

"Please tell them that I'm truly happy for them," Robin said.

"I will. So that's Alyssa, Gina *and* Joan," Jules said. "What do they say—good things come in threes? It's going to be an exciting spring."

It was going to be, indeed.

"Hey, do you know who came over and dragged me to a meeting this morning? This is going to blow your mind. Will Schroeder."

"The reporter," Jules said.

"The reporter who saved your life," Robin clarified. "Yeah. He showed up at ten—way early—with his kid—his niece, Maggie—she's a hoot and a half. You're going to love her. Anyway, Will was like, *okay, I did some research and found a ten-thirty meeting down the street. After last night, Chadwick, you definitely need to go*. He was right. I really needed it. I'm still jonsing a little—I don't know, maybe it's the whole holiday thing. This is my first Thanksgiving that I haven't gotten tanked and . . . Yashi's dad and Cos's mom are going with me to another meeting tonight, God bless them."

"One hour at a time," Jules reminded him.

"I know," Robin said. "I'm doing it. I'm strong, babe. I am. I didn't tell you that so you would worry. I just . . . wanted to be honest about how this staying sober shit isn't as . . . easy as I sometimes try to pretend it is."

"I *want* you to be honest with me," Jules said. "Like . . . even when your show gets cancelled . . . ?"

"Ah, crap," Robin said. It figured that Jules had found out about that. "I was going to tell you in the cab to the airport, but . . . I didn't want you worrying about it while you were over there."

"Are you okay?" Jules asked. "You must be so disappointed." He knew how much Robin had loved working for Art.

"It hurts," Robin admitted. "But it's showbiz. Jobs end." That's the way it always was for an actor. "The good news is that Art called me this morning, asking if I'm interested in starring in another project—something about a movie star who lives in Boston. He's going to fax over the pilot this weekend. We can look at it together—see if it's something I want to do. I suspect, though, that our answer is going to be yes."

"If you want to do it," Jules said, "you know I'm with you."

"Yes, I do know that," Robin said. "Of all the things I'm thankful for today, babe, I'm most thankful that you're in my life."

Jules laughed softly. "Okay, so I was sitting here, feeling a little sorry for myself because I missed the party. But then you go and say that and . . . suddenly I'm having the best Thanksgiving ever."

"Me, too," Robin told this man who was the love of his life. "This one's going to be damn hard to beat."

PART FOUR

the good, the bad and the uninvited

THURSDAY, NOVEMBER 29
BOSTON, MASSACHUSETTS

THIS WASN'T GOING TO BE GOOD.

Will could come up with only one reason why he'd been called into his editor Paul Rigatta's office—and that was because he'd flatly refused to write about his Thanksgiving dinner with Robin Chadwick.

The public's limitless fascination with the TV star was bordering on the grotesque, and when Will had responded to Paul's e-mail request for a Thanksgiving piece by writing back, *While the turkey was a tad dry, the gravy was delicious and more than made up for any overcooking. The end.* Paul had zapped him back a quick response: *Keep going, a-hole.*

To which Will had countered, *I was invited, as a guest, into Chadwick's home. And even if I didn't have issues with taking advan-*

tage of his kindness, I'm NOT a food or arts & leisure or even a feature writer. Remember me, the hard-hitting investigative journalist?

Paul's response: *Tough shit. I want the story. Write it.*

Which had led to Will's somewhat regrettable *Bite me.*

So here he was, dead man walking, making his last excruciatingly long trek to Paul's corner office, so that his editor could not just bite him, but, in fact, fire his ass.

Paul's administrative assistant wasn't at her station, and his office door was ajar, so Will not only knocked on it, he also poked his head in.

His editor was at his desk, on the phone, as usual—a high-tech earpiece and mic attached to his bald head and faintly cherubic face. He waved Will in as he kept his phone conversation going, giving him a narrow-eyed look, no doubt because Will wasn't able to contain his massive disbelief at Paulie's freakish outfit.

Instead of his usual rumpled suit, jacket off and sleeves rolled up, tie comfortably loose, the man was actually wearing bike racing gear—tight-fitting black pants and a neon blue and yellow long-sleeved shirt. Considering Paul wasn't built like Lance Armstrong, it was a questionable fashion statement. In fact, with his phone appendage, he looked quite a bit like Danny DeVito's slightly taller superhero-cyborg brother.

Will sat down in one of the purposely uncomfortable chairs in front of Paul's desk, stretching his legs out in front of him, feigning ease.

"I want it via e-mail in five minutes, I don't care who you have to kill to get it," Paul ordered the poor schlub who was on the other end of that phone call. "I was supposed to go out biking during lunch, so just shut the fuck up."

"I didn't say anything," Will pointed out when he realized that the last sentence was directed to him. It could be disconcerting talking to

Paul because he switched back and forth between phone calls and live conversation seemingly indiscriminately. If you didn't pay close attention, you wouldn't notice when he answered his phone. It was programmed so that it wouldn't ring in the room, only in the man's ear.

"The shit hit the fan with this NFC rape story," Paul told him. "You heard about it?"

"Of course." A Newton Falls College co-ed—one of the very few who'd stayed on campus over the holiday weekend—had been raped and beaten last Saturday night. Her roommate came back to their dorm, found her, and dialed 911. The cops beat the paramedics to the scene, but when they ID'd the victim, they found an outstanding warrant for credit card fraud. Instead of receiving medical care, the girl was arrested—taken from her dorm room in handcuffs and locked in a cell for forty-eight hours, without access to a rape kit or the morning after pill—forget about psychological support.

"We got a tip that the charges of fraud were going to be dropped," Paul told him. "And sure enough. But get this—turns out the girl's a victim of identity theft. She knew nothing about the credit cards. All she knew was she was attacked, and then she was in jail. Eighteen years old."

Will sat up. God. "What can I do?"

"Bite me," Paul said.

"Come on," Will argued. "This is my kind of story and you know it. Do you have someone talking to the university's security? When I went to school, the police never came on campus without a security escort. Let me dig around, see if this school has similar rules, and if so, who was on call that night. Maybe they were understaffed because of the holiday. It's at least worth asking why some kind of campus authority didn't demand medical care for an injured student, regardless of past warrants. This kid got raped twice in one night—let's give her more people to sue."

"That's a good idea," Paul said. "Belinda, have Matt Jablonski give me a call in about ten minutes." He was speaking into his phone again.

"It's *my* idea," Will stood up, the better to loom menacingly over his boss. "You're giving it to Jablonski?"

"You can share the by-line," Paul said. "You're busy—I'm giving you something else. Siddown. Yeah, B., thanks, send him in."

"Something else?" Will repeated.

"Sorry I'm late, Paul." The voice was familiar, and sure enough, Will turned to see Jules Cassidy coming through Paul's office door. Oh, damn. "Traffic was insane."

"No worries," Paul said, getting to his feet. "Come on in. You know Will Schroeder, of course."

"Nice to see you," Jules greeted Will with a firm handshake. "And thank you. I'm pretty sure I owe you my life."

"I was glad to be of help."

"I've been walking around today hyper-aware that my funeral probably would've been held this morning," Jules told him. "Kind of puts things like gridlock into perspective."

"I bet," Will said.

Jules turned to Paul, reaching across the desk to grasp the editor's hand. "*You* have lost a *lot* of weight. You look fabulous."

"Thanks, yeah, the biking's been working." Paul patted his still rotund stomach. "I don't know what I'm going to do when the snow starts piling up, though."

"Rock climbing," Jules suggested. "There's a gym just a couple blocks from here. Now that your weight's down, you should try it. It's really fun—great upper body workout. Robin and I go all the time. If you want, you can come as our guest—give it a try."

"I'd like that," Paul said. "Thanks."

Jules turned back to Will, who was no doubt radiating impatience. "You didn't ask him yet." His words—not quite a question—were directed to Paul.

"I don't ask, I tell," Paul countered. "He wants a paycheck, he takes the assignments he's given."

"What assignment?" Will asked, with dread. As if he didn't already know.

"Mr. Cassidy and his famous fiancé have graciously decided to give the *Globe* exclusive coverage of their upcoming nuptials," Paulie told him, very smugly. "It is an event of national interest, which President and Mrs. Bryant will be attending. You'll be covering the story in a daily column, right up until the big day—think of it as a printed blog."

A *daily* column, for nearly two weeks? On a subject that deserved a single sentence on the social news page?

"We have society reporters," Will pointed out. "Any one of them is better qualified for this than I am." They'd also probably knife fight each other to get this plum assignment. Plum for anyone but him, that is.

"Mr. Cassidy has decided that they want you." Paul was a little too happy about that.

Will turned to Jules. "With all due respect, sir, if this is supposed to be some kind of payback for my help with the Jack Lloyd thing . . . ? Please don't do me any favors. I really don't want—"

Jules laughed. "With all due respect," he interrupted. He was still smiling, but his eyes were no longer warm. "I don't give a shit what you want. You may have saved my life, but you've only just *begun* to pay us back for coming into our home, uninvited, for lying and taking advantage of Robin's generosity. You do realize that this pig mask thing will *never* go away . . . ?"

Will nodded, unable to meet his eyes. "I know, and . . . I'm sorry."

"Personally?" Jules asked. "I think it's absurd, but Robin doesn't.

He feels awful that he said it, and he hates that it's still—*still*—getting airplay."

And *that* was Will's fault. He'd thought it would help to get the recording of his conversation with Robin out into the public. But that had backfired. The *National Voice* article would've quickly faded away. But sound bites of Robin's voice were still getting played—and mocked—on hate-mongering radio shows.

"If you're trying to guilt me out," Will admitted, "it's working. But a daily column? *The President and Mrs. Bryant will be attending* . . . That's it. After that, there's nothing more for me to say. There's no story here."

Jules Cassidy smiled again. "And that is exactly why you're the man for this job. Because we don't think there's a story either. We're all on the same page. You'll have full access—but please call Dolphina and set up any visits in advance. If there's something you need, just ask."

He took two files from his briefcase, handed one to Paul and one to Will. "Here's a schedule of events, as well as bio information for both Robin and me. The schedule is for your use only—if you print it or publish it online, we'll change it immediately—and our arrangement will instantly end. I do *not* take Robin's safety lightly. He's a celebrity, there are people out there who want a piece of him, and I don't share well. You fuck with me on this issue, and you are gone."

Gone, and no doubt badly bruised for quite a while. Not to mention out of a job . . .

Jules closed his briefcase with a crisp snap. "After you have a chance to review the file, please contact Dolphina, so we can set up a time for an interview. She's prepared to work closely with you, to make this ordeal as painful as possible." He blinked. "Did I just say painful?" he mused. "That's kind of funny, but I really *did* mean painless."

Yeah, right.

"Feel free to bring Maggie with you to any of the social occasions on the list, including the wedding," Jules continued. "All of the parties will, of course, be alcohol free." He did a round of handshakes again. "It was great seeing you, Paul—I've got to run—Will, I'm sure I'll see you soon."

With that, Jules Cassidy was gone, leaving Will staring down at a schedule of dates, the first of which was *Bachelor Party, Saturday, December 8th.* That was a week from this coming Saturday.

Were they really having a bachelor party, like, with strippers jumping out of a giant cake?

Bring Maggie, Jules had said, so probably not.

At least *she* was going to be orbiting the moon, getting an invite to *the* celebrity wedding of the year.

She would be happy, too, to see Dolphina again. She'd been talking about her nonstop, ever since Thanksgiving.

Yeah, *Maggie* was the one who was going to be happy to see Dolphina again.

Right.

"You're really going to make me do this?" Will asked Paul.

"I'll need your first column by noon Monday," Paul said. "Yeah, Matt; no, the timing's great. Lookit, Schroeder had a story idea, but he's tied up with something else." He smiled sweetly at Will. "Shut the door on your way out."

MONDAY, DECEMBER 3

The doorbell rang at the worst possible time.

Every day brought a new potential disaster—and okay, maybe that was just Dolphina's tendency to be overly dramatic coming through. But today's calamity was, without doubt, an ugly one.

As she sat at her computer in Jules and Robin's home office, opening the morning mail and inputting the latest batch of responses from wedding invitees—stragglers, all of them having missed the deadline to RSVP—Dolphina saw that the trend was finally broken.

Everyone on the guest list—everyone—was coming to this wedding.

Except for Robin's father and his newest wife.

The doorbell rang again, and Dolphina went to answer it, only to find Will Schroeder standing on the porch, his hands in his pockets, shoulders hunched against the wind.

"Hi," he said, and she closed the door in his face.

Robin picked that very moment to come down the stairs. "Wasn't that Will?"

"He's early," she said.

"I'm pathologically punctual," Will shouted from behind the still-closed door. "That means, yes, I sometimes arrive early."

Dolphina opened the door to give him a withering look. "Two *hours* early?"

"It's sad," he said, with what he no doubt hoped was a winning smile. "I know. I'm trying hard to overcome it."

Sure he was. On Friday, when Will had called to set a time to discuss his latest assignment, she'd made the mistake of telling him their Monday morning schedule, and asking him to wait to arrive until after Robin had left for a casting session at Urban Studios.

Apparently Will wasn't going to follow the rules. Including the one she hadn't told him yet—about not looking at her as if she were something he wanted from the dessert cart.

Or maybe he *was* aware of that rule, because he tried to make his smile less about hunger and more about friendly teasing. "I had no idea we were dressing for our little meeting," he quipped. "I would have worn my top hat and tails."

"This is how I dress for work," Dolphina informed him coolly, despite the fact that she *had* taken extra care with her appearance this morning. She'd foolishly believed—after Friday's somewhat lengthy phone call—that Will had moved out of the liability column and over into the assets. But it was definitely a different kind of ass who showed up two hours early. Wearing jeans and sneakers, and badly needing a haircut, to boot.

"For God's sake, come in," Robin said. "Don't leave the door open. It's freezing out there."

"California Boy thinks thirty-seven degrees is freezing." Jules now came down the stairs, tying his tie, as Will came in and Dolphina reluctantly closed the door behind him.

Her cell phone rang, and she glanced at the number, immediately silencing it as she saw who was on the other end. Just what she needed right now—Mr. I Need to Talk to Jules or Robin Immediately, Regardless of the Fact That Neither of Them Wish to Speak to Me. Let him get bumped to voicemail, because no, she had *not* spoken to Jules or Robin yet this morning. It was one of the other issues she had intended to discuss with them—before Will had shown up early.

And before she'd received the mail.

"Will should come back later," she told her two bosses, neither of whom paid her the slightest attention.

"It's *much* colder than that with the wind chill," Robin was defending himself to Jules as he moved to the little table by the front door and flipped through the latest stack of catalogues.

"Wait until January, sweetie," Jules told Robin with a laugh. "*Then* we'll talk about wind chill." He headed for the kitchen and the coffee, even as Will took off his overcoat.

Oh, no. No, no. Leave that on. "I really do need you to come back later," Dolphina tried speaking directly to Will.

Of course, this was when Robin glanced up. "He's here now, what's the big?"

The big *is that your freaking father isn't coming to your wedding, and someone—probably me—is going to have to show you that awful note that he wrote.* Things not to say in front of a reporter. Dolphina gritted her teeth, and said, "We *do* have some business to discuss before you go."

"How many Pottery Barn catalogues do two men need, anyway?" Robin mused.

Enough was enough.

"Reporter in the house!" Dolphina shouted at the top of her lungs, and both Will and Robin turned to look at her in varying degrees of surprise.

Jules even came back from the kitchen, no doubt to see if she'd completely lost her mind.

"Sorry," she added at a more normal level, in that special tone she reserved for when she wasn't feeling particularly apologetic. "But I just feel as if there should be some kind of warning—maybe a red light flashing when he's here? Guys, he's not your new friend Will. He's a reporter for *The Boston Globe*. He's here to write about you. Don't say anything stupid."

"You mean, like, *Hey, Dolph, things got a little rambunctious last night and my pig mask broke. Will you be a sweetheart and order me a new one?*" Robin said. "*In fact, better get two.*"

Jules cracked up as he went back to his single-minded coffee quest.

"Glad to see you have a sense of humor about that," Will told Robin.

Who shot him a look. "Barely."

"Where should I put this?" Will asked Dolphina—*this* being his coat.

"Back. On," she said, even as Robin asked, "Where's the rest of the mail?"

Oh, hell.

He went into the office before she could stop him or otherwise try to distract him—where was Jules when she needed him? But now her job was to get Will out of there before the mail hit the fan.

"I'll take that." She snatched his coat from him, tossing it over the newel post as she grabbed his arm and pulled him toward the living room. "Why don't you go into the kitchen and get yourself some coffee?"

"*Son* of a *bitch,*" Robin expleted from the other room.

"Seriously, Will," Dolphina said when he seemed more interested in Robin's outburst than the coffee, hoping against hope that the man who'd been so kind to her on Thanksgiving morning was somewhere in those sneakers and that surprisingly soft green sweater. "Please go into the kitchen. Now?"

Will had no clue what was going on, but whatever he saw in her eyes made him nod, and head more rapidly in that direction.

But Robin came to the office door and stopped him. "Don't go anywhere, Will." He looked at Dolphina. He was trying hard to pretend that he wasn't upset. He was good. The man could act his butt off, but *she* knew better. "What's the point? Everyone's going to find out sooner or later, anyway. I'd rather have it be a news item now, than on our wedding day."

Oh, dear. She raised her voice. "Jules, could you please come here for a sec?"

Robin tapped the response card with one of his long, graceful fingers as he told Will. "My father's not coming to the wedding."

Jules, of course, heard him as he came back out of the kitchen. "Oh, sweetie," he said. "I'm sorry to hear that." He looked at Dolphina to verify. "We finally got his response?"

She nodded, reaching to take his mug of coffee from him as he went to Robin's side. "He wrote a note, too," she warned him, and as she saw a solid *oh, no* in Jules's eyes, she nodded. It was bad.

"Apparently, we're making a mockery of the sanctity of marriage." Robin laughed. "Jesus. This is the man who's filed for divorce seven times due to 'irreconcilable differences'—which translates into him wanting to have sex with someone else. Then he gets married again—until he gets bored and divorces *her*. Which he can do easily, since he always makes them sign a prenup." He shook his head, talking now to Jules. "We shouldn't have invited him. I knew he'd do something like this."

But he'd hoped otherwise.

Robin turned back to Will. "Why don't you write one of your columns on the fact that Jules and I don't have a prenup? He wanted to, but I refused. You can tell everyone that I'm marrying him because I love him, because I *want* to share my life with him. And it's only fair that he gets to share the good stuff, since he's also forced to endure *this* kind of bullshit that I bring with me to the table."

Jules gently took the response card out of Robin's hand and tore it in half. "We don't need this."

Dolphina leaped forward to take it from him, and he smiled his thanks even though his eyes were sad.

"May I state for the record," Robin still had more to say, and Dolphina crossed her fingers, hoping that he remembered this really *was* on the record, "that in just a few weeks' time, I'm marrying this man because I want to be with him *forever*." He looked at Jules. "We do this, and I'm never letting you go. This is not some two-year experiment, a la Dad. This is it. We make it work. Even when bad shit happens—we don't quit. *I'm* not going to quit."

"I'm not either," Jules said evenly. "I'm in this forever, too."

And there they stood. Looking at each other, gazes locked. Dolphina wasn't sure what Jules silently said to Robin in that moment, but whatever it was, it took the edge off his anger. Which maybe wasn't such a good thing, at least not with an audience, because without it, Robin couldn't hide his hurt.

"Come here," Jules said as he pulled Robin with him toward the privacy of the office. "This note from your father . . . it's really just . . . terribly sad. He's obviously tried so hard to find happiness. But it always escapes him because he still doesn't have the slightest clue what love really is."

"I know that," Robin said. "I do. It's just . . . You have such a great family, babe. All I've got is Janey. And Cos, and his mom, sure, but . . ."

"Well, now you've got me, too." As Jules closed the door behind them, Dolphina heard him say, "And you *know* that my mother adores you."

She could hear the halting murmur of Robin's voice in reply as she turned to Will. "Let's get some coffee." In the kitchen. Way on the other side of the house.

He nodded. "Okay."

He followed her in silence, watching as she tossed the torn-up response from Robin's father in the kitchen trash. She could tell he wanted to see it, but he managed to restrain himself from diving in after it. In fact, he didn't even move from where he'd propped himself against the far counter.

"Coffee's self-serve," Dolphina said. Best to teach him the house rules now. "Mugs are in here. Sugar's over here, if you need it. Milk's in the fridge."

"Thanks."

She glanced at him as he came to her side of the kitchen, waiting while she poured her own mug of coffee.

"I'm sorry," Will said, "that I, um, made that more stressful for you."

She looked at him again, this time letting him catch and hold her gaze. He wasn't kidding. He was truly apologetic.

He smiled slightly. "That must've sucked—opening the mail to find that?"

Dolphina nodded. She wasn't sure what kind of reaction she'd imagined Robin would have. And all she could think now was *thank God Jules had been home.*

Will was thinking along the same lines. "He's really good for Robin, isn't he?" he said. "Jules."

"Yes, he is."

He broke their eye contact, looking down into his empty mug. "When I got married, I thought it would be forever. She, um, had other ideas about what marriage meant."

He looked back at her, and now it was Dolphina who couldn't meet his gaze. "Maggie told me about your divorce."

Will laughed. "Of course she did. Did she tell you . . . ?" He answered his own question. "All the gory details. She is so dead."

"What's so awful about the truth?" Dolphina asked, unable to keep from laughing, too, at his mock outrage. "You were the injured party."

His smile faded, and for the briefest moment, she saw something uncertain in his eyes. In that instant, he seemed vulnerable, and about ten years younger. "I was the fool." He said it quietly but absolutely, and something twisted in her stomach.

Because she knew exactly how he felt. And yet, she felt compelled to disagree. "For believing in forever?" she asked him.

"Do you honestly think it's possible?" he countered.

"For Robin and Jules?" Dolphina asked. "Absolutely. In fifty years, I am going to be organizing their golden anniversary party." She finally relinquished the coffee pot, giving him space to pour.

He laughed. "If you survive whatever catastrophe the rest of today brings."

Dolphina shot him a look. "It's not always so dramatic around here."

Apparently, Will, too, drank his coffee black. He continued to gaze at her as he took a sip. "Why don't I believe that?"

"How *is* Maggie?"

"Changing the subject," he mused. "All right. She's great. In fact, she wants to know if you want to have dinner with us. Maybe some time this week."

Maggie wanted to have dinner. Dolphina gazed back at Will. "I don't think that's a good idea."

"Oh, come on—"

"I actually try to relax during dinner," Dolphina informed him. "To be honest, when I'm around you, I'm . . . on my guard."

She'd obviously surprised him. "It'd be off the record."

She shot him a disbelieving look. "And if something I say during dinner shows up in one of your columns . . . ? Which it will. Then I'll be furious and this truce we've managed to form will be over, and the next few weeks will be a living hell. For both of us."

He nodded, because he knew she was right. "Have I mentioned how much I hate this assignment?"

"Friday," she said. "On the phone. Yes." He'd gone into some detail, in fact.

"I hate it even more today." Will snorted. "I can't *wait* to see what tomorrow brings."

"Next topic," she said, putting her mug down on the center island, and pulling over a pad and pen she'd set out in anticipation of this discussion. She'd jotted down a short list of matters to discuss, and she quickly reviewed them now. "I'd like to read your columns in advance of your submitting them."

"Read?" he asked. "Or censor?"

"Read," she repeated. "Fact check."

No way. She could see it clearly in his eyes as he pretended to consider it, gazing into his coffee. "No, but thank you," he said, as if she'd offered to do him a favor. It was remarkably diplomatic. "I'll check my own facts. I've already handed in today's piece—it's a reworking of my original article. I managed to squeeze two days out of it, so I'm good until Wednesday."

Dolphina didn't try to argue. She just crossed it off her list. "Next topic. If you give me a list of possible subjects for future columns, I can help—"

"Steer me toward the ones that are least problematic for you," he finished for her. "Sure, why not? But I already know one thing I'm going to be writing about. It's occurred to me that with the President attending the wedding, the entire guest list is going to have to be screened by . . . who? The Secret Service or the FBI?"

Great. If Dolphina had made a list of topics that she, Jules and Robin most *didn't* want Will to start nosing around about, that one would've been right at the top.

"I'm afraid I can't discuss that," Dolphina said, as her cell phone rang.

Oh, double great. The number two topic of discussion that Dolphina most *didn't* want to have with a reporter was calling her again. Again, she silenced her phone.

"So what do you have to do in this situation, call everyone up and get their social security numbers?" Will asked. "That's kind of invasive and awkward, isn't it? Anyone refuse?"

"Yes, it is," Dolphina agreed, "and no they haven't. Which reminds me, I'll be needing yours and Maggie's. Unless you want to see what happens when *you* refuse . . . ?"

"Good idea, but no. My editor told me to play nice."

Showing up two hours early was his idea of playing nice?

"Has anyone on the guest list been red-flagged yet?" Will asked. "And if so, how do you handle that? Uninvite them?"

"No comment," she said. "Seriously, Will, I'm asking you to go in a different direction, please."

"You're kidding, right? This is one of the few interesting stories here," he countered. "What *is* the protocol when the President attends your wedding and crazy Uncle Frank gets red-flagged?"

It was a very good question, and one they were currently dealing with, since one of Jules's very good friends, a man named Davis Jones, had come up on the President's private "no fly" list. So to speak.

Dolphina didn't yet know how this problem was going to be solved, but knowing Jules, he was far more likely to uninvite the President than uninvite his very good friends Dave and Molly Jones.

"I'd like to talk to Jules about this," Will said. "As an FBI agent, he's surely got some insights. And I want to set up a time to talk to Robin about the new series he's working on with Art Urban. Plus, I'm going to need some fairly regular blocks of time to sit down with both of them, together. Please let them know I'll be taking pictures at those times."

"You'll be taking them? Doesn't the *Globe* usually send over a real photographer?" Dolphina glanced up from the notes she was taking, and the look he gave her was cryptic.

"I am a real photographer," he finally said. "At least I am now. I guess Maggie didn't give you *all* the gory details about my divorce. My ex was my photographer. And after . . . I just . . . now prefer working alone."

"It's hard to trust anyone after getting hurt like that," Dolphina agreed.

"Spoken like someone who's been there, done that," Will mused. "So who exactly was this Simon guy?"

Dolphina laughed her surprise. "Maggie does have a very big mouth, doesn't she?"

"Yup, so who was he?"

"It's not like he's dead," Dolphina protested.

"*Is* implies you're still hung up on him," Will pointed out.

"I'm not." She was *not* talking about this with him. She tapped her pen on her pad. "Next topic?"

"That's why you were so pissed when you thought I was what's-his-name," Will realized. "Kuhlman. Robin's real estate agent. You thought you were getting hit on by another married dickhead—No, that must happen to you a lot . . ." He laughed as he figured it out. "You were pissed because you thought you were *attracted* to another married dickhead."

Dolphina couldn't believe him. "You have an incredible amount of nerve—"

"Oh, come on," he scoffed. "What, you want to just pretend it doesn't exist—this crazy chemistry between us? I'm very attracted to you, too. Very."

The heat in his eyes made her take a step back, and he laughed.

"Don't worry," he continued. "I'm not going to kiss you. But, for the record, it's not because I don't want to. I want to make that absolutely clear."

Dolphina found her voice. "This is . . . inappropriate."

"No, it's not. Inappropriate would be me kissing you again, the way I did in my apartment. God, that was sweet. I could've kissed you like that for hours . . ." His voice trailed off. "Next topic?"

He was mocking her, she knew that, but she desperately wanted to change to a safer subject, so she looked down at her pad, which didn't help because she was suddenly unable to read her own handwriting. *God, that was sweet* . . . Dear God, indeed.

"Oh, you know what else I was thinking?" Will said, snapping his fingers, as if their conversation hadn't just swerved, hard, into the danger zone. "For one of my columns? I thought it would be interesting to talk to what's-his-name." He took a little leather-bound notepad from his back pocket, flipping through it. "The actor. Wyndham." He found the page he was looking for. "Adam. I did some research last night, and I read an interview he did where he said that he's Jules's ex—that's how he got the audition for the part in that movie he was in with Robin. *American Hero.*"

Dolphina tried to hide her horror, which was hard, because she was still so distracted by . . . "I'm not sure Adam is a good candidate—"

"Are you kidding?" Will said. "He's perfect. He knows them both, probably quite well . . ."

A little too well. Jules and Robin would've hooked up several years ago, if Adam hadn't purposely come between them. More things not to say to a reporter. Although, Dolphina suspected if Will dug deeper, he'd find out the whole story. It hadn't solely been Adam's fault. Robin and Jules had both made their share of stupid mistakes as they were finding their way to their happy ending.

But the last thing either of them would want now would be to give Adam an engraved invitation to once again screw things up.

As if on cue, her phone rang again. And yes, again, it was Adam. She was going to have to go into the bathroom to call him back. This was one conversation she didn't want Will to overhear.

"You need to get that?" he asked her now.

"No." Dolphina finally just turned her ringer off. "You know, there are other people to talk to," she said, trying to convince him. "Robin's sister, for example. Jane. She knows Jules really well—he handled the FBI investigation when she received those death threats a few years ago. She's the reason why Robin and Jules met—that's a great story."

Will didn't seem convinced. "One that's been told before."

Jules shouted from the foyer. "We're out of here. I'm dropping Robin at the studio. Dolph, you need anything before we go?"

"Just . . . call me later please," she said, not daring to look at Will.

But something in her tone made Jules come into the kitchen to ask, "Everything all right?"

"She doesn't want to tell you about the latest catastrophe in front of me," Will answered for her. He put his empty coffee mug in the sink. "Which is why I'm going. To pick up sandwiches for lunch." He looked at Dolphina. "I'll be back in about an hour with food—does that work for you?"

Considering it would then be close to the exact time of their scheduled appointment? Still, she found his offer gracious. "Thank you."

Jules looked at his watch as they followed Will back into the foyer. "Robin, I'm going to be a few minutes. If you need to go . . ."

"Actually," Dolphina said, "I have a couple of . . . questions for him, too."

Will glanced at her—he wasn't fooled.

Nor was Jules. But he waited not just until the door closed behind Will, but until the reporter was off the porch and on his way down the sidewalk.

Only then did he turn to Dolphina and ask, "What's going on?"

Robin's day went from crappy to full-out shitty, as Dolphina cleared her throat and said, "So. Adam Wyndham called me last night. He said he's been trying to reach you."

Goddamnit. "I'm not interested in talking to him," Robin said from his seat on the couch, even as Jules said, "I left him a voicemail. I was quite clear about . . ."

Jules realized it at the same moment Robin did, and turned to look at him in surprise. "Adam's been calling you, too? Why didn't you tell me?"

Robin bristled because, crap, they'd run this pattern before. Jules was going to get jealous, and . . . He did *not* want to do this right now. Besides . . . "Why didn't *you* tell *me* he was calling *you*?"

"Um, guys," Dolphina started.

Robin stopped her. "No," he said. "I'm curious. Why am I the bad guy here? Why is it okay for Jules not to tell *me* when his ex has been calling for the past two weeks?"

"Two *weeks*?" Now Jules was extremely not happy. "Maybe because he's only been calling me for two *days*."

Oops. Robin saw in Jules's eyes the accusation that he was too classy to say aloud, at least not in front of Dolphina. *And he was* my *ex a long time ago—a lot longer than it's been since he was* your *ex.* And *have you forgotten that you ended your relationship with him because you thought he might be falling in love with you . . . ?*

Jules turned to Dolphina. "Will you excuse us for a minute?"

Robin put his head in his hands. *Here we go . . .*

She sighed, clearly frustrated with the both of them. "Yes," she said, "but before I do that, may I just point out that Adam said he was calling because he received what he described as *kind of weird, vaguely threatening fan mail,* which also mentioned Robin. He didn't go into much detail when I pressed him, which made me a little suspicious—he just kept saying that he wanted to talk to either one of you. Now, what I know about Adam is that he appears to like nothing more than to cause trouble." She looked from Robin to Jules and back, beseechingly. "Please don't let him do that."

"Call the service that handles Robin's mail," Jules ordered her. "Have them send over anything unusual, anything that fits that description."

She hesitated. "Jules, it's probably just—"

His voice was sharp. "Just *do* it. Please."

"Yes, sir." She closed the office door quietly behind her.

Robin spoke first, because Dolph had been right—Adam was probably rubbing his hands in glee right now, thinking about this very fight that Robin and Jules were about to have. He took a deep breath and kept his voice evenly pitched. "I should have told you when Adam first called. I just . . . I thought I was handling it."

Jules was silent, standing by the fireplace, either unable or unwilling to look at Robin. He was a picture of tension.

He gets really jealous, Adam had once told Robin, talking about Jules, and boy, he wasn't kidding. *I know you think he's perfect, but he's not. He's extremely possessive. It used to drive me crazy . . .*

But it didn't drive Robin crazy. He loved the way Jules touched him, the warmth of his hand on Robin's back, solid and, yes, very possessive. Despite the fact that Robin was taller, Jules was the alpha in their relationship. And Robin loved it, loved him.

"Please don't think I was trying to hide it from you," Robin said now, "because I wasn't. I was ignoring him. I was hoping he'd just . . . go away."

"For two weeks," Jules repeated.

"If it went on," Robin said, "I was going to change my cell number."

Jules turned to face him. "And tell me . . . what?"

"The truth." Robin let a little more affront into his tone than he'd intended, because this was *his* hot button—Jules's implication that he could have—*would have*—lied. He closed his eyes. *Can we please not fight today?* He clenched his teeth around the words because they *weren't* fighting, they were talking, and yes, one of the reasons why he *hadn't* told Jules that Adam had been calling was because he knew Jules would be jealous. And the reason he'd be jealous was because he was afraid of losing Robin, which was both ridiculous and flattering, and Jesus, now Jules was standing there, hiding his fear and hurt behind anger, trying desperately hard not to show just how vulnerable he was feeling . . .

"I love you," Robin said, bringing it all down to the bottom line. "You know that. And I *would* have told you if it kept going. Look, he first called me when we got engaged—when the news went public. It was just . . . *hey, how are you, congratulations, I'm glad things are going well* . . . That kind of call. We chatted, maybe for ten minutes and . . . Then he called me again, a few days later. And then he called a few days after *that,* and yeah, it started to feel inappropriate. He was making me uncomfortable, so I was honest with him. I said it was nice to be in touch every now and then, but there was . . . too much history between the three of us to be friends."

Jules had this way of listening with every cell in his body, and he was doing that now.

So Robin went on. "So then he waited an entire week before he called again. At that point, I told him that *wasn't* what I meant, that a week between phone calls is *not* now and then, and no offense, but I was going to stop answering his calls. Which is what I did."

"You should have told me," Jules said, but then looked as aghast as if he'd farted loudly during a particularly somber moment at a funeral, no doubt due to his accusatory words. *You should have* . . . He corrected himself to make his statement be more about himself. It was beyond clear that he was trying hard here, too. "I mean, I just . . . really wish you'd told me."

"Yeah, I wish I had, too, babe. I really do. But it seemed to work," Robin went on with his story. "At least for a while. But then Adam called me again—this was about two weeks ago. I've set my phone so that it doesn't ring when he calls, so he left a voicemail—something along the lines of what Dolphina said. Was I getting weird letters from some crazy fan. I checked the service and they had nothing stranger than usual. It was obviously an attempt to get me to call him back . . . And I didn't want to, so . . . Since then, I've just been deleting his messages."

Now Jules was pissed for another reason. "Messages about a potential threat? You should have told me about *that.*"

Robin shook his head. "And teach Adam that all he has to do to get us to come running is whisper the words *crazy fan?* No thanks. You know what this is about. He's mad that we didn't send him an invitation to the wedding."

"As opposed to, he's checking in to see if you're having any doubts?"

Robin laughed, but Jules wasn't even smiling, so he said, "If that's the case, he's going to be disappointed. I'm a million percent doubt-free—you know that, right?"

Jules nodded. "Yeah." But then he shook his head. "Most of the time," he amended himself. "Sometimes . . . I get crazy."

"Talk to me when that happens," Robin said. "My God, I lean on you for so much."

Jules nodded again. "It's hard to . . . But I'll try." He managed to force a smile and roll his eyes. "Fuckin' Adam," he said.

"I'm really sorry about this," Robin said again.

"I am, too. I'm . . . very sorry."

"Why didn't *you* tell *me* that he called you?" Robin asked again, more quietly this time.

Jules came over and flopped down on the sofa beside him, his legs stretched out and his head back. "I guess I figured I was handling it, too. I didn't listen to the message he left—I just assumed, yeah, that he was bitching about not getting invited. God."

"I'll tell you if he ever calls again," Robin promised.

Jules turned his head and looked at him, some amusement finally back in his eyes. "If?"

"When," Robin agreed. Because with Adam, it was definitely a *when.* He grabbed Jules by the tie and manhandled him in for a kiss. Mmmm. He wrapped his arms around Jules, pulling him back so they were lying together on the sofa. "Let's just cancel all our meetings today and stay home. Damn, I was already exhausted from that crap with my father."

"I wish I could," Jules said with a sigh, his head against Robin's shoulder, his fingers playing with the buttons on his shirt. "But I can't. Ah, God, I'm already late." And yet he didn't leap to his feet.

"I've got to get going, too," Robin said, also very much not moving, because yes, this was extremely nice—just relaxing here like this. Problem was, he had a meeting with Art that began in forty minutes. It was kind of important, considering they were starting filming tomorrow and they still hadn't found an actor to play his fictional father. Wasn't *that* ironic? "I'm just . . . doing some heavy-duty wishful thinking."

"We're not done with Adam," Jules reminded him, his hand warm against Robin's stomach. "Do you want me to take care of it—check out these e-mails he's received? Keep you out of it?"

Robin didn't like that idea very much—Jules spending time with Adam? "I get jealous, too, you know. You used to be in love with him."

Jules turned his head to look at him. "That was before I knew what love really was." He smiled. "When I met you, Robin, God . . . I had to redefine everything. You know, there was this country song my mother really liked. It used to annoy me, I was in my technopop phase, but lately I just . . . I find myself thinking about the lyrics all the time. *That was a river, this is the ocean* . . . I thought I loved Adam, and I did, but . . . It wasn't even close to this incredible ocean that I feel for you."

Robin laughed as his heart did a slow flip. "You are too fucking romantic," he said, loving the way Jules was looking at him, like he had an agenda. And oh yeah. He definitely did. "You say shit like that to me and I am . . . putty in your hands."

Jules smiled at that. "Hardly," he said.

Oh, yeah. Oh . . .

Yeah.

NEWTON, MASSACHUSETTS

When Will got home, Maggie wasn't back from school yet, which was good because it meant he could get on the computer and access the Internet.

Still, the reason she raced for the computer every day, after dropping her backpack of books just inside the apartment's front door, was one Will could relate to.

So the first thing he did when he signed on was to check their e-mail account. And sure enough, today's e-mail from Arlene was ready and waiting. It was brief—thanks for the package, the weather was getting cold, don't forget to e-mail and report what happened this week on *LOST*—a TV show she and Maggie had always watched together.

Will printed it out so that Maggie could see it that much sooner, and then got down to work.

First things first—Googling the telephone number he'd copied from Dolphina's incoming calls list on her cell phone.

And yeah, that was definitely guilt he was feeling, as he typed the numbers in, starting with the Los Angeles area code. Dolphina hadn't said *Don't snoop through either my cell phone or my computer files* before she'd vanished upstairs to help facilitate the delivery of Robin and Jules's brand-new toilet. But she'd probably assumed it was understood.

Apparently, she didn't know many reporters and . . .

Whoa.

Wasn't *this* interesting? The number he'd copied down belonged to one A. Wyndham. For some unknown reason, Adam had called Dolphina a number of times over the past few days.

This was certainly provident. It kept Will from having to search for Adam's phone number so he could interview him. He stored it in his own cell phone address book.

Next up was the info he'd swiped from a computer file called *Guest List.* Just as he'd suspected—due to Dolphina's reticence to discuss the matter—one of the wedding guests *had* been red-flagged by the Secret Service. And it wasn't just a "check more thoroughly" notice. It was a full-scale, red-alert, screaming-meanie "must not attend."

The guest in question was one W. Davis Jones, who, according to Dolphina's records, lived with his wife, Molly, and their two-year-old daughter, Hope, in . . . Flatulence, Iowa?

He squinted at the words he'd scribbled on his notepad. That couldn't be right.

He had their street address and zip code—as well as their social security numbers, so . . .

Okay. Flat Ridge. That was better. It was a 'burb of Des Moines, which seemed kind of redundant—Des Moines being smaller than some of the suburbs surrounding Boston.

The information he was finding was . . . weird, to say the least. Jones was an insurance adjuster with Northstar Company—which didn't seem too dangerous a profession. Although he *had* been an NCO—a sergeant in the Army—with a relatively recent discharge.

Honorable discharge, so that didn't quite fit either.

He'd served in . . . Southeast Asia, Indonesia, Germany and Kuwait.

Jones's wife, Molly, was almost ten years older than he was. Nee

Anderson, she'd worked overseas for years, for several different Peace Corps–type organizations. Kenya, South America, and—this was interesting—also Indonesia.

Will checked the dates. The record he could access for Sgt. Jones's service was sparse—no details of when he'd served where. But Little Miss Molly had been in Indonesia roughly the same time that Will himself had been there—back around the time of the Bali terrorist bombing. She'd lived on remote Parwati Island, as a member of a relief organization.

It seemed likely, since Indonesia was the common denominator, that Davis and Molly had met there.

Will accessed a search site that wasn't quite legal and . . . Mr. and Mrs. Davis and Molly Jones had paid their taxes on time last year. Good for them.

But damn, an insurance adjuster in Des Moines made even less than a reporter in Boston. Of course, Jones wasn't paying Boston rents.

Molly worked in daycare—either part-time or at slave wages.

Yow. Lookee how much huge-large the Joneses had stashed in their money market savings account. And they owned their own home, outright.

Will flipped back a year to try to find out when they'd won the lottery, and then another and . . . That was odd. Apparently Davis and Molly were newlyweds, married for not quite three years. Prior to 2005, he found tax returns for Molly Anderson—who lived and worked in Kenya, again at slave wages, and before that, yes, Parwati, Indonesia.

He found nothing at all for Davis Jones.

Will searched for William Davis Jones, of which there were only a handful, but none that matched the date of birth. He tried William D. Jones and got pages of hits, but again, no birthdate match.

Didn't sergeants in the Army have to pay taxes?

Unless they didn't exist prior to 2005. Unless their Army records were a fabrication, handed to them along with a shiny new identity.

Hmmm.

Indonesia was more than a pretty ocean nation with jewel-green jungles and turquoise blue seas. It was predominantly Muslim, and populated primarily by people of true faith who were outraged by terrorist violence. But Indonesia also had more than its share of poverty, despair and fear—three of the main ingredients that fundamental extremists needed to succeed.

And terrorists were just one of the many dangerous factions who used Indonesia as their stomping ground. Drug lords had island kingdoms, complete with private armies that often warred with one other. Kidnapping tourists was a lucrative business venture for the average middle-class citizen—and apparently Americans and Japanese got the biggest rate of return. Pirates roamed the open seas—but they dressed more like the kids who hung out at the Copley Crossing mall than Johnny Depp.

Will knew the country well—both its history and its current events.

And just a few short years ago—2005, as a matter of fact, back when Davis Jones had mysteriously first appeared—a major Indonesian presidential political contender named Heru Nusantara had been executed—gangland style—after an ugly story connecting him to greed, murder and intrigue had come to light. In this tale, he was tied to a notoriously violent drug lord named Chai.

Chai had been dead for years, but his reputation lived on. People were still afraid to talk about him—he'd ruled his corner of the world with an iron fist, using imprisonment, torture, death—and his army of mercenaries—to keep the locals in line. His army of mercenaries—which had once included an American ex-pat and former Special Forces NCO named Grady Morant.

Hmmm.

Morant had cut ties with Chai years ago, and pretty much dropped off the face of the earth.

Or did he?

It was funny how the dates lined up. In 2005, after Nusantara's crimes were exposed, Davis Jones had mysteriously appeared.

Coincidence? Maybe.

Maybe not.

Will popped open a can of soda and cracked his knuckles, getting into bear-went-over-the-mountain mode. He typed the names Chai, Heru Nusantara, Grady Morant and Molly Anderson into his search engine, just to see what he could see.

Tucson, Arizona

Adam got another e-mail from the freak.

It made him get up from his computer, close the curtains in his hotel room and put the chain lock on the door.

It was stupid. He knew that. Whoever was writing to him had clearly gone off his freaking meds and was probably unable to leave the protective confines of his mother's basement.

And yet . . .

Is Adam enjoying Tucson?

The motherfucker always referred to him in the third person—no doubt because he thought it would be Adam's evil robot twin who answered his e-mail.

Adam laughed as he poured himself a drink. So what if it was only 9:30 in the morning? He'd worked nearly all night, and wasn't needed on set again until sunset.

Besides, if he got drunk, he could always send his evil twin in his place.

His cell phone rang and he leaped to answer it, because that was Robin's ring. Robin Chadwick was *finally* calling him back.

"Hey," he said, breathless despite his attempt to sound cool. "About time, Einstein. I thought you were never going to ring me. Getting a little intense there in Jules-ville as the wedding approaches, huh? It's not too late to run away . . ."

"It's not Robin, it's me." Oh, hell, it was Jules on the other end, sounding as if he'd accessorized his dark suit today with some extra-crunchy grim.

"Sneaky," Adam said past the disappointment that tightened his chest. "Using Robin's phone to call. Checking up on him, are we, J.?"

"Nope, just fucking with you," Jules said. "Kind of the way you've been trying to fuck with me and Robin ever since you heard we're getting married."

"Right." Adam loaded a ton of patronizing disbelief into that one word. "Let me put your suspicions to rest, G-man. As much as I'd love to tell you he's been seeing me on the side, alas, your golden boy's been true."

"We're getting married, Adam," Jules repeated. "I know he's true. I'm incredibly happy—wow, thanks *so* much for asking."

"I didn't need to ask," Adam said. "I know how happy you must be. I mean, Robin . . . Damn. He always was ready for anything, any time. Did he ever tell you about the night we ran into each other at a party at Susie and Jamaal's house in Malibu?"

"I'm sure he doesn't remember it."

Well, yowch.

But Adam wasn't the only one stinging—Jules's voice was tight. "He made a lot of mistakes before he got sober," he told Adam.

"He's really staying with the program, huh?" Adam was suddenly highly aware of the drink that sat on the table in front of him. Still, that didn't stop him from picking it up and taking another sip.

"Yes, he is. He's . . ." Jules paused, his voice quiet now. "He's really doing well. He's happy, too. We both are."

"That's . . . good," Adam said past the sudden lump in his throat. "Really, Jules. I'm glad. I am. That's . . . really good."

"Yes, it is." He paused again. "So are you honestly getting threatening e-mails?"

Adam sighed. "Yes and . . . no? They're mostly just . . . freaking weird. The threats are . . . more implied than . . . Okay, look. Some days they seem really threatening, some days I can laugh it all off. I've been getting about an e-mail a day for the past nearly, I don't know, three weeks? They're from this guy who calls himself Jim Jessop. Don't laugh, but he seems to think that there are two of me. One is me, and one is, like, a twin. An impersonator. Sometimes he calls it an alien, sometimes a robot." He snickered, he couldn't help it. "And yes, when I say it aloud, I feel incredibly stupid. But he claims he can tell the difference and that my evil twin *is* evil—and a danger to the nonrobot me."

"I'd like to see the e-mails that mention Robin," Jules said. "Can you forward those to me?"

"Yeah," Adam said, stretching the words out. "Well . . ."

"Ah," Jules said.

"Jessop's written about *American Hero*, though," Adam defended himself. "He claims he can tell which scenes were filmed with me and when it was, you know, Adam Evil in the shot. It's only a matter of time before he brings Robin into it."

Jules was silent.

So Adam pressed it, pulling his laptop computer closer and typing in a web address and . . . "Have you seen the website Celebrity Stalker dot-com? Robin's got a page. You ever want to know where he is? Just jump online and, presto, you'll find him. I see he's over at Art Urban's office right now. Looks like you drove him over there—

at least I hope it was you. Whoever it was, Robin apparently soul-kissed him before getting out of the car—"

"I'm aware of the site," Jules interrupted.

Aware, and no doubt driven crazy by it. "I know I'm not as famous as Robin," Adam said, typing his own name into the site search, "but I've got a page, too. It's not as well maintained, though. If you go there, you'll see my last sighting was . . ." He waited for the computer to catch up with him. And . . . perfect. He cleared his throat. "Three nights ago, I was at, um, Big's in West Hollywood. But I'm in Arizona right now, for a three-day shoot, and the e-mail I got from ol' Jimmy J. today? Asking nonrobot me if I'm fricking enjoying Tucson."

Jules sighed. "What's Jessop's e-mail address? I'll check to see if Robin's been getting anything from him, too. But other than that . . ."

Adam knew what was coming. "You can't help me. No, you can, but you won't." He caught himself. "I'm sorry," he quickly said. "I didn't mean that. I know you're busy with the wedding, but . . . I'm just a little freaked out."

Silence.

"What exactly is it that you want me to do?" Jules finally asked.

Victory. But what *did* he want? Besides Robin, back in his life . . . "Can you . . . at least look at these e-mails? Maybe do some kind of computer check of the language and phrasing, like you did back when Jane Chadwick was getting death threats? Make sure I'm not being stalked by some particularly screwed up serial killer?"

Jules sighed again. "All right."

Yes. "Thank you."

"Have you gone to the police yet?" Jules asked.

"Yeah, right. I rushed right over because I love it when they *laugh* in my *face*."

"You have a lawyer, don't you?" Jules didn't wait for him to answer. "When you get back to L.A., bring the e-mails to your lawyer and ask him to call the police. If the police determine that there should be an investigation—and I can't help you there, because as it stands, this is not a federal crime, so I can't open that door—but if the LAPD does, you can request that Celebrity Stalker takes your page temporarily out of cyberspace. After you talk to the police, have your lawyer call the website and make noise about them being brought up on charges of accessory, yada yada, should anything happen to you. Believe me, they'll do it."

"Great," Adam said. "Except this guy can find me without their help."

"The police should also be able to track him down from his e-mail address," Jules said. "It's likely that he's harmless. And probably not entirely crazy." He made a noise that might have been laughter. "I always thought you had an evil robot twin."

Adam laughed, too. "Very funny."

"Actually, no," Jules said. "It *wasn't* funny. Particularly not at the time. And frankly, it's still not. And when you see him, this evil twin of yours? Tell *him* to stop calling Robin, too."

WEDNESDAY, DECEMBER 5
BOSTON, MASSACHUSETTS

"Wow," Jules said, still breathing hard. "Where did *that* come from?" He turned his head to look at Robin, who had collapsed beside him in their bed, equally spent. "Don't get me wrong, I loved it, but . . ." He had to laugh. "Holy shit."

Robin lifted his head from the tangle of sheets, an interesting mix of sheepishness and satisfaction in his eyes. "Sorry about your shirt."

"I'm not," Jules said, up on one elbow so he could kiss Robin before he pushed himself out of their bed. Time was running short. He had to get back to the office.

The suit he'd been wearing mere minutes ago was scattered across the room—his pants dangling from the free-standing mirror in the corner, his jacket and shirt in a crumpled heap by the bathroom door. One shoe had slid halfway beneath the dresser, and his socks, his other shoe and a handful of coins from his pants pocket littered the hardwood floor.

It looked as if he'd exploded out of his clothes—which wasn't that far from the truth.

Jules picked up his jacket. It hadn't been on the floor that long—a few good shakes would get any wrinkles out. But his shirt—new, from Pink—was ruined, the buttons torn clear off.

Robin laughed ruefully as he saw the damage he'd done. "Too bad we don't have a wardrobe department, you know, to come rushing in with a replacement."

"That's not a *too bad* for me," Jules told him with a laugh. "In fact, I think the *too bad* would be if someone *did* come rushing in here right now."

Speaking of replacements, would anyone notice when he went in to tonight's meeting wearing a different shirt—after hurrying home to pick up a file?

Uh, yeah? They were freaking FBI agents. They'd notice.

Jules grabbed his shorts and his pants and went out to use the hall bathroom. One of these days their master bath would have more than the current gorgeous new shower—installed sans bursting pipes, because the water-pouring-through-the-kitchen-ceiling thing was so two-months-ago.

When finished, their bathroom would have their new water-efficient toilet actually installed, instead of sitting beside a capped-off hole in the floor. The rich wood cabinets that surrounded the double sinks would have a gleaming granite countertop. The water-damaged walls would be patched and painted. There would be mirrors and towel racks and hooks for bathrobes.

Jules was no longer hoping that the work would be done by his and Robin's wedding. At this point, to avoid the relentless, repeated disappointments, he'd set his sights on the project's completion far into the future. Say, in thirty years or so? Or how about—optimistically—hoping it was done by their twentieth anniversary? That would be nice.

But right now he had more immediate issues to consider. As he washed up in the hall bathroom, splashing water up and onto his face, he tried to decide whether to wear an entirely different suit to his meeting—maybe pretend he'd had an accident with a Starbucks cup in the car?

The other option was to just *so what* it. Yeah, he went home on an errand, and his incredibly hot lover jumped him and rocked his world. What's the big deal?

Robin had been trying out their new shower when Jules had dashed upstairs to say hi. The pipes were finally hooked up, the caulking had dried and the system was ready to go.

It was beautiful—if you put your hands up to the sides of your eyes and created blinders to keep from seeing the under-construction mess of the rest of the room.

One entire spacious end of the big bathroom was now walled off with pristine, clear glass. With tile on the walls and the ceiling, too, the multiple showerheads sprayed from all directions, and the inset lights made Robin seem to gleam as water cascaded down his lean, hard-muscled body.

Beautiful, indeed.

Jules hadn't made a sound, but somehow Robin knew he was

standing in the doorway. He'd turned, and as he pushed his hair back from his face, he'd opened his eyes.

Jules was frequently surprised by how very blue Robin's eyes were. But something about the light in their new shower made them look different. Even more blue, if that were possible. Certainly hotter—which was saying something, because Robin was particularly talented when it came to looking at Jules and smoldering.

"Come on in," Robin said. "The water's fine."

"I wish I could." And wasn't that the truth. Dang. Robin was obviously getting turned on from watching Jules watch him—and he wasn't the only one. If he'd had even just twenty extra minutes . . . "I gotta go back to work. I have a meeting at eight thirty."

Robin turned off the water, and pushed the glass door open. He stepped out and onto the bathmat, water still streaming off him as he reached for his towel. "What time is it now?"

Jules checked his watch. "Seven forty-five." Their eyes met, and Robin's sparked. Of course, he wasn't the one who had to rush to the office and give a presentation. "I'll be home by eleven at the latest. Can you, um, hold that thought?"

But Robin dropped his towel, clearly more interested in Jules holding the thought in question. "This time of night," he said, "we could make it from here to your office in fifteen minutes. Easy."

"Yeah." Jules knew he should back away. If Robin so much as touched him, his willpower would completely evaporate. "But it's another fifteen minutes for the hike from the parking garage."

"Not if I drive you."

Very true.

If Robin drove, he could drop Jules at the front of the building. Jules could be upstairs and at the meeting site within sixty seconds of kissing Robin good-bye.

Robin was still watching him, just waiting . . .

And Jules nodded, already breathing hard.

Robin had grabbed him, buttons had gone flying, he'd damn near thrown Jules onto the bed and . . .

Holy shit, indeed.

Jules was now standing in the hall bathroom, grinning like an idiot. A very happy idiot.

Robin followed him in, grabbing him from behind in a hug, his arms tight around his chest as he smiled at Jules over his shoulder, into the mirror. "I just want to point out that while privacy is nice, there *is* something to be said for having an authority figure around to call for take two."

Jules laughed as Robin nuzzled his neck. "Take two. Really?" But it was a somewhat unnecessary question. He could feel Robin, thick and warm against him, already half aroused again.

Robin smiled, no doubt because he could see that he wasn't the only one turned on by the idea of a replay. "Your meeting's going to go for a couple of hours?"

"I'll keep it short," Jules promised. If he talked fast, he could get this done in an hour.

"Then I'll drop you and wait," Robin told him. "I'll hang in the car. I've actually got some lines to learn for tomorrow."

His character in this new pilot that Art Urban was filming was in nearly every scene, but up to this point, he hadn't had a whole lot of dialog. It was a fact that Jules found extremely disconcerting—so he tried not to think about it.

Especially not at times like this.

Robin kissed Jules again and reluctantly backed away. "I don't want to make you late," he said as he went to get dressed. But then he was back almost immediately, watching him from the doorway. "That was a lie," he admitted. "I want to make you *really* late. But I won't."

Jules laughed. "Thanks," he said, as he stepped into his pants.

Robin nodded, lingering. "Why don't you wear one of your older shirts, you know, from the back of your closet . . . ? There's one, I think it's got green and white stripes. It's got some fraying on the cuffs . . ."

Jules looked at him, but he wasn't kidding. Oh, my.

"You want me to, um, get it out for you?" Robin asked, his subtext extremely clear. *So I can tear it off you later?*

Jules managed to nod. "Yeah," he said. "Thanks."

"Good." Robin smiled. "Hold *that* thought," he said, and finally went to get dressed.

FRIDAY, DECEMBER 7
SAN DIEGO, CALIFORNIA

Sam wandered the house while Alyssa slept.

He'd just finished reading his book and wasn't up to starting a new one yet. There was nothing on TV but the same old discouraging news, so he woke up the computer and went online and . . .

Brrrring.

You still up? An IM from username Squidward appeared on his screen.

It was one a.m. Pacific time.

Which meant it was four a.m. in Boston.

Yeah, Sam typed back. *What are *you* doing up?*

R's doing a night shoot, came Jules's reply. *I can't sleep. You got a sec?*

Sam didn't bother to type in his answer. He just picked up his phone and dialed.

"Thank you," Jules said as he answered.

"What's up?"

"I got a thing," Jules said, "that you might be able to help me with."

"This about Adam?" Sam asked. Alyssa had filled him in on *that* latest goatfuck. Apparently Adam's crazy-ass fan was indeed a gentleman named James Jessup, of Anaheim, California. Jules had given samples of J.J.'s writing to the FBI analysts, but nothing had set off any alarms, which was good.

Everyone—Sam included—*did* agree that the evil robot thing was pretty weird shit. But when the police had gone to Jessup's home to talk to him, the place had been boarded up, water and power turned off. Which left them kind of at a loss. They knew who Mr. Crazy was, they just didn't know how to find him to make sure it was just a small screw that was loose, instead of a major homicidal one.

"Believe it or not," Jules said now, "no."

If it wasn't about Adam . . . Uh-oh. Sam laughed. "I'm kinda afraid to ask who else might have an evil twin robot."

Jules laughed, too, but he sounded tired and more than a little stressed. "I've got a friend who's coming to the wedding who's . . . got the Secret Service on edge."

Sam didn't hesitate. "How can I help?"

"I love you, you know that?" Jules said.

"Easy there," Sam said. "Just 'cause Lys is asleep and Robin's out all night—"

"Yeah, yeah," Jules said. "Ha, ha. I know. Real men don't express themselves honestly without making stupid jokes about it—"

"I love you, too," Sam interrupted. "Can we move on to why you're not sleeping?"

"That's . . . something entirely different," Jules said.

Sam braced himself. "Something named Robin?"

"No, it's all me this time," Jules admitted. "Ah, Jesus, Sam. I messed up. When I found out Adam had been calling, I got a little . . ." He cleared his throat. "Upset. We . . . got through it—in fact, Robin was really patient with me, and I apologized, which was . . . well received. But—"

"Squidward, you've got to keep in mind that if *you're* stressing about the wedding, Robin's got to be—"

"No," Jules said. "That's just it. He's not. He's great. Things are . . . God, it's really, unbelievably great." He laughed, but it was filled with despair. "Except for the fact that Robin's starting to wonder why I don't want to watch the DVDs of the dailies that he brings home from the studio."

"Dailies, like the day's scenes?" Sam clarified.

"Mmm-hmm."

"I don't get it," Sam said. Why didn't Jules want to watch them? He'd always thought that he got off on seeing Robin acting in his movies. Well, except for *American Hero* . . .

And, okay, light dawned and Sam got it. In *American Hero,* the one movie of Robin's that Jules absolutely hated to watch, Robin and his co-star, that same fucking idiot Adam Wyndham, had had a number of extremely intimate scenes.

"So this character that Robin's playing, what's his name?" Sam asked.

"Joe Laughlin," Jules tersely supplied the information. "It's basically Robin—if Robin lived in an alternative universe, where he hadn't come out of the closet or gone into rehab—if he just kept making movies."

"So Joe's a big-time movie star slash alcoholic," Sam confirmed.

"Substance abuser," Jules corrected.

"Plus he's gay, and no one knows it. Not his family, not his friends."

Jules laughed, but not with humor. "Yeah. No one knows. Aside from the small army of men that he has sex with. In the pilot alone—I read the script—there's, like, an entire platoon cycling through his condo."

"Yeah," Sam said slowly. "I do see the problem." Some of those dailies would definitely include physical scenes that Jules was apparently afraid to watch.

"It's stupid, I know. It just . . . it bugs me. Just . . . tell me I'm crazy, and I'll shut up."

"You're not crazy," Sam said. "And even if you are, I don't think you can just discount what you're feeling. Crazy or not, you're feeling it." He paused. "Is it going to freak you out too badly if I call this . . . thing that you're feeling by it's technical name?"

"Jealousy," Jules said.

"That would be the word I was going for," Sam said.

His friend laughed. "I guess that's not a big surprise."

"Yeah," Sam said. This was not the first time Jules had struggled with similar issues in terms of his romantic relationships, and it would probably not be the last. "It doesn't help for you to know that it's fiction—that Robin's only acting?"

Jules sighed. "It should, but . . . No, it doesn't. The really stupid thing," he continued, "is that I was just getting ready to bring up the subject with Robin. Like, *Hey, sweetie, wow, this new character that you're playing is really complex, and, boy, I know how much you're enjoying the role, but I've got to be honest—I'm freaking unable to think about anything else except how much it bothers me.*" He laughed his disgust. "That's going to go over well. But I've got to say *some*thing, right? But then Adam reappears and my brain shorts out, and yeah, Robin *was* extremely cool about it, but he's *not* going to be cool if it becomes this incredible, pain-in-the-ass, daily ordeal that we have to wade through—who's Crazy Jules jealous of now?

So I'm just keeping my mouth shut, because if I don't, Robin's going to be like, *Wow, you're insane. I'm not sure I want to be married to* that *bullshit*."

Jules finally took a breath, which gave Sam an opportunity to speak. "Robin's a drunk," he pointed out.

"Recovering alcoholic," Jules corrected, a tad sharply.

"That's the PC term that you fairies use," Sam said. "It's just a polite way of saying that he's a fucking drunk. You sure you want to be married to *that* bullshit?"

Jules laughed softly. "Point taken."

"Talk to the Boy Wonder," Sam advised. "You know, I bet if he knew the ulcer this was giving you, he'd think twice about taking the role."

"That's what I'm afraid of," Jules admitted. "That he'll walk away from doing something that he loves."

"What he loves is you," Sam pointed out.

"He shouldn't have to choose. God, he's *so* happy, and . . ." Jules sighed. "I just need to learn how to deal with this. I can do this."

"Step one kinda seems to be talking to him, whatever the outcome."

"Yeah." Jules sighed again. "Can we focus on my Secret Service–challenged friend for a minute?" he asked.

"Just a wild guess," Sam said, "but might this friend's name be . . . Jones?"

"That's him," Jules said. "Max has pretty much convinced the head of the President's security that Jones and Molly will behave themselves during the ceremony. He and Gina are friends with the Joneses—they'll enter the church together, limit their movements, sit in a specially designated area . . . Max'll even be armed. Yashi, Deb and George, too. They'll all be nearby—which is ridiculous. Can I just say how ridiculous this is? Jones is my *friend*. Even if for some unknown reason he *did* want to harm the President—which he could easily do at his own leisure, might I add—he wouldn't do it at my wedding."

"It is pretty fucking ridiculous," Sam agreed. "But coming as I do from the personal security industry, I can see the Secret Service's side, too. Not everyone knows Jones as well as you do."

Jules was silent, no doubt in agreement, but too pissed to acknowledge it. "So here's the thing," he finally said. "I gotta tell Jones. Don't I?"

"Yeah," Sam said.

"Rats," Jules said. "I was hoping you would say that I didn't have to."

Apparently Jules *was* extremely tired. "Like he won't know what's going on, even from out on the street?" Sam pointed out. "Cassidy. Think about it. The man's an experienced operator. He's going to notice, especially when he sits down in the church and sees the sniper aiming the rifle directly at his forehead."

"That's not going to happen," Jules snapped. "I won't allow it."

"It's your party," Sam drawled. "You can cry if you want to, my friend—but you can't tell the Secret Service where to place their snipers."

"Shit," Jules said because he surely knew that Sam was right. He laughed his disgust. "I hate this. I hate . . . the idea of having to tell Jones, *Hey, you know how we gave you a new identity and a chance to start with a clean slate? Except not so fast there, pal, because when we said* clean slate, *we didn't really mean it.*"

"Is he coming to the party this weekend?" Sam asked.

"Yup."

"I'll tell him for you," Sam said.

"No." Jules sighed. "Thank you. Really. But . . . I'll talk to him. Just . . . Will you do me a favor and . . . try to recruit him?"

Sam laughed. Do Jules a *favor*? Sam had wanted to add Jones to the Troubleshooters Incorporated team since Jules first told him the man was back in the States. "You said I should stay away—that he wasn't interested."

"He's not," Jules said. "But just . . . do it anyway. I want to make sure he knows that *someone* respects and appreciates him."

"I'll make him feel the love," Sam said. "Except, of course, when Lys and I are kicking his ass out on the gallery's game room floor."

"Jones won't play laser tag," Jules warned him. "He never does."

"Yeah, we'll see about that," Sam said.

"Alyssa's really going to play?" Jules asked.

"Oh, yeah," Sam said. "And can I warn you in advance? If anyone makes a *bigger target* comment, they may not survive." He lowered his voice. "Her hormones are a . . . tad unbalanced—and God forbid you repeat that—I'll deny having said it. Talk about evil twin robots . . ." He laughed. "Last time I used the H-word, she damn near laser-beamed a hole in me with her eyes. It's kinda funny in a twisted way—apparently a symptom of her pregnancy's hormonal inbalance is being completely unable to acknowledge the hormonal inbalance."

The biggest problem of all, in Sam's opinion, was that when Alyssa got pissed off or impatient, she got full of attitude and sharp, dry humor. She totally cracked him up, especially when she got indignant—and she thoroughly turned him on. He was walking around these days in a perpetual state of *do me now,* and she was collapsing into bed at night, too exhausted to do much of anything but sleep.

"I can't wait to see you guys," Jules said.

"Back at ya, Cassidy," Sam told him. "Hey. Today, we're in single digits. Nine days and counting until Chadwick marries you—and all your annoying bullshit."

Jules laughed, as Sam hoped he would. "Yeah, but at least I don't have an evil twin robot."

"That we know about," Sam pointed out.

"Later, SpongeBob." Jules was still laughing as he hung up the phone.

PART FIVE

ghosts of christmases past

SATURDAY, DECEMBER 8
BOSTON, MASSACHUSETTS

WHEN THE BULK OF U.S. NAVY SEAL TEAM SIXTEEN arrived at the party, Jules came over and put his hand on Robin's back.

He just rested it there lightly, hooking one finger into one of the empty belt loops on Robin's cargo pants as the wave of testosterone entered the huge lobby of the laser tag gaming hall.

Robin had to smile. It was so Jules. He was smiling and as friendly as ever, but staking out his territory.

He did it again, seeking Robin out when a group from Art Urban's studio made the scene. Although this time, he pulled Robin even closer, his arm around his waist.

Robin put his hand over Jules's, interlacing their fingers and holding it there, firmly in place. *Yes, that's right, babe, I'm yours.* Interestingly, the look that Jules flashed him was faintly apologetic.

Whatever he was sorry about was fine with Robin. Jules was . . . extremely creative when it came to his apologies.

It was interesting to see the two worlds collide—SEALs, FBI agents, and Troubleshooters operatives mixing and mingling with actors, set dressers and makeup artists—not to mention a smaller group of spouses and significant others.

It was interesting, too, to be in this kind of party setting with nary a drop of alcohol in sight. Jules had been adamant about that, all throughout the planning stages. Their wedding, and everything surrounding and leading up to it—this so-called yet extremely co-ed bachelor party, next Thursday's rehearsal dinner, and especially Saturday's reception—would all be completely dry. They'd toast their lifetime commitment to one another with sparkling apple juice.

It was weird, though, to be in a blow-out party setting like this with music playing and people talking loudly, and *not* have a drink in his hand. No, one in *each* hand. Robin always had been efficient.

"You okay?" Jules asked him now, his voice low, as usual, able to read Robin's mind.

Robin nodded. "Yeah. Although if one more of your friends introduces themselves to me and gives me that *you hurt Jules and I will hunt you down* look, I might start taking it personally."

"Oh, God," Jules said. "Please tell me you're kidding."

"It's fine," Robin said, cursing himself as Jules's tension level got even higher. He shouldn't have said anything. "It's that old AA trust thing." One of the things he'd learned in rehab, and was reminded of nearly daily in the AA meetings he attended, was that everyone had different rules and time limits, and a recovering alcoholic had to be patient when it came to re-winning their trust. "I've earned it. Plus, I'm secure in knowing that even though *my* friends won't hunt you down if you hurt *me*, they *will* give you a bad haircut if you ever stumble into their makeup trailer."

Jules laughed. And didn't kiss him. Even though they both knew he wanted to.

"Oh, come on," Robin said. "You're going to kiss me in front of everyone next week at the wedding." He had a sudden twinge of doubt. "Aren't you?"

"Jules, excuse me." Dolphina appeared at Robin's shoulder, keeping Jules from answering. "You asked me to let you know when the Joneses arrived? They're here."

"Thank you," Jules said. He looked at Robin.

"Go," Robin said. This was about the problem that the Secret Service had with Jules's very good friend Davis Jones. Jules had been losing sleep over it for a week now. They'd talked about it, and Jules was adamant about pulling Jones aside and talking to him privately, without Robin or even Jones's wife, Molly, as an audience.

But before he went to handle what was, at the least, an extremely awkward situation, Jules grabbed the front of Robin's shirt and pulled his head down for a kiss that was neither short nor sweet.

Jay-sus Lord A'mighty, someone grab the fire extinguisher. The crowd of friends around them noticed, of course, and started to whoop and holler.

"I'm not just kissing you at the wedding," Jules told Robin over the applause, as he finally let him go, smoothing Robin's shirt back down, his hands warm on his chest. He was actually blushing slightly, which was completely adorable. "I'm kissing the shit out of you."

"Hey, now," Robin said to Dolphina, who looked as surprised as he felt, as they both watched Jules walk away. "Is he hot, or is he *hot*?"

"He's hot," Dolphina agreed. It *was* almost criminal how good Jules looked today in his jeans and a T-shirt. Particularly walking away.

But this entire party here at Laser-Mania was a snug-fitting T-shirt fest, with an entire team of Navy SEALs on hand to model the latest in camouflage wear.

A trio of them—Izzy Zanella, Jay Lopez, and the impossibly young and blue-eyed Tony V.—hadn't been shy about letting her know that they were checking her out. Although young Tony just seemed to be along for the ride. Maybe it was Dolphina's imagination, but he appeared to be far more interested in checking out Jules.

And Lord save her, she had to be completely crazy, but despite the SEAL eye-candy, she found herself watching the door.

For Will Schroeder.

For crying out loud.

"Sam Starrett's organizing a laser tag game called Balls over by the playing area," Dolphina told Robin as the door opened and someone who wasn't Will came inside.

"Of course he is," Robin said with a laugh. "You gonna play?"

Dolphina gave him a look. Not a chance. It was, from what she gathered, an elimination contest between closely-tethered-together two-player teams, hence the earthy name. The object was to survive a pitched laser tag battle on a course vaguely reminiscent of a classic *Star Trek* set—with plenty of fake rocks and pretend ruined buildings to hide behind.

Apparently Sam and his wife, Alyssa, were the reigning champions. They had never been beaten. Not ever. Not by anyone.

"It's fun," Robin urged her.

When Sam had explained the rules in his perpetually amused-sounding Texas drawl—*there are no rules*—he'd also been extremely vocal in his opinion of why he was the king: It was because sharpshooter Alyssa was his queen. She was, in his words—at least when small ears weren't around—*fuckin' great.*

"Sam always sets it up so that there're three different skill levels," Robin continued. "Everyone's welcome, and there'll be plenty of us in the beginner group. And if you can't find a beginner level partner, say, if you want to team up with, oh, maybe Captain Biceps, Commodore Six-Pack or even Admiral Pecs over there— Well, forget the admiral, Dolph, he's . . . not your type. But say you and Cap'n Zanella hit it off, you can team up to play Balls at the beginner level, but the Z-man'll need to handicap himself."

"How's he going to do that?" Dolphina was skeptical. "Hop around on one leg?"

"Maybe. Jules and I once teamed up to play my sister and Cosmo's mom." Robin laughed. "Lot of shrieking involved in that game. Especially since Jules tied his ankles together and his hands behind his back—you know, to bring him down to our amateur-hour level. So there we are, attached to each other—you put on a harness, and there's a bungee cord that stretches to about three feet, total, connecting you to your partner and . . . I was laughing so hard, I was totally useless. It wasn't just Jules flopping around like a fish, but Cos's mom—she screamed and did this little dance every time she pulled the trigger. She told me later that she was pretending to be one of Charlie's Angels. I'm telling you, Janey and I were *crying*. So there's Jules with his weapon behind his back, right? And he was still a better shot than the three of us put together."

"So who won?" Dolphina had to ask, grinning at the picture Robin had painted.

"Cosmo's mom killed us all—starting, of course, with Janey, her own teammate."

"Speaking of Cosmo's mom," Dolphina said. "Yashi's dad is here." She singsonged, "He asked me where she wa-as."

"Oh, *really*?" Robin was intrigued. He'd told Dolphina on Thanksgiving that he thought he'd noticed a spark between the two older members of their dinner party. Dolphina hadn't noticed it then, she'd been too busy dodging Will, but this afternoon, Yashi's dad had been just a *smidge* too casual when he'd asked about Mrs. Richter.

"Have you seen her?" Dolphina asked Robin now.

"Not since she arrived," he said. "But knowing Cos's mom, she's queuing up to play Balls—probably trying to talk Commander Jacquette into being on a team with her."

SEAL Commander Jazz Jacquette was about seven feet tall—a very big, very black, very handsome man who rarely smiled. She couldn't imagine him teaming up with Cosmo's mom to do anything, let alone play Balls. And yet . . . Cosmo's mom was so infectiously upbeat—Dolphina had never seen anyone say no to her.

Maybe it was time to wander up to the spectator loft . . . "If you see Yashi's dad," Dolphina started.

"Cosmo's mom and Yashi's dad," Robin mused. "They must've had real names at *some* point in their lives . . ."

"Lois and Clark," Dolphina said, and at Robin's disbelieving look, she confessed. "I don't know what Yashi's dad's name is, but Cosmo's mom is Lois."

"I kind of liked thinking of her as *Mom*," Robin admitted. "But now, all I'm going to be able to picture—whenever I talk to her—is her flying through the night sky, with Yashi's dad in a Superman suit."

They both laughed, because Yashi's dad was an exact replica of Yashi, only older. Both men were deadpan and slow-talking, but with a dry sense of humor. There had been times, during Thanksgiving, that Dolphina had wanted to check Yashi's dad for a pulse.

"Thanks *so* much for that, Dolph," Robin continued. "I gotta find Jules . . ."

"That's why you pay me the big bucks," she called after him as he went in search of his partner, no doubt to make sure that Jules, too, would forever carry that image of Cos's mom and Yashi's dad in his head.

"Hey."

Dolphina turned, and there they were. Will and Maggie. "Hey!" She focused her sudden quick rush of pleasure on the girl, who was dressed in warrior gear, including a cammie-print bandana, worn biker-style on her head. She held out her arms, and Maggie gave her a warm hug. "How are you? You look ready to play Bah—laser tag. I'm glad you could come."

"Are you kidding?" Maggie radiated excitement. "I can't believe I was invited. Where's Jules? I want to meet Jules."

Dolphina stood on her toes and scanned the room and . . . Oh. Jules was still in the corner, by the door, in deep discussion with the much taller, dark-haired man who obviously had come only as a spectator, dressed as he was in khakis and a polo shirt. He looked like an insurance adjuster from Iowa, and not at all like someone whom the Secret Service believed posed a threat to the President.

"He's still talking to Jones," Robin answered for Dolphina as he reappeared, and Will stood on his toes to look over at Jules.

"Lot of people here," Will told Dolphina as she looked at him. "Gotta start learning names."

Oh, God. She fished in the bag she was carrying on her shoulder, pulling out a set of labels she'd made for the occasion. *I am a Boston Globe Reporter,* they read. She stuck one on the front of his T-shirt, aware of how solid he was beneath her hands.

Will laughed as she turned him around and put one right in the center of his back as well.

Robin, meanwhile, was giving Maggie a low five. "You came to play, huh, hot shot? You want to head over to the gaming area and partner up?"

"With *you? Yeah.*" She turned to Will. "Can we go over there?"

"I think I'm going to just stand right here," he replied, "and let Dolphina cover me with labels." He looked at her. "Don't stop with only two—I'm enjoying this."

"I'm done," she said. And great. She was blushing now.

"Are you sure?" he teased. "Because they're not very big. You might want to put a few more on me, just to be safe—"

"Come on, Maggie. Let's leave these kids to their squabble and go kick some butt," Robin said, but then turned to Will. "If it's okay with you . . . ?"

"Go wild." The reporter looked hard at his niece as Dolphina jammed her sheet of labels back into her bag. "But Mags—"

"I know." The girl was clearly long-suffering. She began to recite, with plenty of eye rolls as accompaniment: "I don't leave the building, I don't give anyone my phone number or e-mail address, I leave my cell phone on so you can call me if you need me, I don't bother anybody, I don't ask any embarrassing questions . . ."

"Embarrassing questions like what?" Dolphina heard Robin ask as he led her toward the gaming area.

"Change the subject, Mags," Will shouted after them, but it wasn't clear if she'd heard him. He looked at Dolphina and rolled his eyes, too. "I guess he asked for it."

"I'm a little afraid to ask," Dolphina said.

"Isn't it weird to film a love scene? What's it like be naked in front of all those people? What if you really *hate* the person you're kissing?" He did a dead-on imitation of Maggie. "What if they think you weren't really acting and later they knock on your trailer door? What does *Jules* think when he watches a movie where you're kissing someone else?" he said. "The list goes on. And on. So where's *my* hug?"

Maybe it was that same insanity that had her watching the door for him. Or maybe she wanted to throw him into the same kind of chaos that she was feeling.

But she did it. Dolphina actually hugged him, enjoying the flare of astonishment in his eyes.

But then he wrapped his arms around her and hugged her back, even as he laughed with a mix of surprise and appreciation. "I guess I should stay away from you more often," he said, his breath warm against her ear.

Ever since that first day when he'd shown up early, he'd been careful to keep to his scheduled appointments with Robin and Jules—none of which had brought him out to the house.

Will had e-mailed her, though, numerous times throughout each day—and even on the weekend—sometimes just a brief line with a link to an article or a YouTube clip that he'd thought would make her laugh, but usually a longer, charming, chatty note, in which he'd written, surprisingly candidly, about himself.

He wanted to write a book—nonfiction. He had a number of ideas, and quite a few leads on what he believed would be not merely a great story but also a timely subject.

Living with Maggie had turned his world upside down—in a good way. It had raised his respect for his sister enormously. He remembered back when Maggie was seven, Arlene had lost her job. He'd been so blasé. *So? Get a new one.* Now *he* was the one worried about what the next few months were going to bring. It was eye-opening and humbling.

On top of his e-mails, Will's columns in the *Globe* had been both interesting and respectful—his two-part article on Robin's father's decision not to attend the wedding had turned into a charming profile on a local Boston couple—two men who'd been together since they'd met in the Navy during the Second World War.

The next day, Will profiled Robin's father's dismal marriage track record, then filled the remaining space with a list of other so-called "defenders of marriage," mostly senators, congressmen and right-wing pundits who had married and then discarded their first, second and sometimes even third wives.

He ended the article by stating that the elderly couple that he'd profiled the day before, who had stayed together through sickness and health for sixty-two years, had celebrated the third anniversary of their legal marriage this past May.

As icing on the cake, Will had sent Dolphina another e-mail just yesterday, telling her that Monday's column would be focused on Greater Boston PFLAG's Safe Schools Program—one of Robin's favorite charities.

All discussion about the Secret Service's perusal of the guest list had ceased. As had any request for Adam Wyndham's contact info.

"I was thinking about your . . . dinner invitation," Dolphina admitted now as she pulled back from their embrace. She suddenly felt shy. Awkward. What if he'd stayed away because he'd decided he wasn't interested after all? "I mean, if you still want to have dinner—"

"Very much," he said. He hadn't let her go, his arms still around her, and as he tugged her even closer, she didn't know where to put her hand. "Very, very much."

She knew where she *wanted* to put it—on the back of his neck, her fingers in the softness of his too-long hair. Instead, she touched the sleeve of his T-shirt, the warmth of his arm. "Because I was thinking, you know, the wedding's next Saturday. Maybe . . . we could make plans for . . . Sunday?" She looked up into his eyes, and God, she was in trouble.

Because he was looking at her the exact same way she knew she was looking at him.

With all of this crazy attraction right there in her eyes. With heat and desire and, yes, even fear . . .

But also hope.

"Uhn," he said—an exhale that was more a sound than an actual word, yet still managed to express exactly what he was feeling. She knew because she felt it, too.

And Dolphina couldn't help it. She put her hand on his neck, but instead of kissing her, he grabbed her. He pulled her back with him to the shadows at the edge of the room, where he yanked her into his arms and finally did capture her mouth with his.

Unlike that gentle kiss in his apartment, this time he kissed her hungrily, pulling her tightly against him as if he wanted every inch of her touching every inch of him, as if he wanted to absorb her, to fuse together so he'd never have to let her go.

Or maybe that was just what she wanted.

It was crazy.

And it was a darn good thing they were standing here, in a crowded room. If they'd been alone, there was no telling how much of their clothing would've been on the floor by now.

Which *was* crazy. And totally unlike her.

Of course, she'd been so careful with Simon, and look where that had led.

In the end, it was Will who stopped kissing her, resting his forehead against hers, breathing hard. His voice was rough. "Now I know *exactly* what I want for Christmas."

She started to laugh, but he kissed her again, and it was a searing promise of heart-stopping, mind-blowing sex. God, God, God . . . It was weeks until Christmas. "Maybe we should celebrate Chanukah this year," she told him. Chanukah had already started.

She'd surprised him—again—and he laughed as he looked at her. "Yeah," he said, but it was strange, as if he weren't responding to her, but instead coming to a conclusion. "Yeah."

"So . . . dinner on Sunday, then?" she asked. "Maybe just the two of us . . . at my place?" Her audacity made her voice sound a little tentative, so she added, "I don't make that kind of invitation very often." That is, if *not very often* could be defined as *never.*

But somehow Will knew, because his eyes were soft now, and as gentle as the hand he used to tuck her hair behind her ear. "I would love that," he said. "But I'd also love to take you out, so if you decide you'd rather . . ."

She kissed him again, and he made a sound, low in his throat. "Or we could skip the whole dinner and dating thing and just get married."

He was smiling at her, clearly kidding, or . . . Was he? There was a glint in his eyes that seemed deadly serious. Of course she really didn't know him very well, so maybe this was how he teased. So Dolphina laughed, and reached for him again, but this time he kept her at arm's length.

"We're both supposed to be working here," he reminded her. "I've got to go interview a Navy SEAL or two, and check out this game that Robin and Maggie are playing and . . . you're looking at me as if you want to kiss me again and I'm never going to leave this corner of the room if you don't stop that."

"Well, maybe *you* should stop looking at *me* like you want to kiss *me* again," she countered.

"It can't be done," Will confessed. "I've been looking at you like this ever since I crashed the shower. I always thought love at first sight was a crock of shit. But, God—I feel as if I've known you forever. And I've never been so certain of anything before in my life. You're the one."

Dolphina's heart was in her throat. He was serious. He was . . . She nodded. "You had me at *crock of shit*," she told him and he laughed. "But would you mind repeating that very last part . . . ?"

His smile faded, but it didn't disappear. It just morphed into something tender, something heartfelt. Something she'd been afraid she'd live her whole life without ever seeing. "You're the one," he whispered as he searched her face, no doubt looking for that same wondrous something.

And finding it in her eyes, he kissed her again.

The party was winding down.

At least this part of it was. Tonight, those who could stay were coming back to the house for pizza, and to help trim the Christmas tree.

Most of the SEALs and Troubleshooters had left, off to do some combined training. Jules knew that he could thank the commanding officers of both groups for setting up what had rapidly become their yearly tradition—cold weather training in the mountains of New Hampshire—during this, the week of his and Robin's wedding.

It would have been impossible for so many of the SEALs to arrange leave all on the same day. And catching a flight to Boston would have been another challenge. This way, they were within a relatively short drive of the festivities, with all of next Friday night and Saturday scheduled as downtime.

Of course, there were no guarantees that SEAL Team Sixteen wouldn't have to go wheels up before the wedding. Heck, there were no guarantees that Jules wouldn't have to do the same—if a situation arose that was dire enough.

But Jules had learned, as Robin had, that it was often best to take life one day at a time.

And today had been a very good day.

Even with that crappy conversation Jules had had with Jones, back at the start of the party.

Jones was now sitting with his arm around his wife, Molly, on one of the sofas in Laser-Mania's spectator loft. Their two-year-old daughter, Hope, was angelic in sleep, with her head on her mother's lap.

Jones looked over, as if he felt Jules's eyes on him, and smiled, shaking his head slightly as if to echo the very words he's spoken earlier. *You worry too much, Cassidy. Did you really think I didn't expect the Secret Service to mark me? I'm fine with however you want to handle it—including watching the ceremony off-site, via webcam. I want to be there, you know I do, but we both know it's more important that the President attends.*

Despite Jones's reassurances, Jules knew that it was going to bother the man to sit in the church surrounded by an armed security team—like he was some kind of monster.

A monster who leaned over and sweetly kissed his wife, after laughing at something she'd said to Cosmo's mom.

Who was sitting on one of the sofas perpendicular to the Joneses', discussing her favorite rap artists—unbelievable, but true—with Yashi's dad, who was named Greg, not Clark.

Although Lois Richter did seem to be looking at Greg Hirabayashi as if he might, indeed, wear a giant S on his chest, beneath his gray Boston College sweatshirt.

Jules had to smile at the Superman image Robin had put in his head, and then he was just thinking about Robin and grinning like a fool.

Alyssa, who was curled up at the other end of that third sofa where Jules was parked, poked him with her toe. "That's some smile," she said.

He met her eyes, still grinning. "So did you ever think you'd be best man at my wedding?"

She thought about it. "I think I did. I didn't think it would be Robin you'd be marrying, but . . . I'm glad it is. I also didn't think it would be a *wedding* wedding, more like a commitment ceremony."

"It's not the same thing," he told her. "It's just . . . not."

"If you move out of Massachusetts," she started.

"I know," he said. In most states, his marriage wouldn't be considered legal. "It's incentive to stay."

"Have you . . ." Alyssa started, but Jules shook his head and she stopped. She knew not to press him on the issue of his plans after his current temporary assignment ended. Instead, she gave him a sudden brilliant smile. "I think the thing I find most astonishing is that I'm sharing my best man duties with Sam. I still wake up sometimes in the night and see him in bed next to me, and . . ." She laughed.

"You think, *Holy shit,*" Jules spoke for her, because he knew exactly how that felt. "*How'd I end up here?* But it's a good *holy shit.* It's the polar opposite of waking up in a ditch, or in jail. I mean, I'm just guessing, since I've never done either of those things. Well, there may have been a ditch once, back when I was in college."

"You? Never." She poked him again.

"No fair, I'm ticklish," he said, grabbing her feet.

"Remember how nervous I was when Sam and I got married?" she asked.

Jules nodded. He did remember, and he answered her next question before she asked it. "No, I'm not nervous at all."

"You're such a liar."

"I am," he agreed. "I'm extremely nervous. This is a huge fucking deal." He looked over at little Hope and winced, but he was in luck, she was still asleep. "Kind of like having a baby," he pointed out. "I mean, look at you, Lys. Yikes. You're already huge—that thing's only going to get bigger, and *then*? It's going to want to come out. Have you thought about that? I mean, good grief—have you taken a long look at Sam? He was no mere seven-pound baby. You're going to be giving birth to a . . . a *Texan.*"

Alyssa was laughing. "I'm aware of how tall Roger is, yes, thank you."

"Do you really still call him Roger?" Jules interrupted himself to ask. Sam was just a cowboy-style nickname. Starrett's given name was, indeed, Roger. "Like, when you're . . . you know."

"Sometimes," she said, laughing, because now he was trying to tickle *her* with his feet. "Yeah. It's his name. You got a problem with me calling my husband by his given name?"

"How'd we both get so lucky?" Jules asked.

"It ain't luck," Sam's voice drawled, extra heavy with the High Plains Drifter, and they both looked up to see him holding out a vest and harness to Alyssa. "It's pure, unadulterated skill. Come on, Sweet Thing, we got us some more Yankee ass to kick."

Alyssa looked at Jules. "He knows this is the only time he can call me that, when he's pretending to be Macho Texas Guy. He claims it helps psych out our opponents."

"And yet," Jules pointed out, "you call him Roger whenever your little heart desires."

She grinned. "Yes, I do." She held out her hand so that Sam could pull her to her feet. She spoke in a shock-TV-announcer voice. "Who has the *Balls* to challenge the champions?"

"I do." Jules turned to see Will's niece, Maggie, playing right along. She held her laser weapon at ready and tried to scowl menacingly. Her freckles and impish nose ruined the effect.

"Mighty Mouse here needs a partner." Sam turned to Jones. "You. Couch Potato. You've done nothing but sit around and watch all day. It's your turn."

Jones shook his head. "No, thanks."

"What are you, heartless?" Sam pulled Maggie closer. "Look at that sad little face."

Maggie went from scowl to poor little waif quite effortlessly.

"Jules'll play," Jones said quietly.

"Jules is about to become very busy comforting the Boy Wonder," Sam said, "as soon as he crawls off the gaming floor where Mouse and I teamed up to crush him and his pitiful excuse for a bodyguard."

"Dolphina's not his bodyguard," Maggie said, giggling as she corrected Sam's obviously intentional gaffe. "She's his personal assistant."

"Ah. That explains the ease with which we crushed them, then," Sam teased her back.

"Now I want to go against the great Sam and Alyssa." Maggie turned to Jones. "Sam said I don't stand a chance with anyone but you."

Jones looked at the girl, then over at Sam, and then back at his wife.

"Oh, go on," Molly said. "You know you want to."

As Jules watched, Jones looked around the room, his gaze stopping only briefly on Will Schroeder, who was still wearing Dolphina's warning labels. *I am a Boston Globe Reporter.*

Jones looked at Maggie again, and then at Sam, and then once more over at Jules.

And then he smiled.

Uh-oh.

"All right," Jones said, pushing himself to his feet. "Come on, kid. Although I've got to warn you—it's been years since I've done anything like this."

As Maggie led Jones down to the gaming floor to put on the vest, harness and tether, Jules moved closer to the railing, to get a closer look at the action that would be unfolding below.

From where he stood, he could see Jones talking to Maggie. She was laughing as she nodded enthusiastically.

"This should be good." Robin joined him at the railing, leaning on it with his elbows, making his shoulders the perfect height for Jules to slip his arm around. He was radiating body heat from his recent round of play. His hair was rumpled, and his face was damp with sweat, and his smile was wide—he wasn't just radiating heat, he was radiating sheer happiness.

But as he met Jules's gaze, something shifted in his eyes, turning his joy into something hotter, yet truth be told, no less joyful. "Yeah, and you better stop looking at me like that," Robin murmured. "We've got guests coming over for dinner—and a Christmas tree to trim. I'm not getting you naked until midnight, babe—and that's at the earliest."

Jules smiled happily back at him, because, yikes, he loved the anticipation, and Robin knew it. For Jules, the entire evening would be foreplay. Every time their eyes met, even from across the room . . . Every time their hands touched . . . By the time they finally did fall into bed, the heat between them would be nuclear. "It'll probably be more like three a.m."

"You're so mean," Robin said, laughing. He was far less patient than Jules, and far more into immediate gratification. Spontaneous combustion.

When they went home, they would have to shower quickly, and get changed for dinner. Well. Provided they timed it right . . . Jules sneaked a quick look at his watch. Yeah, if they got out of here in the next, say, fifteen minutes . . . the showering part could well end up being a little less quick because, knowing Robin, he'd use the opportunity to grab some immediate gratification.

Meanwhile, Jules could stand here and anticipate *that*, too.

"That is one hell of a smile," Robin mused, but even before he finished saying the words, he'd figured it out. "Ooh, you're going to let me jump you in the shower, aren't you?"

"Pretending I didn't just hear that," Will announced as he joined them at the railing, to Jules's right. "Dolphina said to tell you she's going back to the house. She wanted to be there in case the pizza delivery guy came early."

"Thanks," Jules said.

"Why are you blushing?" Robin asked him. "You think Will

doesn't know just from *looking* at me that I'm all over you, every chance I get?" He gazed pointedly at the reporter. "Kind of the way we can tell, just from looking at him that he's got a major thing for our Dolphina?"

"Although a big clue," Jules agreed, "was the way they kept sneaking away, all day, looking for each other."

"To suck face," Robin added. "Imagine my surprise when I dash to the men's, and there in the shadowy corner by the pay phones is my personal assistant in a lip lock with the evil *Boston Globe* reporter."

"That was my fault," Will said quickly. "It was me. It wasn't . . . She was trying to . . . I'm completely to blame."

Jules looked at Robin, who looked back at him, amusement dancing in his eyes. They both looked back at Will, who wasn't just embarrassed, but also worried now that he'd gotten Dolphina into some kind of trouble.

"You got any problem with Dolphina being happy, babe?" Robin asked Jules.

"Nope," Jules said. "But I've got a problem with her being *un*-happy." He put a little FBI into his tone as he asked Will, "Are your intentions honorable?"

"Very much so," the reporter answered.

But then all conversation ceased as, from the gaming area, the buzzer sounded, signaling the start of the round.

As Jules watched, the two teams—Sam and Alyssa, and young Maggie and Jones—leaped into action.

And Maggie literally leaped. In what was clearly a planned move, Jones dropped to his knees and the girl scrambled onto him, so that he was carrying her piggy-back style.

It was brilliant, because her position there on Jones's back kept her front target—in the very center of her vest—protected from the other team's laser blasts.

Jones moved easily despite the extra weight, heading swiftly for one of the faux rock formations, firing at Sam and Alyssa as he went.

He seemed to know exactly where they were going to be, narrowly missing them both with every shot he took. It was possible that he was rusty. But probably not.

"If he goes over into that corner, he's going to get trapped," Robin said.

Jules shook his head. "He's not looking to win, he's looking to break the second place survival record," he pointed out. "Yeah, he and Maggie'll be trapped there, but they'll also be able to hold Sam and Alyssa off." The reigning champions wouldn't be able to attack Jones and Maggie without being targets themselves.

"But they'll get Jones and Maggie with the twenty-second rule," Robin said. That rule was designed to prevent teams from hunkering down, out of range of their opponents. After twenty seconds with no major movement from at least one team member, the computer would shut down that team's weapons. The rule kept the game from stagnating.

"Just watch," Jules said, as on the gaming floor Jones—and Maggie, too—held Sam and Alyssa off for as long as possible before leaping behind the protective cover of the rock formation that would, indeed, trap them.

After twenty-something seconds—Jones stretched it as long as he could—sure enough, he alone came out from behind the cover. It was a sacrificial act which reactivated Maggie's weapon, even as it got him "killed."

And then it was Maggie's turn to keep firing, keeping Sam and Alyssa at bay for an additional twenty seconds, which—yes!—gave them best survival time *ever* among all the second placers that Sam and Alyssa had slaughtered.

Maggie was beside herself. Jones was laughing—a sound Jules

didn't hear often enough. Sam and Alyssa, too, were loudly appreciative of both the skill and knowledge that had gone into Jones's plan.

But it was Will who caught Jules's attention, as he frowned at the computer screen that allowed participants and viewers to replay a simulation of the battle, to analyze and improve upon technique.

"Damn," he said.

Jules went to look.

"He was nine and a half centimeters from ending the game in three seconds." Will replayed the segment, pointing to the screen which showed that Jones had gotten off two nearly dead-accurate shots, one at Sam and one at Alyssa, right after the buzzer. Each had been, indeed, nine and a half centimeters from the targets on their vests.

Will used the computer keyboard to request a more detailed analysis. Out of all the times Jones had fired his weapon, there were eight different instances where he'd come nine and a half centimeters from "killing" either Sam or Alyssa.

Okay, not exactly nine and a half centimeters every *single* time. Twice he'd missed by nine point four seven centimeters, once he'd missed by nine point five three centimeters.

One clearly wild shot was nine point three eight centimeters from Sam's target.

"You have interesting friends," Will commented to Jules. "A roomful of counterterror experts, and an insurance adjuster from Iowa can kick everyone's ass."

Jules reached over and pushed *escape*, clearing the information from the computer screen. "It's just a game."

"If it were just a game," Will pointed out, "why go to such effort not to win?"

"Not everyone's been as lucky as you, Will," Jules told him. "Not everyone gets to go to an Ivy League school and live in a world that's black and white. Good and evil. Wrong and right. Some people are pushed into a place where there are only shades of gray. Most of them don't ever make it back out into the light. And those who do . . . They tend to have different priorities. Winning a game is outrageously unimportant to Jones."

"FYI, I'm going to approach him, see if he'll talk to me," Will said.

Jules shook his head. "No, you're not."

It wasn't a response Will was used to getting and it clearly made the reporter's hackles rise. "That wasn't a request. It was an announcement of my intentions. I was being courteous—"

"Look." Jules tried diplomacy. "We're having a party tonight. He's got a flight out in the morning. Whatever questions you think you have for him . . . Just let it go."

Will nodded. "Questions like, what was it like to work for the most notorious Southeast Asian drug lord of the twentieth century? And what exactly did he do to get the United States to erase all charges against him—to earn his new name?"

Shit.

"How does he feel about being red-flagged by the Secret Service?" Will continued. "Probably not surprised since the U.S. had no qualms about letting him get tortured for over two years in a jungle prison, simply because acknowledging his presence there would have been politically uncomfortable for them. Oh, and I'd love to find out if it makes him nervous to know that, despite the new name, his true identity is still known among high ranking members of an administration who've outed covert operatives for political gain."

Jules sighed. So much for his pre-dinner shower.

"I suspect Mr. Jones will be interested in making time to talk to me," Will continued. "Or should I call him . . . Mr. Morant?"

"Dear Lord." Jones's wife, Molly, had been leading her sleepy daughter toward the ladies' room, but now she stopped, having clearly overheard Will.

And now it wasn't merely Jules's shower that was in jeopardy. It was the entire rest of the evening. Thanks to Will, Jules was probably going to miss the trimming of the Christmas tree. He looked over at Robin, who'd had his plans for their first Thanksgiving disrupted, too.

Damn Will Schroeder.

Of course, Jules could also thank Will—and fellow reporter Jack Lloyd—for his being alive to enjoy this season's Christmas tree. Without their help, Jules—and Max, too—would surely have been killed. And heck, the man *was* some amazing investigator to have dug up all that accurate information on Jones in such a short amount of time.

But Molly was standing there with her jaw on the floor and horror in her pretty brown eyes. Jules could only imagine what she was feeling. She was surely picturing not just her evening, but her entire new life slipping away from her.

Sure enough, she got in Will's face. "Who else knows? Who else have you told?"

The tension in the room was like a living thing.

Sam was tempted to call in the Ghostbusters, because it seemed to hang above them all—a dark, swirling cloud of unhappiness, anger and frustration.

Jules had jumped immediately into negotiator mode back at Laser-Mania, which was the only reason the dickhead reporter was still breathing. He'd commandeered Sam and Alyssa, putting Will Schroeder into their custody, so to speak, instructing them to get him into their car and over to this office in their house in thirty minutes. No sooner, no later.

They'd had to drive around the block a few times, but when they'd walked in, right on the dot, Jules already had Molly and Jones sitting on the sofa. Robin and Dolphina were in the room, too.

Out of those five unhappy faces, Dolphina won the prize. Molly was clearly worried and upset, but Dolphina's face was a thundercloud. If looks could've killed, Will would've gone toes up instantly.

In the car, on the way over, Sam had spent some time wondering if Dolphina had been working with the reporter. He'd seen them together at the party, and they'd seemed really friendly. Extra friendly, in a *let's pretend we're friends so everyone won't know how badly we want to have sex* way. Which, in the entire history of mankind, had never truly fooled anyone.

But now it was clear that Dolphina had been used.

And here Sam had been thinking he was going to be needed to prevent *Jones* from wrapping his hands around Will's skinny neck.

"You son of a bitch," Dolphina put voice to her feelings as she glared at Will. "What the *hell* is wrong with you?"

Fa la la la la, la la la la.

Sam looked over at Jules. Who apparently was curious as to how Will was going to answer Dolphina's question.

"Dolph," Will said. "I know what you're thinking, but you're wrong."

"I can't believe you would do this," she said. "I'm such an idiot. I'm *always* surprised."

"Please let me explain."

"Please do," she said. The guy who'd penned that "hell hath no fury" phrase had known exactly what he was writing about. She was practically snarling in her outrage. "That's why we're all here, isn't it? Instead of enjoying Jules and Robin's party? So you can *explain*?"

"You want us out in the hall?" Alyssa asked Jules quietly.

"I'd like you and Sam to stay." It was Jones who answered her.

Out of everyone here, he was least visibly upset. Which, as Sam well knew from his own experience, didn't mean shit.

Still, Sam hid a sigh as Alyssa closed the door behind them, sealing them here in the temple of doom. And sealing them *off* from the sounds of merriment and the delicious aroma of perfectly cooked New England–style pizza wafting in from the kitchen, where Robin's sister, Jane, and her husband, Cosmo, had taken Hope and Maggie and apparently gotten the party started.

Sam found a chair under Robin's butt and evicted him from it, bringing it over to his pregnant wife.

"Sorry, I wasn't thinking," Robin apologized.

"Thanks," Alyssa said to Robin as she sat down, even as she gave Sam a darkly amused look.

"What?" he said. "I was just helping him think."

"I'd like to start by making it clear that no one else knows about any of this." Will looked at Molly. "I understand your concern— "

"You have *no* idea," she told the reporter.

"Yeah," he said. "Actually, I do. I used to live in Indonesia, Mrs. Jones. I was a . . . guest in the same prison where your husband spent quite a few years. Fortunately, my sister raised the money and arranged my release before they removed too many of my fingernails." He looked at Jones. "I can't imagine what it was like to be in there with no hope of getting free."

"You say no one else knows," Dolphina's voice shook as she rewound the conversation slightly, "but just a few weeks ago, your computer was hacked."

"I've been careful this time," Will said. "I've upgraded my entire system. Dolph, look, I know what you're thinking . . ." He took a step toward her, but she took a step back. "This wasn't supposed to happen like this." He spoke to Jones. "I'm not going to write a news story about you. It was never my intention to out you."

Jules proved that his good listener skills were still his forte. He'd caught the nuance of Will's wording. "What *are* you going to write?" he asked the reporter.

"A book." Will turned to Dolphina, imploringly, as if he still thought he had a chance at getting laid tonight, fool that he was. "I told you I wanted to write a book. I wasn't keeping this a secret from you."

He turned to Jones, no doubt realizing that getting laid would be permanently off his "to do" list if he were dead. "It wasn't my intention to frighten you or your wife. I was hoping to talk to you in a . . . less public setting, but . . . Sergeant Jones, I really want to write your story. It *needs* to be told."

Jones just sat there silently, an impassive stone.

"Where did you get your information, Will?" Jules broke the silence by asking. "Dolphina said you were interested in finding out if the Secret Service had flagged any of the guests, but that she didn't provide you with that list."

"She didn't," Will said quickly. "She had nothing to do with it. When I said that to you, before, about Jones being on the Secret Service list, I was just bullshitting. I was guessing. I didn't even know for sure that Davis Jones *was* Grady Morant. Not until Mrs. Jones's reaction . . ."

Deck the halls with lying liars. Sam wasn't sure what it was about Will's delivery that didn't ring true, but it seemed glaringly obvious to him that the reporter wasn't giving them the truth, the whole truth and nothing but the truth. He glanced at Alyssa and she met his eyes in silent agreement.

"I'm so sorry," Molly murmured to her husband.

"It's okay." Jones came to life to reassure her, and he even managed to smile. "We'll get through this."

"Will's lying again. What a surprise," Dolphina announced. As he'd been talking, she'd been accessing her laptop computer and now she pointed to it. "He absolutely got access to the Secret Service list from me. Not intentionally, but . . . I'm at fault. It says here that the file was opened on Monday afternoon, but I hadn't touched it since the previous Wednesday. I mean, why should I? It was a list with a single name." Her fingers flew across her keyboard. "The guest list file was also opened at that same time—1:34 p.m. on Monday. It must've been while I was upstairs, dealing with the toilet delivery." She squared her shoulders as she faced Jules. "I have a computer password, but I didn't activate that function before I left the room. I didn't close any files. I just . . . left the reporter in the room with my laptop. It's my—"

"It's *not* her fault," Will started, but she cut him off.

"Just don't," she told him. "It *is* my fault and nobody wants to hear your excuses. Nobody believes you anyway—why should they? You're a liar." She turned to Jones. "He knows where you live. He knows your phone number. That was the extent of the info I had on the guest list."

"I know significantly more than that about you now," Will admitted. "Some was theory, but, um . . . It's really only because I spent so much time in Indonesia that I was able to piece it together. I honestly don't think there are many people who could have connected the dots the way I did."

"An egotistical liar," Dolphina mused. "What *was* I thinking?"

Will turned to her. "I'm just trying to reassure them that they're still safe." He turned to Jones. "You need to tell whoever's in charge of your new identity to create tax forms for W. Davis Jones—from before you and Molly were married. A more detailed service record would help, too. At the risk of sounding, yes, egotistical, most experts on Indonesia's politics don't have my investigative skills so, again, in my opinion, you're extremely safe. And that's not taking into consideration that the Indonesian factions who might still carry a grudge and want to harm you are no longer in power. Frankly, I believe that you're hiding from a threat that doesn't exist."

"That's what I believe, too," Jules said.

But Jones didn't. Sam could see the man's doubt, his fear for his family, his unwillingness to take an unnecessary risk.

"You know the really stupid thing about all this?" Jules asked. Sam wasn't sure if he was talking to anyone in particular, or just the room in general. "It's that after Robin and I got back from our honeymoon, I was going to call you." He was speaking to Jones now. "You've been talking about writing a memoir for a while—organizing your notes. I've been impressed by Will, and with his background knowledge of Indonesia . . ." He shrugged. "It seemed like it would be a good match."

"I'd be interested in collaborating on the project," Will told Jones. Sam had to give the guy credit. He didn't know the meaning of the word *quit*. "I didn't realize you wrote, but . . . Either way, I'd love to see your notes."

Jones looked at Will. "Give me one good reason I shouldn't just kill you right here."

Again, to his credit, Will didn't wet his pants with fear. He just kind of smiled back at Jones. "Her name's Maggie, and she's in the kitchen. Although maybe if you *did* kill me, her mother would get to come home from Iraq. If I could get that guarantee in writing, I'd say go for it."

Dolphina made a noise. "I think we should check to make sure he really *has* a sister in Iraq."

He looked at her. "What? Do you think . . . Maggie's just some kid I hired . . . ?"

"With you, anything's possible," Dolphina snapped back.

And there they stood, glaring at each other.

Molly spoke up. "Why are you so interested in writing this book, Mr. Schroeder? With your credentials, surely you could write about anything. Anyone."

"Your husband's story needs to be told," Will said again, quietly now. "A frighteningly large percentage of Americans currently believe that torture is acceptable, when, in fact, it's what the bad guys do. As a country, we've got to be better than that. Maybe if people get a chance to read about what your husband lived through, they'll begin to understand what torture really means."

"What it *means*?" Jones was no longer impassive. In fact, he was up and on his feet—as was Sam. But Jones wasn't going for Will. He was just unable to sit still. "How are you going to make anyone understand what it *means*?"

He was up in Will's grill, but the reporter held his ground. "I know what it's like to be afraid of it," he told Jones. "I do know that. I've gotten the crap kicked out of me for information a time or two—I know what that's like, too. I haven't had your experiences, but . . . I'm better informed than most people. I think the answer to making readers understand is to make your story personal." He paused. "And show them what it's like to carry the scars that I know you must have. God knows *I* still have nightmares about that prison. I can only imagine what yours are like."

"Yeah," Jones said. "And they all start the same way. With some asshole finding out who I really am. They end the same way, too. Back in that torture room—every goddamn night—with Molly and Hope being killed in front of me—" He broke off, turning to look at his wife, chagrin in his eyes.

Molly had gotten to her feet, her own eyes filled with disbelief and concern. "You told me you were sleeping better. That the nightmares had let up . . ."

Jones nodded, unable now to meet her gaze. "I know. I'm sorry."

"Oh, Dave . . ." She put her arms around him, and the way he grabbed her and held onto her so tightly made Sam avert his eyes. He'd held Alyssa exactly like that—at the times he himself was fighting tears.

Jules had the same idea as Sam, moving toward the door. "Let's clear the room, give them some space," he said quietly, and Alyssa stood up.

But, "Wait," Molly said. "Don't leave. Please." She pulled back from Jones and spoke to him. "Something's got to change. It has to. Maybe . . . I don't know, but, what if . . . Will's a gift? His being here. His knowing." She wiped her face with her hands. "Maybe you still need to write about what happened to you." She looked at Jules. "We *did* talk about it, about Dave's writing a memoir, around a year ago. The nightmares were so bad . . ." She looked at Will then. "He started making notes, writing things down, and it seemed to help." She looked at Jones, clearly skeptical now of his honesty in regard to this topic. "Or did it?"

"It did," he said. "Really. But then . . . it didn't."

"Because you stopped writing," she accused him. "I offered to help, but he didn't want me to read what he'd written. He said it was bad enough that I'd have to read it once—after the book was finished. But the book never even got started. And now . . . Apparently, the nightmares are back."

"They may never go away." Robin spoke up for the first time, from where he was leaning against the fireplace mantel, over near Jules. "Some nightmares . . . just always come back."

Sam looked at the happy couple, and it was beyond obvious the Boy Wonder hadn't yet told Jules about *his* nightmares. Which no doubt started, *I'm a kid, maybe seven years old, and I come home and I know right away that my mother's been drinking . . .*

As Sam watched, Jules took Robin's hand, interlacing their fingers. Once upon a time, that would've really freaked Sam out. But now it seemed as natural as Molly reaching for Jones. Or Sam reaching for Alyssa.

"If that's the case, if the nightmares never leave, so be it," Molly said just as quietly as Robin. "We'll just have to learn to cope. But . . . maybe they *would* fade if we stopped hiding." She turned to her husband. "If *you* stopped pretending you were happy."

Okay. Now it was *really* time to leave.

"I am happy," Davis Jones protested. "Being with you and Hope—"

"You're happy when you're home," Molly agreed. "I know." She saw Sam sneaking for the door, and she turned and pointed at him. "Don't you leave. I saw you talking to Dave this afternoon. You were offering him a job with your Troubleshooters, weren't you?"

Sometimes there was nothing to do but stand tall and confess. "Yes, ma'am."

"I turned him down," Jones told Molly. "There's no way I would do that to you."

"Do *what* to me?" she asked. "Be happy in your work? Right now, you live for six o'clock, for the weekends. You pay our bills, but that's all you're doing. When you leave each morning, it's as if you turn out the light in your eyes." She shook her head. "People should love what they do—they should care about it, passionately. Dave, oh, honey, you should have seen your face when Sam was talking to you about working with him." She turned to Sam. "Does the offer still stand?"

"Of course," Sam said. He didn't risk a look at Alyssa, for fear he'd piss himself with excitement. Jones had been on his personal dream team wish list for years now. Alyssa and Jules both teased him mercilessly about having a man-crush on the guy, and yeah, if deeply admiring a fellow operator was defined as having a man-crush, then he definitely did.

"The past few years served a purpose," Molly was telling her husband now. "We both needed a rest—time to just be together. And that was wonderful. Those first few months . . . Maybe if we had all the money in the world we could do it—just both stay home all day and raise our children. But vacation's over. It's time to get back to the real world. And maybe we can help to change it, while we're at it."

Jones was looking at his wife, a little smile at the edge of his lips. "You always were a do-gooder."

She lifted her chin as she met his gaze. "You always were, too." She crossed her arms. "As far as I'm concerned, the only thing left to decide is between Florida or San Diego." She turned to Sam. "Where is the Troubleshooters office in Florida?"

"Sarasota," he told her.

"I'm leaning toward Florida." Molly looked at Jones. "How about you?"

He shook his head. "I don't care where I am, as long as you and Hope are with me." He looked at Sam. "Am I really going to be able to get the clearances I need to work for you?"

Sam let Alyssa, who was, in fact, his boss, answer that one. "We'll take care of that. We'll also make your new identity more complete."

Jones was looking at Molly again.

"Wake me up when you have nightmares," she told him, and he nodded. "So," she added. "Florida." She turned to Will. "That's probably more convenient for you, too, since you'll be helping Dave with his book. Right?"

Will looked pretty damn unhappy for a man who'd just gotten exactly what he'd wanted.

Oh. Except Dolphina, with her thundercloud face, was making it pretty obvious that his personal happy ending was going to be, well, euphemistically speaking, happy-ending free.

It was then that Jules chimed in. Once again, he'd been paying careful attention to word choices. He looked from Jones to Molly and back again. "Did you say *children*?" he asked.

Molly smiled, her hand on her stomach. "Yes, that was a plural," she admitted. "I knew when it slipped out that you were going to catch it."

"Sweetie, congratulations." Jules gave both Molly and Jones a hug.

Jones looked at Sam. "How's Troubleshooters' medical insurance?"

Sam tried his best not to grin his ass off. "For prenatal care? So far, so good."

"Are any of your friends *not* pregnant?" Robin asked Jules.

It was possible it was just a coincidence, but it was right at that very moment that Dolphina burst into tears and rushed out of the room.

Will tried to follow Dolphina, but his path was blocked by Alyssa, who was ten times scarier than her former-SEAL husband. Although as Sam came to stand beside her, he was pretty damned intimidating, too.

And then there was Jules, who looked as if it wouldn't take much incentive for him to rip out Will's throat, either.

But it was Robin who grabbed Will by the front of the shirt and uttered words that at first made him laugh. Bad move. But it was just that *Did you get Dolphina pregnant?* was the last question he'd been expecting to be asked here tonight.

"You think that's funny?" Jules asked him with outrage in his voice, and Will knew if he didn't talk fast, he was going to get the hell kicked out of him by two very angry gay men.

"No, it's not funny," he said. "And no, I haven't . . . We haven't even . . . No. I mean, unless Mommy was wrong and you *can* make babies just from kissing." He sighed. "Just hit me anyway, guys. We'll all feel better."

"I think it's time for you to go," Jules said. "You got what you wanted. I'll make sure Jones has your contact information. Oh, and after you leave here? You decide to change your mind and write an article exposing Jones?"

"I won't," Will said.

"Good," Jules said, leaving all threats silent but strongly implied.

Damn, but this had gone completely wrong. Will had been so proud of himself, too—especially at the party. Everything had been going so right—starting with him finding a parking spot right outside Laser-Mania's front doors. Maggie had had a great time, and Will had, too.

The teasing he'd gotten from the SEALs had been good natured and friendly. He'd even managed a face-to-face with an old nemesis—Troubleshooters operative Jim Nash, who'd been one of the many men to share Will's ex-wife Jackie's bed. Will had met Nash and his pal Larry Decker several times while chasing a story, and seeing Nash had always pissed him off. But today, Will's blood pressure hadn't been even slightly elevated as he'd greeted the man.

He'd felt nothing. Nada. Not even a hint of the old animosity.

Because Will was having dinner on Sunday with Dolphina. At her place.

He was, without a doubt, on top of the world.

But not anymore. And it was his own stupid fault.

Robin now handed him his coat. "Maggie's welcome to stay. We'll drive her home later—say, 9:30?"

"Thank you," Will said, humbled by their generosity. "Yeah. I just . . . I need to, you know, talk to Dolphina before I . . ."

Jules looked at Robin, who slipped out the door. He came back almost right away. "She's not interested in talking to you."

Will nodded. "Okay." He put on his coat, as if he were just going to walk out the door without an argument, without a fuss. Just walk away from the best thing that ever happened to him . . .

But Jules had him by one arm, Sam by the other as he went out into the foyer, as if they knew he was just faking his passive accord. And Will knew that Dolphina was out here somewhere—Robin had come out and back in so quickly. She was probably sitting on the top of the stairs that angled up and around, maybe on the second floor landing.

"Dolph, I made a mistake," Will called, knowing that she could hear him, hoping that she would listen. "I lied and I shouldn't have. I did it because I was afraid you would get in trouble. I wasn't thinking—I was just trying to protect you, and . . . it was stupid. If I could do it again, I'd do it differently. All of it. I'd tell you to lock your computer before going upstairs, because I know myself, and I couldn't not look. I should've told you what I found out about Jones. I should have told you what I was hoping to do. I should have been honest with you about everything . . ."

The door closed behind him with a gentle click, and Will found himself out on the porch, in the cold.

Honest about everything—not just about the way she made him feel. *You're the one . . .*

If Dolphina had heard him, she didn't respond.

And she didn't respond.

Will stood there a long time, his hands in his pockets, before he turned around and finally dragged his sorry ass home.

Sunday, December 9

"Do you . . . ever have nightmares?"

Jules looked up from the file he was reviewing as Robin slipped into bed, next to him. He'd brought an entire box of paperwork home on Friday, even though he knew he wouldn't have an extra second of time all weekend long to read any of it.

But the last of their guests were finally gone. The party had been a raging success—despite the Will Schroeder goatfuck. And who could know? Molly might well have been right—the Jones/Schroeder collaboration could well work out as a double win.

Plus, it had been fun to see Sam walking around like he'd just won the lottery, having successfully recruited Jones. He'd been so happy, he hadn't seemed to mind knowing that, had Jones wanted to, he could've beaten Sam and Alyssa at Balls. But only, Jones had humbly said, because he'd been sitting there for hours, watching them play game after game, with the area set in that specific configuration. Change the gaming area—and he probably wouldn't have stood a chance.

Or so he claimed.

The evening had improved greatly after Will had left the house, although Dolphina had never quite returned to full speed. Still, the tree had been trimmed, the pizza consumed, carols sung, cookies baked. All that, and—thank God—by driving Maggie home, Jules had conveniently "missed" the viewing of the promo for *Shadowland*, Robin's new TV series.

"Sometimes," Jules answered Robin's question about nightmares, tossing the file onto the floor, ready to give Robin his full attention and finally do it—talk about his feelings of jealousy. He'd gone so far as to poke his head into the bathroom while Robin was brushing his teeth and had said, super casually, *When you're done in here, I've got a question for you about the rehearsal dinner, and . . . there's some other stuff.* Yeah. *Some* other stuff. "They're not really nightmares. They're more . . . disturbing than scary. Like my father'll be there, and I'll know in the dream that he shouldn't be, that he's dead. And I'll wake up a little weirded out."

Robin had propped himself up on one elbow, head in his hand, his eyes serious. "That's it?" he asked. "You've lived through a lot of really bad shit . . . I mean, this past Thanksgiving alone . . ."

"I don't dream about things like that very often anymore," Jules admitted. "I don't know why. I mean, yeah, I've lived through some nightmare scenarios . . ." The worst had been that terrible, awful day last year when he'd believed that Robin had drowned. He reached out and touched Robin's arm. "Maybe I'm just really good at letting it all go."

"You're, like, the most well-adjusted person I've ever met," Robin said.

Jules laughed as he took his hand back. "Yeah, I don't think so . . ." It was the perfect segue. *Speaking of well-adjusted people, one of which I don't consider myself to be, considering my issues of intense jealousy . . . have you noticed that I haven't been able to watch any of the filmed footage from* Shadowland?

"I have nightmares about my mother," Robin said. "Usually a couple times a week."

That was news to Jules, and he sat up. "Really? About . . . the car accident?" he asked.

"No," Robin said. "I, um . . . have these nightmares where she, um . . . hits me."

"Oh, sweetie," Jules said. "That's an awful thing to dream."

"Yeah," Robin agreed, looking down at the blanket. "I'm pretty sure I dream about it because, well, she, you know, used to. Hit me. Not very often. Maybe once a month. Not because I'd done something wrong, but just . . . kind of randomly."

Dear God. Once a month for eleven years was *not very often*?

Robin looked up, meeting Jules's eyes only briefly before looking away again. "It was when she was drunk, so—"

"Don't make excuses," Jules sharply cut him off. "There's no excuse for that. None at all."

Robin nodded, the muscle jumping in his jaw. "Yeah, I know." He shifted so that he was lying down, his head on his pillow, as if telling Jules about this had exhausted him. "It was funny," he continued with his eyes closed. "I was talking to Sam, months ago, and it just kind of slipped out, you know, about my mother. And he told me that I had to tell you. But I've been putting it off because . . ." He opened his eyes and looked at Jules. "I guess I didn't want you to know. Like, Jesus, aren't I already screwed up enough without throwing child abuse into the mix?"

"Ah, baby," Jules breathed, as he pulled Robin close, wrapping his arms around him. "No. You're not responsible for that. My God . . ."

"I don't know what I was so afraid of," Robin said as he held Jules just as tightly. "I know you don't think I'm perfect and you love me anyway. I know this. So why am I scared to talk about it? And why am I still so hurt by that stupid note that my father wrote? Why does that make me feel so goddamn sad?"

"Because you have an optimistic soul," Jules told him, his heart in his throat. "Because you know that everyone deserves parents who take care of them, who protect them. Because you believe that fathers should love their sons the way my father loved me."

Robin's eyes filled with tears. "The world you grew up in was so different from mine."

"Well, you're in my world now," Jules whispered.

"I have a really vivid memory," Robin said. "I don't know, I must've been . . . maybe eight? And I was just . . . coloring, I think. I remember I was trying to be quiet, because my mother was on the phone. But she was really upset and . . . She threw it, and it hit me, but then it hit the floor and it broke, and God, she slapped me so hard. I think I fell and hit my head because I got a bloody nose. And that really freaked her out, and she did what she always did after she hit me like that. She started to cry and to hug me and to tell me how much she loved me. And I'm just bleeding, all down my shirt, but she's too drunk to help me. And I look up, and I see my father. He's standing out on the porch, on the other side of the sliding glass door, like he was about to knock. And I knew, from the look on his face, that he'd seen the whole thing. And do you know what he did?"

Jules nodded. He could guess, but he couldn't speak past the lump in his throat.

"Yep," Robin said. "He walked away. He fucking *walked away.*"

Jules just held him.

"He avoided me for years after that," Robin continued, his voice tight. "And then, when my mother died, and I had to go live with him . . . He never spoke of it. Like it had never happened. Or it was somehow my fault. Maybe I keep dreaming about it because I'm still trying to figure out exactly what it was that I did that was so wrong."

"You dream about it because you were traumatized," Jules told him. "Oh, Robin . . ."

"I think you're right about not having nightmares because you process the information properly," Robin said. "You never blame yourself for things you're not responsible for. You're so . . . secure in your . . . you-ness. You know who you are, and you like yourself. God, Jules, you have an accurate read on your abilities and skills—you see yourself as part of the picture, instead of, like, a blot on the picture. A stain."

"Is that really how you see yourself?" Jules was both bemused and horrified. "As a *stain*?"

Robin shrugged. "No. Yeah. I don't know. That's not quite right . . . It's more like, *you're* part of this massive group doing tai chi, and you're in perfect sync, in harmony with the entire world. You just move effortlessly, like you've got a place, a role and you understand it and are at peace with it. Meanwhile, I'm over here doing the watoosie, in the middle of a stampeding herd of buffalo. At least that's what it feels like."

"Can you really do the watoosie?" Jules had to ask.

Robin managed a laugh. "What do *you* think?"

"I think you could do anything that you want to," Jules told him. "Absolutely anything at all."

Robin shifted to face him, to gaze into Jules's eyes. "God, you have such faith in me," he finally whispered.

"I'm amazed by you," Jules admitted. "I know you see yourself as broken, but . . . I see only incredible strength. To have survived what you survived and still be so alive, so . . . joyful. So, yeah, I have faith in you. Infinite faith. And every time I turn around, I discover that I love you even more."

The tears were back in Robin's eyes, but instead of turning away—the way he always did, because he hated to cry in front of anyone, even Jules—he hung in.

"I like being in your world," he told Jules. "I think I'm finally ready to leave mine behind and, um . . . I was wondering if you'd mind if I . . ." He cleared his throat. "Took your name next Saturday. I won't if you don't want me to," he quickly added, no doubt because of the utter shock on Jules's face.

"No," Jules said. "I'm just . . . surprised."

Back when they'd first gotten engaged, they'd had about a ten second conversation about potential name hyphenation. Some gay couples combined their last names when they married, but Chadwick-Cassidy or Cassidy-Chadwick just seemed too unwieldy. Keeping their own names had seemed the way to go.

"Chadwick's some . . . dick who walked away from his kid," Robin told Jules now. "I'd rather be a Cassidy."

"Won't the studio want to . . . Have you talked to your agent about this?" Jules asked.

"No, but they'll want me to keep the Chadwick as a middle name, at least for a while," Robin said. "I'm okay with that—Robin

Chadwick Cassidy. Maybe eventually we can phase the Chadwick out, go to Robin C. Cassidy and then just . . . Robin Cassidy." He smiled, no doubt at the expression on Jules's face. "It does have a ring to it, doesn't it?"

Jules managed to nod. *Robin Cassidy* . . .

"It's okay with you?" Robin asked, as if he actually thought Jules might not want to share his name.

"It's very okay," Jules told him.

Robin kissed him. "What was it that you wanted to talk to me about?" he asked.

Jules just shook his head as he kissed Robin back. *Robin Cassidy* . . .

It could wait.

PART SIX

attack of the evil twin robot

THURSDAY, DECEMBER 13
LOS ANGELES, CALIFORNIA

SOMEONE HAD BEEN IN HIS CONDO.

Adam had been home for about ten minutes when he saw the pictures that had been left on his kitchen table.

They were Polaroids—who the hell used Polaroid instant film these digital days?

At first he thought it was something his cleaning lady had left behind, but then he saw what they were pictures of—one was a handgun, the other was ammunition, both bullets and clips.

Go back where you came from had been written on the bottom of the photo of the gun in creepy psycho-style printing. The son of a bitch had signed it, too. *Jim Jessop.*

The hair went up on the back of Adam's neck as he grabbed the remote control and muted the TV that he'd turned on when he'd first entered his kitchen. He stood absolutely still, held his breath and listened.

But it was hard to hear much of anything over the pounding of his heart.

Get out of the house. Adam could hear Jules's voice in his head, an echo from all those times they'd discussed personal safety. Jules wasn't just possessive, he was obsessive about safeguarding what was his. *If you ever think someone's broken in, get out, get to safety and call the police from there.*

After a while, Adam had tuned him out, but apparently, some of what Jules had said all those years ago had stuck.

He grabbed the photos and ran.

ARLINGTON STREET CHURCH
BOSTON, MASSACHUSETTS

"Any questions?" Pastor Stevens asked, as Jules's pants started to shake.

Shit. He hadn't turned his cell phone all the way off as they'd gone into the church for the rehearsal, because there was trouble brewing again in Afghanistan. He hadn't mentioned it to Robin, who no doubt had figured it out for himself, on account of Jules having to "just run in" to the office this morning, on this, the first day of his three week leave of absence.

Jules could feel Robin's eyes on him now, as he stepped aside and took out his phone and . . .

Nice. It was Adam. What a surprise that *he* would call, two days before the wedding.

Jules slipped his phone back into his pocket and smiled at Robin, who didn't look any less worried.

"I got a question," Sam was saying. He and Alyssa were standing up for Jules as his best men, so to speak. Jane and Cosmo were doing the same for Robin. "What happens if Jules's mom can't get out of Chicago?"

His mother had been flying into Boston from her home in Hawaii, and her connecting flight out of Chicago had been delayed due to bad weather in Milwaukee. The storm had swiftly moved east and now nothing was leaving O'Hare. Forecasts had lake-effect snow crushing Chicago until well into Saturday morning.

"We'll have to postpone the wedding." Robin didn't hesitate. "We'll wait until she *does* get here."

"Actually," Jules said. "I spoke to Mom this morning. I think she's trying to hire a dogsled, she's that determined to get here. But in the event that the snow doesn't let up . . . Sweetie, she doesn't want us to postpone."

"Tough shit," Robin said and winced. "Excuse me, Pastor. Jules. This is a beautiful church, and I understand that we only have access to it for a limited time on Saturday, but . . . I'd rather get married at the Dunkin' Donuts on the corner if it means that your mother can be there."

"I'm with you," Jules said, as Sam stepped aside to either make or take a phone call, Jules wasn't sure which. "I want her there, too, and I'd rather, you know, have the Coffee Coolatta and Turbo Hot decor, if it means she *can* be, but . . . You should probably talk to her. She made it *very* clear to me that the President's attendance is more important to her than just about anything." His mother was very aware that Bryant's attendance was an endorsement of equal marriage—of Jules and Robin's right to have the same rights as everyone else in America. "She was adamant."

Robin nodded. He'd gotten to know Jules's mom pretty well over the past few months, so he understood adamant. But he didn't like it. "Then what *is* our backup plan if she's not here to walk down the aisle?" he asked.

"Some couples choose to enter the church by these doors," the pastor pointed to two arch-shaped doors on either side of the church. "When the music starts, you would both step out and meet at the altar. The wedding party could process as planned, with the two of you standing at the front of the church."

"Works for me," Jules said.

"Your mother just . . . better get here," Robin said as Jules's phone, again, began to shake.

Los Angeles, California

Adam could get a restraining order against Jim Jessop.

He sat in the police station, staring at the officer who'd just made that genius suggestion.

"Nobody knows where Jessop is." He managed to keep from shouting. "What good is a restraining order going to do? No one's going to be able to find him to warn him away from me." As if a restraining order ever worked in the first place. It was just a piece of paper. It didn't create a bulletproof shield. "Look," he said. "Jessop broke into my house. He committed a crime. These pictures are proof."

"They might've been evidence," the police officer said, "but you removed them from the scene, so . . ." He shrugged, obviously enjoying himself just a little too much.

So Adam took out his cell phone, and accessed its voice recorder. "This is Adam Wyndham and it's Thursday, December thirteenth, and the man, Jim Jessop, who's made it clear via e-mail that he's stalking me, left a Polaroid of a deadly weapon on my kitchen table. Apparently Officer Rolande, that's R-o-l-a-n-d-e, first name Frank, is amused by my attempt to report this crime." He shut and pocketed his phone, smiling sweetly at the police person. "This way, after this nut-job kills me? The studio will know exactly who to sue." He gathered up the photos. "Thanks so much for your time and concern."

As Adam left the police station, he tried calling Jules again, but again, Jules didn't pick up.

Goddamn it, what had his life come to that the only people who would care if he were murdered were those who worked for the studio that currently employed him? And, face it, they'd only care about recouping the losses from having to replace him halfway through a movie shoot.

No one would miss him. No one would mourn.

As Adam stepped onto the sidewalk, the hair on the back of his neck was on full alert again. Damn it, ever since he'd run out of his condo, he'd had the creepiest feeling—as if someone were watching him.

It was probably his overactive imagination. Except he hadn't felt this while he was safely inside the police station.

He stood there on the corner, uncertain, flipping through his cell phone address book. There was no one to help him—no one who didn't charge him by the hour, like his good friend Lawyer Bob.

Adam gave up and tried calling Robin's phone. No answer.

Of course not.

This was his fault. Somehow he'd become the boy who'd cried wolf.

He knew Jules would believe that Jessop had broken into his house and put those photos on his kitchen table. He knew Jules would see those photos as a real threat, as the serious danger that they were.

The problem was in getting him to pick up his phone.

Adam tried Jules's number again, and was pushed right to voicemail.

He snapped his phone shut and stepped off the curb, hand held high to flag down a miraculously empty approaching cab.

He climbed in. "LAX," he told the driver, even as he opened his phone, and dialed his travel agent. "Yeah," he said as the line was answered. "I need to catch the next flight out of L.A. to Boston, Massachusetts."

BOSTON, MASSACHUSETTS

"Lemme get this straight, Squidward," Sam said with a laugh as he sat in the coffee place that was around the corner from Jules's house. They had a couple hours before the rehearsal dinner was set to start. Alyssa was back at the house, napping, and Robin was . . . off doing whatever Robin did when his sister and her family were in town. "You're worried—because you're having the best sex of your life. I'm sorry, but that's pretty fucked up."

But Jules wasn't laughing. In fact, he wasn't just upset, he was also embarrassed, so Sam tried harder to understand. But it did not compute.

"What aren't you telling me?" Sam asked him.

But Jules stayed silent, staring down into his mug of coffee, apparently unwilling to go into any detail more specific than "best sex of my life."

"This isn't locker room talk," Sam reassured him, and Jules actually smiled at that.

"At least not any locker room that *you* hang out in," he pointed out. But his smile faded and he still hesitated.

So Sam said, "This is between you and me. It goes no further. I won't even tell Alyssa." He leaned across the table, lowered his voice. "You know, past few weeks, I was struggling with some kinda weird shit myself. Everything I did, it seemed that Lys ended up pissed off at me. There was obviously something going on with her hormones, from the pregnancy? I told you about that. But when I tried to talk to Alyssa about it—like, *hmmm, guess we need to find you someone to kill*—she got even madder. And then I realized—it was like this fucking eureka moment—that she was frustrated. I'm talking sexually. Which, in hindsight was partly my fault. A lot my fault. But she was always so tired in the evening, and mornings were kind of questionable, with her varying nausea levels, and then we were at work . . . and I made the mistake of thinking, *okay, she's pregnant, I guess I'm just never having sex again.*" He laughed. "Instead, she's walking around pissed off because she wanted to, um, get it on during what she considered to be inopportune times of the day. And hey, you know me. *Inopportune* isn't in my vocabulary. In short, I installed a new lock on her office door. I say, *Tracy, hold Alyssa's calls, I got an important matter to discuss*, and . . ." He shrugged. "Problem solved."

Jules was hiding his smile behind his hand. "Sex in the office," he said. "That's . . . so not Alyssa."

Sam nodded. "Little Miss Do-No-Wrong is very happily breaking some of her rules. Thank God."

They sat in silence for a moment, just sipping their coffees, Jules not eating the cookie he'd bought. He looked tired, as if he still wasn't doing too well when it came to sleeping.

Of course, the potential problems in A-stan were adding to his tension—to Robin's as well. It was going to be rough for Robin when Jules went back out into the field. Sam's own anxiety levels had been through the roof when Alyssa had gotten back into the game after a near-death experience.

"Your turn," Sam finally broke the silence.

Jules looked up at him. "You really want to hear this?" he asked.

"Is it more embarrassing than me not having the sense to know that Alyssa would *never* want to not have sex?" Sam asked him.

Jules managed a smile. "It might be."

"Well, good," Sam said. "Then I won't be the only fool sitting at this table."

Jules cleared his throat. "I've been trying really hard not to let it bother me," he said. "The fact that Robin's playing this character. Joe."

"You haven't talked to him about this?" Sam couldn't believe they were still dragging *that* shit through the mud. "What's wrong with you? I thought talking things out came with the gay gene."

"I'm afraid to bring it up," Jules admitted. "And it just keeps getting more complicated. Joe Laughlin's a great role—I see that, I know that. I just . . . It was different when Robin was Jeff O'Reilly. Yes, he did a lot of love scenes, but it was always with women and . . ."

"Now he's doing it with men," Sam said. Okay, bad word choice. "Acting," he reiterated. "He's not really . . . You know what I mean."

"Yeah, thanks so much. But you're right—it *is* acting. I know that. I do." So why was he saying it as if he were trying to convince himself? Jules went on. "And the pilot hasn't been sold yet, it may not even be bought so . . . Who am I kidding?" He rolled his eyes. "If it doesn't get picked up by HBO, Showtime's gonna grab it. Robin is amazing. And, Sam, God, I know that he loves me."

"But?" Sam asked.

And Jules nodded. There was definitely a *but*. "It began a couple weeks ago," he continued. "After they started filming the pilot. I came home to pick up a file and Robin was there. He was in the shower and . . ." He smiled. "*Inopportune*'s not in his vocabulary either."

He paused, and Sam just waited.

"So," Jules finally said. "It was . . . unbelievably hot, and kind of rough—not in an *I'm going to hurt you* way, but more like *I need you right now.* It was, um . . . extremely erotic. He was totally in charge, right from the start when he . . ." He cleared his throat. "Literally ripped off my shirt."

Ee-doggies. Sam found it best to stare at his feet. This all fell into the column under the heading *things about Jules that he really didn't want to picture.* He *had* asked, but yeesh.

"Sorry if that sounds like TMI," Jules apologized, "but it pretty much happened again when I got home later that night and it was . . . just as great. And Thursday was . . . also really, *really* . . . Just trust me. It was . . . Past two weeks, just . . . crazy great sex."

"I'm still struggling," Sam said carefully, "with the concept of this being a problem for you."

"It's a problem," Jules said a touch snittishly, "because I finally watched one of the DVDs that Robin brought home. It was a promo for the show and . . ." He laughed, but it was with despair. "It was so good. Scary good. But there was this one sequence—it was really well done, nicely edited, but oh my God, Sam. It was Robin. Just . . . cut after cut of him . . . kissing and then ripping the shirts off of all these different guys, like he's getting ready to have—guess what?—kinda rough, very hot sex with them."

He broke a piece off of his cookie but he didn't eat it, he just crumbled it.

"The stupid thing is," Jules continued quietly, "that it really worked, you know, to show that the character, Joe, is both promiscuous and desperate. It was like . . . the sex is virtually identical in all of these snippets of scenes, but his partners are different, like they're on a conveyor belt—just one after another—and Jesus, watching it bothered me."

Sam shifted in his seat. "You don't think that Robin really—"

"No," Jules said. "I know he was acting, but . . ." He exhaled hard. "All I could think was, *this* was what he was doing all day that first time that we . . . That he . . . I thought he was hot for me, but hey, maybe he was just hot. Yeah, we had great sex, but look what he did, first, with a dozen other guys. I guess *that* pretty much got him primed."

Damn. "I'm not an actor," Sam said, "so I don't have a clue how actors do this kind of thing, you know, separate the fiction from reality, but Jules, it's part of the gig. At the risk of sounding like a fucking broken record, man, you're going to have to talk to him about this. This is not just you being a little irrational and getting jealous because, well, face it, you happen to be wired for jealousy. This is something you need to handle, either by saying *Have you thought about a career in landscaping—*"

"I can't do that," Jules said tightly.

"Sure you can."

Jules rephrased. "I won't, okay?"

"Okay." It wasn't as if Sam hadn't expected that response. "Then you're going to have to educate yourself. Talk to other actors before you talk to Robin if you think that'll help. There are lots of actors out there who go to work every day and lock lips with someone who isn't their significant other. And despite all the Hollywood fuckups out there, there are plenty of couples who make it work. But bottom line? You're eventually going to have to talk to Robin. I don't know him all that well, but I do know that the last thing he'd ever want is to hurt you."

"And vice versa." Jules sighed, and his body language was so tense that Sam braced himself. There was something else that he hadn't yet revealed. "This is going to sound weird, but . . . Ever since he started filming the new pilot, Robin has . . . seemed different. Just a little, and . . . Okay, I'm just going to say it." He took a deep breath and exhaled hard. "I think, for the past two weeks I may have been having sex with Joe Laughlin."

For a second, Sam didn't know what the fuck Jules was talking about. And then he got it. Joe Laughlin as in Robin's character. Robin's *fictional* character.

This entire situation was getting more and more tangled in a knot, because Sam realized what Jules had told him. "Best sex of your life," he repeated. As in even better than the sex Jules had been having when Robin was just Robin.

"Yeah," Jules said a tad sharply, probably due to the amusement Sam hadn't kept from his voice. "How do I start *that* conversation? *Hey, babe, would you mind very much bringing your work home with you tonight?*"

Sam couldn't help it. He began to laugh. "I don't want to piss you off, Squidward. And I don't mean to be disrespectful, but is it possible that this isn't really a problem?"

Jules had so clearly lumped everything about Robin's acting career into the con side of their relationship. He needed to dust some of this shit off and look at it a little more closely. Because in Sam's book—which was a clearly hetero tome, which might have made a difference, although he doubted that—this was not just something for the pro column, but a big, happy plus, with a check mark, four hearts and a smiley face all written next to it.

"People role-play all the time," Sam told his friend. "You know. In the bedroom. Maybe you should step back and try to look at this from a different perspective."

"Role-play," Jules repeated, and it was so obvious from his frown that he was stuck here in this dark place that he'd dug for himself. Trapped inside the box, so to speak. Which was unusual for Jules, because he was one of the best outside-the-box thinkers Sam had ever met.

"Yeah," Sam said. *Come on, Squidward. Shake yourself loose.* "It's usually not as specific as . . . Joe Laughlin. Usually it's the meter maid, or the pool boy. Little Red and the big, bad wolf." He waggled his eyebrows at Jules. "That one's Lys's favorite. She loves it when I put on my little red riding hood."

Jules finally laughed, slipping into a far more receptive place.

So Sam stopped joking. "You know, Robin might be . . ." What was the best way for him to say this? "*Learning* a thing or two from playing this character. Joe apparently likes it—" he cleared his throat "—rough, Robin's paying attention to what he's doing on set, thinking, *Hmmm, that might be fun. Jules might go for that* . . . He brings it home, tries it out and . . . Did you let him know you, um, enjoyed what he did?" He answered for Jules. "Of course you did. Robin's a smart guy, so now he's probably thinking, *Gee, what else can I try?* But he's not just smart, he's also kind of, well, gentle. Sweet. So maybe he does bring a little bit of ol' Joe home with him at times, to give him the courage and the edge he needs to, uh, boldly go. To rock your world the way he wants to rock it, because he's crazy about you."

Jules was staring at him. "I never thought of it like that."

Sam shrugged. "Maybe you should. Think about it more. Try this perspective on for size, see how it feels."

Jules was shaking his head, but this time it wasn't because he disagreed. "You missed your calling," he told Sam. "You should have been a therapist."

"Shit," Sam said. "Just kill me now."

"Seriously," Jules said. "That was pretty freaking profound . . ."

"For a guy who wears cowboy boots and blows shit up," Sam finished with him. "I know. Will you please do me a favor and talk to Robin about this? Sometime between now and, oh, say, eleven hundred hours, Saturday, when you're marrying him?"

Jules's phone rang, and he picked it up off the table. "Cassidy."

His face and voice softened immediately. "Oh, hey, sweetie." He glanced at Sam, mouthing, *Robin.* "No," he said into his phone. "No-no, that's . . . That's *great.* Of course I trust your . . . No, it does. It sounds like . . . Yeah, *exactly* the color we were looking for . . . *How* many?" He cracked up, and told Sam, "Robin just bought twenty new towels for our finally fucking finished master bathroom. Yeah," he said into the phone. "I'm having coffee with Sam." He laughed again. "Robin says to make sure you know that they're bath sheets, not towels and . . ." As he listened to Robin on the other end of the phone, his smile faded and he swore. "You, too, huh? *Seven* times? God*damn* him . . ."

The him in question had to be Adam. Jules had told Sam that the little bastard had started calling him again. Right during the wedding rehearsal. It was highly unlikely that *that* was a coincidence.

"He said *what*?" Jules's voice went up an octave, and he turned to look at Sam. "Son of a *bitch.* Adam left Robin a voicemail. He says the stalker—evil twin robot guy—broke into his house, left a threatening note. He said the police aren't taking him seriously. So he's catching the red-eye to Boston."

Sam gently took Jules's phone from his hand. "Hey, Robin," he said, speaking both into the phone and also to Jules. "It's Starrett. Alyssa and I are going to take care of this for you guys, all right?" He looked at Jules, nodding slightly to encourage him to nod, too—which he finally did. "You can cross Adam off your list of things to worry about," Sam continued. "He's not going to fuck up your wedding. I won't let that happen."

"Thank you." Robin's gratitude was heartfelt, but across the table, Jules wasn't looking quite as convinced that Sam could just abracadabra Adam away.

"We'll take care of it," Sam said again, as he hung up Jules's phone and handed it back to him.

Jules managed a smile, but damn, the tension was back in his shoulders and neck. "Maybe he won't be able to get a flight, with all the delays in Chicago." He laughed. "No, you know what's going to happen? He'll go through Dallas or Atlanta, and he'll get here tomorrow. The one person I *don't* want at my wedding is going to be here, and the one person I most want *won't*."

Sam reached across the table and put his hand on Jules's arm. "Squidward. Look at me." He waited for eye contact. "Your mom's coming in tonight. She'll be here in time for the rehearsal dinner."

"What?" Jules said. "How . . . ?"

"I called in some favors," Sam said. "I got her on a flight that . . . I can't tell you about, but she's landing at Logan . . ." He looked at his watch. "In about ninety minutes. It was going to be a surprise, have her walk into the restaurant tonight, blow your mind, but . . . You look like you need . . . at least one less surprise right about now."

Jules started to cry.

And as he did, Sam realized that out of all the years he'd known Jules, the times he'd seen the man cry had been few and far between. He hadn't cried when Adam had left him. Nor when he'd gotten the news that another ex, Ben, had died in Iraq.

And he was crying now the way Sam cried—with his hand over his face, trying to hide it. He was actually laughing, too, as if he realized how absurd it was that he was crying at all. But relief was such a funny emotion. A man could be stalwart through anger and hurt and even bitter grief. But relief was a bitch to fight.

Jules wiped his eyes as he looked up at Sam. "Thank you so much for that," he said. "It's the best gift you've ever given me. And you've given me some . . . pretty wonderful gifts these years that we've been friends."

Aw, hell. Now Sam was getting misty-eyed, too. "I'm glad I could help."

Jules took a deep breath. Exhaled. "Let's go home and see Robin's towels."

"Bath sheets," Sam reminded him. "What kind of gay man are you?"

Jules laughed as they went out the door. "The kind who can kick your ass, SpongeBob, and don't you ever forget it."

Dolphina was crying again.

The entire rehearsal dinner was, for her, one sob-fest after another.

Jules had neglected to inform her that his mother had safely arrived. It was possible Dolphina was the only one who was surprised when Mrs. Cassidy walked into the restaurant.

The way Jules had hugged his mother had made Dolphina tear up. But it was the way Linda Cassidy greeted Robin with such love and approval that had really gotten her going.

Alyssa and Jane had both made funny, wonderful, heartfelt toasts to the happy couple—and again, Dolphina had cried.

Robin had arranged for a piano and a sound system, and after dinner, he'd sat down and played, singing right to Jules. He sang two songs—"This Boy," an old Beatles ballad that was incredibly romantic, and an oldie called "Hooked on a Feeling," which seemed kind of an odd choice for a recovering alcoholic. Jules, however, seemed to love it. He laughed when the song started, and smiled his way through it, watching Robin sing and play with such love in his eyes.

Dolphina just sat off to the side as the last of her mascara washed down her face.

Of course, it didn't help that she'd spent most of the past week crying. For no apparent reason.

Robin and Jules had both rather gently suggested that she at least listen to what Will Schroeder had to say. He'd called, he'd e-mailed, he'd FedExed letters, he'd even shown up at the door.

But she'd shut him out again and again.

He'd even been here tonight, waiting in the restaurant lobby as she'd arrived early to make sure everything was ready for the rehearsal dinner. He'd looked awful, as if he wasn't sleeping, either. He'd actually shaved and put on a suit and tie, with real dress shoes instead of his stupid sneakers.

Because she'd been early, she *had* listened to what he had to say.

"I'm sorry I lied," Will told her. "I've spent a lot of years lying, and it's . . . a hard habit to break. I was afraid you'd get into trouble, and I just opened my mouth and . . . It came out. It was wrong. I was wrong. It was a huge mistake. I've got this . . . book I'm working on now, and . . . I thought that was what I wanted, and I was wrong about that, too. I would trade it, in a heartbeat, for another chance with you."

And then he'd stood there, looking at her as if he actually hoped she'd say, *Okay. Sure. You can have another chance. And maybe this time, I'll be stupid enough to* sleep *with you before you break my heart. Again.*

Instead, she said, "You used me. You were trying to get me to go out with you. You were attracted to me and you knew I . . . felt the same and yet . . . I was only upstairs for a few minutes that day. Apparently you didn't spend very much time wrestling with whether or not you should help yourself to my computer files."

"No, I didn't," he admitted quietly. "But I should have."

"You, of all people," she said. "After what your ex-wife did . . ." She'd found out more about Will's break-up via Google. It hadn't just been ugly, it had been public, as well.

Apparently, his photographer wife had used him to gain access to people and places. She'd used his research skills, too, to snap a series of award-winning photos that had propelled her to a new level—at which point she'd dropped Will like a stone, all but flashing him an L-for-loser sign as she walked out the door.

"I was wrong," Will said again now. "I've been thinking about it and . . . I think I've been living for so long in this cutthroat world where it's . . . every man for himself. It's hard to not do unto others what's been done unto me."

"So let me get this straight." Dolphina crossed her arms. "It's hard for you to not lie, and it's hard for you to behave like a considerate human being. I should fall into your arms because . . . ?"

"Because I love you," he said quietly. "That's got to be worth something to you, because it's everything to me."

But she was already shaking her head.

"I'm not perfect," he said. "I know that."

"Understatement," she said.

He laughed softly. "Yeah. I wouldn't want anything to do with me, either. It's just, you make me want to be . . . more than I am. You make me want to be a team player again, Dolphina."

She almost caved at that one. He almost had her. But she just kept on shaking her head. "I can't do this," she said. "I just . . . I can't."

Will was looking into her eyes, and he nodded. "I'd be too scared, too. It's scary—"

"I'm not too scared," she said sharply. "I'm too smart."

"Ah," he said. "I thought you were . . . scared. My mistake. I . . . make a lot of them, apparently."

"You should go," she said. "The guests will be arriving soon."

"Right," Will said. He turned away, but then turned back. "We have one last photo session scheduled. For tomorrow afternoon. I never got a picture of the guys in their tuxedos—Robin wanted me to wait until he got his haircut, you know, for the wedding."

Robin had needed to keep his hair shaggy and long while he was filming Art Urban's new pilot. He'd finally gotten it cut that very afternoon, immediately after the wedding rehearsal. He looked amazingly good—and it was clear to Dolphina that Jules had thought so, too. He'd come home from having coffee with Sam and had found this shiny, clean-cut, blindingly handsome version of Robin in his kitchen. He'd circled his fiancé about a half a dozen times, and then pulled him upstairs to check out the new towels in their finally completed master bathroom.

Right. As if towel viewing always took the better part of an hour.

"I'll make sure they're ready for you," Dolphina told Will. Tomorrow—Friday—had purposely been a lightly scheduled day. Friends would be arriving for Saturday morning's wedding. Plans included nothing more strenuous than a sleep-late morning, and a casual evening get-together at the house.

Will nodded. He looked as if he wanted to say something more, so she'd waited. Impatiently.

"I'll see you tomorrow, then," he finally said, and went out the door.

Friday, December 14
Boston, Massachusetts

Robin's brother-in-law's crazy mom had reassured everyone that she would be able to get a cab from Logan Airport when her flight arrived much, much too early in the morning, on the day before the wedding.

She hadn't wanted to intrude on yesterday's rehearsal dinner despite Robin's assurances that he'd love for her to come out early with Jane, Cosmo, and Billy, and join the party.

Instead, she'd taken this later flight, insisting she was perfectly able to make her own way to Robin and Jules's house in Boston's South End.

Which was why Cosmo and Jane had gone to red alert when, an hour after her arrival time, she'd failed to appear at the front door.

"She's not answering her cell phone," Cosmo reported.

"She probably forgot to turn it on when she landed," Janey suggested.

"Should we try to page her at the airport?" Robin had shuffled into the kitchen in his bathrobe, to grab a mug of coffee for Jules, who was still upstairs in bed, trying desperately to pretend that little Billy's breakfast temper tantrum hadn't blasted their day's sleep-late plans clear out of the water.

Nothing like luxuriating in bed, knowing that their first appointment wasn't until the afternoon, while being serenaded by *But I want to! But I need to! No! NO!*

Robin loved his nephew, but *Jesus*. The kid had a pair of lungs.

"Sorry about the Cheerios thing," Janey murmured as he yawned his way over to the refrigerator.

"That was about Cheerios?" he asked, eyeing Billy, who was still sniffling as he sat in his high chair, a slumped picture of misery, suffering the parentally-decreed injustice of having his right to eat at the "big boy" table taken away from him due to his failure to act like said big boy. Damn, what would the noise levels have been like if it had been about Lucky Charms or Cap'n Crunch? And then he realized that that *was* what it had been about. Billy had wanted some of the high-energy-inducing cereal that Robin and Jules kept in their cabinets.

Someone—thank you, Jules—had taken out the box of Corn Pops last night, no doubt to have a snack, and left it on the counter for Billy to see at oh-my-God-o'clock, when he'd woken up.

"Sorry," Robin told his sister as he finally unburied the cinnamon bread and put two slices into the toaster.

"I can't believe you still eat that sugary . . . stuff," she said.

"It's Jules's," he told her as he got out a plate and a tray to carry the coffee and toast upstairs. He gave her a wicked smile. "He likes things that are . . . extra sweet."

Janey laughed as she gazed at him over the top of her coffee mug. "With your hair like that, you look like you did when you were twelve."

Robin bent down to look at his wavery reflection in the microwave window. His newly cut hair would indeed have won the gold medal in the Bedhead Olympics this morning. He rubbed his unshaved chin. "Not quite."

"Yeah," Jane agreed. "Back then, you walked around with this . . . perpetual expression of anxiety. Robbie, it's wonderful to see you looking so happy."

The cinnamon bread popped out of the toaster, and Robin put it on the plate, then grabbed a knife from the drawer. "I'm not just looking happy," he told his sister as he buttered the toast with that organic soybean spread stuff that Jules liked. "I *am* happy."

Her smile got tremulous. "I'm so glad. Robin, you can't know how proud I am of you."

"Stop." He made a cross between them, with the knife and his finger. "This kitchen has a weeping limit and Billy used up the morning's allotment."

Jane laughed. "I just wanted you to know," she said, this incredible woman, this half-sister who'd so fiercely loved the little abandoned boy he'd once been. She'd saved him with her attention and affection—even when it sometimes had its downsides. Like the time she'd used him—in her defense, he had been a willing volunteer—to see if syrup of ipecac truly worked.

For the record—it did.

Jane leaned closer now, lowering her voice, mischief in her eyes. "I still can't believe you scored Jules Cassidy. If I were a guy, I'd turn gay for him, too."

Robin looked at her. "I didn't *turn* gay," he said. "I always was gay and yeah, okay, you're just being a jerk."

"Don't you get tired of always correcting reporters?" she asked, grinning at him.

"*My sexual orientation never changed,*" Robin recited. "*I merely stopped pretending that I was straight—pretending to myself as well as everyone else.* Yeah, I don't even need to think anymore, I just open my mouth and the words come out, I've said it so many fucking times." He glanced at Billy and winced. "Sorry."

Fortunately, the kid was paying attention to something his father was quietly telling him.

And then Jane was smiling over Robin's shoulder. "Good morning."

"Morning." Jules had thrown on sweats and a T-shirt and was bee-lining for the coffee. He rarely added the *good* until he'd caffeined up.

"I already poured you some, babe," Robin told him. "I was going to bring it up." He gestured to the tray, and Jules stopped short and his morning blear turned to wonder.

"You were bringing me breakfast in bed," he realized. "You are *so* sweet."

Robin shot Jane a *See?* look, and she laughed.

"I think he was trying to make up for screaming nephew syndrome," she said as Jules came over and gave Robin a kiss. "We *are* checking into the hotel for tonight and tomorrow. I know you both have been trying to convince us that it's okay to stay here, but . . . This latest bout of boundary testing can get really loud and we can't back down—it's a battle we can't afford to lose. I've already packed up our things—we'll be out of here shortly."

Robin looked at Jules, and Jules looked back at Robin.

"Strangely, I feel no need to argue with you," Jules told Jane. "So, thank you."

"Yeah," Robin added. "If anyone's going to be screaming *But I want to, but I need to* on the morning of my wedding day, it's going to be me."

Jules laughed as he picked up a piece of the toast Robin had made for him. "Has he always let whatever he's thinking just . . . fly right out of his mouth?" he asked Jane before taking a bite.

"Pretty much," she said, laughing, too.

"God, this is good," Jules said with his mouth full. He'd moved slightly, so that he was close enough to touch Robin's leg with his own, to put his bare foot on top of Robin's as they stood there talking to Janey across the kitchen's center island. "I can't believe you made me breakfast in bed."

"It's just toast." Robin put his arm around Jules, tugging him even closer. "Besides, you know what happens when you drink coffee on an empty stomach, babe." He made a face at Jane. "Coffee farts."

Jules turned and gave him his *what-the-fuck* face. "Yeah, hello, that would be *you*, thank you very much."

"As of tomorrow morning we'll be married," Robin pointed out, trying to gross his sister out. Old habits died hard. "And my farts will be your farts, forevermore."

"Robin, ew," Jane said. *Score.*

But Jules just laughed as he smiled into Robin's eyes. "It must be love, because I'm actually okay with that."

"Janey, I'm on hold with the airline," Cosmo said from across the room, frustration ringing in his usually fluster-proof voice. "Will you try calling my mom's cell again?"

"Of course."

"What's going on?" Jules asked, as Jane opened her own cell phone and dialed.

"Cosmo misplaced his mother," Robin told him.

"Hang on, Jane," Cosmo said. "I've got her on call waiting—she's beeping me right now. Mom," he said into the phone. "Are you all right?"

Cosmo's mom was a still youthful fifty-something, but she could be a real space cadet at times. Still, Robin adored her.

"She's fine," Cosmo reported, and they all breathed a sigh of relief. "You're *where*?" he said into the phone. "South Boston."

Robin started to laugh.

"No, Mom," Cosmo said, with the patience of a saint. "South Boston is *not* the same as the South End."

And wasn't *that* an understatement? The South End, where Jules and Robin lived, was Boston's gay neighborhood. South Boston, however, was near Dorchester, where Robin's character Joe Laughlin had grown up. It was blue collar and heavily Irish Catholic—not exactly a part of town where Robin and Jules would be able to stroll down the street, hand in hand.

"Just hang tight," Cosmo told his mother. "Stay there, we'll come and get you." He paused. "No, you stay inside the coffee shop where it's warm. If we get there, and you're waiting outside . . . Mom. Robin has enough to worry about today without putting the possibility of you freezing to death on his list, all right? Good. Just order a cup of tea. We'll be there soon." He snapped his phone shut and shot Robin a desperately amused look. "Apparently, Mom likes you best."

Robin laughed as Cosmo lifted Billy out of his high chair. "Come on, Buddy, let's go find your grandma," the SEAL said to his son. "You need to hit the head before we get into the car?"

"Yeah, but . . . Gwamma likes Unca Robin best?" Billy asked, clearly worried about that.

"Nah, I was just teasing," Cosmo told his son. "See you guys tonight. Let us know if you need us to help with anything," he said to Jules and Robin, before turning his attention back to Billy. "Grandma loves everybody best—she loves you and me and Mommy and Uncle Robin and Uncle Jules."

"And Unca Izzy?"

"Yup, even Uncle Izzy . . ."

Robin sighed as he watched Cosmo carry Billy out of the kitchen.

"That's one lucky kid," Jules murmured, putting voice to Robin's thoughts. "Having a dad like him . . ."

Jane laughed. "You guys are freaking me out a little—standing there ogling my husband."

"I'm not ogling," Jules said. He looked at Robin. "Are you?"

"Not in a gay way," Robin said. "But definitely in a God-I-wish-you'd-been-*my*-father way." He smiled at his sister. "Maybe you and Cosmo could adopt us. Take us camping."

"God, no. I hate camping," Jules said.

"Really?" Robin looked at him.

"Uh-oh," Jules said. "You didn't know that?"

"No," Robin said.

"I used to like it," Jules said, "but lately . . . I'm totally camped out."

"How could you be camped out?"

"I take it you like camping," Jules said.

"Yeah," Robin said, pulling him close. "And I bet you I could get you to like it again, too."

Jules laughed. "Sweetie, there's not much that you *couldn't* get me to like, if you put your mind to it."

"My mind?" Robin teased.

"Among other things . . ."

And, ooh, the look that Jules was now giving him was not a conversation-in-the-kitchen-with-Robin's-sister-listening look. And sure enough, Jules had forgotten that Jane was standing there. "Yikes," he said, glancing over at her. "Sorry."

But she was laughing. "I bet if you run upstairs really fast, I could talk Robin into bringing you the rest of your breakfast in bed."

"I suspect he won't need any encouragement," Jules told her, even as he blushed.

"I suspect he won't either," she said, reaching across the island to ruffle Robin's hair, the way she used to do when he was little. "Seriously, guys, it's not even seven. Go back to bed. We'll lock the door behind us when we go, okay?"

Robin nodded. "See you tonight."

"Yes, you will." Jane ruffled Jules's messy hair, too. "Thank you for loving my little brother."

The smile Jules gave her was beautiful. "Thank *you* for loving your little brother, too."

Adam stank.

The trip from L.A. had been horrific, with a too-short layover in Phoenix that had made him miss his connecting flight. He'd then had to wait seven *hours* for the next flight to Boston—via Dallas, Atlanta *and* Newark.

He was exhausted, he was starving, and yes, the cold sweat he'd manufactured back in his kitchen in L.A. had not improved with age. His T-shirt was ready for a toxic waste dump and he could smell his own feet, even while standing up.

The jacket he was wearing was barely suitable for a cold day in

Southern California, let alone winter in Boston, but he hunched his shoulders against the wind and put his hands in his pockets as he bypassed the luggage carousels and headed for the door to the taxi stand.

Please God, let the cabs here in Boston take credit cards . . .

The line was long and, damn, it was cold, but Adam stood there, because cold was better than lying dead on the floor of his living room, with a hole blown through his extremely nonrobot head by some mental case with a newly purchased gun.

He took out his phone and turned it back on, checking to see what time it was because he had absolutely no clue, other than it was daylight.

It was nearly noon, which was good. It was also the day before Jules and Robin's wedding, which probably wasn't as good, although certainly better than being the day *of*.

Adam keyed in Jules's cell phone number with his thumb and was just about to press *talk*, when a voice spoke in his ear.

"Close the phone, Wyndham."

It was a male voice, a rich baritone with a faint Western accent.

Adam turned and found himself looking up at . . . *not* Jim Jessop, but Jules Cassidy's good friend Cowboy Sam.

"Oh, thank God," Adam breathed, even as his phone was taken from his hands by someone standing on his other side. It was the cowboy's wife, Alyssa, whom Adam had always thought to be much too gorgeous, much too smart, and much too not-white to have hooked up with a good ol' boy from Texas.

Of course, Sam *did* ooze pure sex appeal, with his rugged good looks, sun-streaked hair, and long, *long* blue-jean-clad legs. The cowboy boots and sheepskin-lined leather jacket he was wearing this afternoon really worked for Adam, too.

"Jules is a little busy today," Alyssa said, checking his phone to see that, yes, he had been about to call Jules. In fact, as Adam watched, she deleted both Jules's and Robin's numbers from his address book.

Hello, she was pregnant, which oddly enough didn't make her look any less capable of thoroughly kicking his ass.

"Congratulations," Adam said, but it was like talking into a void.

"He and Robin are both very busy," Sam told him. "They don't want to talk to you. They don't want to *see* you. And they *really* don't want you fucking up their wedding. So why don't we all just go on back into the terminal and get you onto a flight back to L.A.?"

Alyssa was thorough as she went through his phone. She also deleted his incoming and outgoing call logs before she handed it back to him. "You really need to go home and sleep this off, Adam," she said, her tone far more kind than Sam's had been as she, too, took hold of his arm.

"I'm not drunk," he said. "And I'm not going anywhere, so take your hands off me." He smiled at Sam. "Honey, you can put *your* hands a whole lot lower if you want."

"No, thanks," Sam said, as Alyssa countered with, "Adam, you smell like a distillery."

"I had a few drinks on the flight," he admitted. "I spilled one of them." He started to reach into his jacket pocket for the photos, but Sam bristled, tightening his grip on Adam's right arm. Adam laughed. "You seriously think I'm reaching for a weapon? I just got off a plane." He reached again, and this time Sam let him. "I'm not here to sabotage the wedding, despite what you think." He handed Sam the photos. "I'm here because my stalker got himself a new toy."

Sam was silent as he looked at both photos. He didn't say a thing. He just handed them over to his wife.

Alyssa looked at them. Looked at Sam.

"You get any more e-mail from this Jessop guy?" Sam broke the silence to ask Adam.

"I haven't had Internet access," he said, holding his breath. Please God, let them believe him . . . "Not since yesterday morning."

Sam and Alyssa seemed to reach some kind of consensus, with Sam nodding and Alyssa saying, "We're going to find the nearest Kinkos. You're going to get online and check your e-mail. And then we're going to figure out what to do."

As Robin always used to say—*score*.

"You're not serious," Robin said.

"I'll be back in forty minutes," Jules said, as Dolphina heard the front closet open.

"This is what Adam wants," Robin pointed out.

Dolphina could tell, even from here in the office, that he was trying very hard not to lose his temper.

"He wants you to jump when he says jump," Robin continued. "And here you go, jumping."

"Sam and Alyssa have some concerns," Jules said. "*They* asked me to look at the photos. I'm going to meet them at the coffee place, because I don't want Adam here."

"And I can't go with you because . . . ?"

"You can get started with Will," Jules said, as if that were his real reason for wanting Robin to stay behind. "You know he's going to want photos of you by yourself—you're the movie star."

Robin laughed. "Why don't you just admit that you don't want me to go with you because you're jealous of Adam, because you're afraid I'm going to . . . what, Jules? Take one look at him and go *Gee, how could I have been so foolish to agree to marry a man whom I deeply love, because hey now, if I didn't, I could still be having a cheap sexual relationship with some loser I used to fuck when I got drunk enough not to care who I was with. I'm sorry, Jules, the wedding is off. I'm running away with Adam."*

There was silence then.

"I don't want you to go with me," Jules finally spoke, his voice so quiet Dolphina almost didn't hear him, "because, yes, I'm jealous of Adam. Because I hate seeing you with him. Because I *really* hate picturing you with him."

More silence, then, Robin: "Thank you for being honest with me. Call me if you're going to be more than forty minutes, okay?"

"I'm sorry," Jules said. "I hate that I—"

"Shhh," Robin cut him off. "Just go, baby, and come back as quickly as you can."

"Yeah," Jules said.

Dolphina heard him come farther into the foyer. He let himself out the front door without saying anything to her at all.

Robin, however, came into the office. "I'm going upstairs," he said. "I've got a headache—I gotta lie down, take a combat nap. We woke up way too early this morning, then never got back to sleep so . . ."

"Okay," she said, turning from her computer to face him. "Can I get you anything?"

He *did* look tired. "No. Just . . . wake me up when Will gets here, all right?"

"All right," she said.

"Seriously, Dolph," Robin told her. "Wake me. Don't wait until Jules gets back. I don't want you to have to sit here with Will all that time. And you know he's going to get here early, so . . ."

"Thank you," she said.

He turned to go, but then he turned back. "You heard all that, huh?"

"Kinda hard not to," she said.

"I get jealous of Adam, too," Robin said. "And when I do, Jules goes *what I had with him was a . . . a . . . puddle, what I have with you is an ocean,* and . . . I believe him. I do. He said it, he meant it, and I believe him. So why doesn't he believe me when I tell him the same thing? Why do we have to rehash this, over and over? What does he want me to do?"

"Reassure him?" Dolphina suggested.

Robin sat down on the sofa. "I know I should just be grateful that he trusts me at all. God knows I made some huge mistakes. That YouTube thing. I watch it sometimes, just to remind myself how incredibly magnanimous Jules is." He met Dolphina's eyes. "How much do you want to bet that all of the cable news stations play a ten second clip from my drunken YouTube-memorialized binge when they announce our wedding on Saturday?"

"They'll play at least ten seconds," Dolphina agreed.

"Somehow," Robin said, "Jules found it in himself to forgive me after that. It had to take—it still has to take—an incredible amount of courage to put your heart on the line for someone you know is capable of hurting you."

Dolphina narrowed her eyes at him. "Are we still talking about you and Jules?" she asked.

"I'm just saying," Robin said.

"Go take a nap, Boy Wonder."

Robin laughed as he stood up. "What did I do to deserve that nickname?"

"You met Jules," Dolphina pointed out. "He's kind of like Batman. But gay and much cuter."

"Batman," Robin repeated as he went up the stairs. And light dawned. "Holy shit, I finally get it. As in, I'm Robin, the Boy Wonder, and Jules is Batman. But with a sexy new twist. Jeez, it took me long enough. Don't forget to wake me when you need me, Dolph."

Will sat on the steps of Robin and Jules's front porch for such a long time that his butt was starting to freeze.

He was early. What else was new?

When it finally came time to ring the bell, he was afraid that Jules and Robin would answer the door, dressed and shined in their tuxedos. They'd let him inside and casually drop the news that Dolphina had stayed home today.

On the other hand, Will had pretty much said all there was to say last night. Except maybe, *Please, please, give me a second chance . . .*

He may well have just sat there forever, if a man hadn't come walking down the street and turned up the front path.

He stopped at the bottom of the steps, just gazing at Will.

He was one of those bald men who could've been anywhere from in his thirties to late fifties, with the kind of round face that wasn't particularly distinctive. His mouth seemed thin and lipless—and his lack of smile certainly helped with that illusion. His eyes were hidden behind a pair of glasses, and his nose was . . . noselike. Kind of bulbish but not overly so. Not like, *Hot damn, would you look at that guy with his* W. C. *Fields monstrosity in the middle of his face . . .*

On the stocky side, he wore an overcoat that made him look like a large rectangle. Odder still than his choice of fashion was the fact that the coat was so new it had all of its tags still on it.

"Can I help you?" Will finally said, wondering what this man saw as he looked back at Will. A too-skinny, angular-faced, redheaded loser in a shabby coat with a frozen butt and a broken heart of his own foolish making.

"Do you live here?" the man asked. "Are you Jules Cassidy?"

"No," Will said. "I'm not. I . . . don't live here. No."

"That's good," the man said. "Because Jules Cassidy may be one of them. That's how you find the nest. You frighten them and see where they go. They always head for the safety of the nest."

Wow. Will was tired. He hadn't slept much in the past week, but even allowing for his potentially fatigue-induced lack of understanding, that sounded to him like some ultra-crazy lunatic ravings.

"No one's home," Will said. "That's why I'm sitting outside. I'm sorry, what's your name? I didn't catch your name."

"I didn't give it."

"Ah," Will said. "That would explain . . . why I didn't catch it." He stood up. "They should all be home by four-thirty," he lied. Damn, he *was* good at doing that, but there were lies and then there were *lies.* "We should both probably come back later."

But the man sat down on the steps. "I'll wait."

Will took out his phone. "Maybe I'll, uh, call Jules and, uh—"

"That's not a good idea."

Holy. Fuck.

Mr. Nameless Newcoat had a gun. It was little, easily concealable, and deadly looking. He didn't try to hide it from any of the neighbors—who were nowhere in sight, damn it. He just pointed it at Will as he held out his hand for his cell phone.

Will's mouth was dry as he handed it over. Please God, let Dolphina have stayed home today. Please God, let Jules look out the window and see this lunatic and his weapon and realize they were in danger. Please God . . .

"They call them cop killer bullets," the man informed him, "because they want to make them hard to obtain. But the truth is, they're the only ones that will pierce the metal exoskeleton. And they're really not that hard to find."

"Metal exoskeleton," Will repeated.

"Of the robot."

Will tried to think, tried to calm his pounding heart, tried to figure out his options. He could run for the street, try to get to a phone where he could call the police or Jules or both. But his doing that could get him shot. Or someone else might be hit when the crazy man fired his weapon.

On the other hand, firing that weapon would certainly get *some*-one's attention. But on the *other* other hand, if Dolphina was inside, she might come out to see what was going on, which would put her in peril.

Will could stand here. And talk to the guy. Stall, and hope some-one would see them, see that gun and call for help.

"So you, uh, really think Jules is one of them?" Will asked, hop-ing he'd gotten the right amount of conspirator into his tone.

But the man didn't answer, because someone—No!—was open-ing the front door.

"It's freezing out here." It was Dolphina. "Are you intending to just . . ." She saw the gun, but damnit, she didn't slam the door shut and run for the phone. She just stood there breathing. "Oh, my God."

"You said no one was home," the man accused Will.

And he shot him.

Robin awoke with a start, his heart pounding. Jesus, what was that?

He'd been dreaming—a good dream. Extremely simple. No dog-headed people dancing the Macarena, or wipe-cuts to little Billy with a moustache, speaking Romanian.

Just Jules. And Robin. They'd been in a club, dancing. Holy DJ, Jules was an amazing dancer, but they rarely went clubbing because of the alcohol factor. Because of Robin. Occasionally alcohol-free party nights would line up with one of their free evenings and they'd go, but those were few and far between.

Robin was looking forward to tomorrow. They'd hired a live band for the reception—a local Boston group called Firefly who specialized in what he thought of as "Jules Music"—a mix of swing, old standards and plenty of pop rock from the 60s and 70s. "Come and Get Your Love," heavy on the cowbell. "Funky but Chic." And, of course, "Hooked on a Feeling." It was going to be great.

So he'd been dreaming, they'd been dancing, Jules had been smiling at him and . . . There'd been the unmistakable sound of a gunshot.

Had he dreamed it? Or . . . ?

Robin now sat up as he heard what sounded like Dolphina's voice coming up from downstairs. "Oh, my God! Oh, my God! *Will!* What have you done?"

What the hell?

Robin got out of bed and went out into the hallway, onto the second floor landing.

Will wasn't dead. He wasn't dead, not yet anyway. Think. She had to stop shaking and crying and think, and somewhere, from deep inside, Dolphina grabbed hold of a strength she hadn't known she possessed.

"There's no one else home," Dolphina told the man with the gun, the man who'd—dear God—shot Will in the leg. She spoke as loudly and as clearly as she could with her quavering voice, praying that Robin would hear her and call for help.

"Bring him inside," the man ordered, and she hesitated.

Will was bleeding, blood seeping through his fingers as he clasped his thigh. His pupils were already dilated as he gazed up at her from where he'd fallen on the steps—he was going into shock. "I'm sorry," he whispered. "I should've tried to grab his gun . . ."

"Shhh," she told him, then turned back to the gunman. "Let's leave him out here. That way I can call an ambulance and—"

"You'll call no one." He pointed the weapon again at Will. "Bring him inside or I'll shoot him again."

Oh, God. She grabbed Will beneath the arms and pulled him into the foyer.

Moving him like that had to have hurt him badly, but he gritted his teeth and tried to swallow his pain, obviously for her sake—which made her start to cry again.

"Don't die," she begged him. "Don't you dare die."

Sam watched Adam, who was watching Jules as he looked at those two Polaroid photos, and then the latest e-mail from Jim Jessop.

It wasn't much of an e-mail—just ten short words. *Run. Run to your nest and I'll kill you all.*

It had made the hair on the back of Sam's neck stand up, and it was clear it was doing the same now, to Jules.

Adam looked like hell, slumped the way he was at the coffee shop table with his unwashed hair and his three days in the same grimy clothes. "I know this is not the right time for this, but I didn't know where else to go," he said quietly.

"What does he mean by nest?" Jules asked.

"It's the same old robot-alien shit," Adam said. "According to the gospel of Jim, we robots come here from outer space and take over people's lives. But we don't show up here all alone. Apparently, I've got some kind of alien posse. We all stay in touch and we all regularly check in at some place Jessop calls our *nest.* It's fricking crazy and I'm sick of it and I want it to stop."

Jules got very still as he looked again at the e-mail. Alyssa noticed the sudden change in him, too. She was always hyper in-tune with Jules, and she sat forward.

Jules looked at Adam then, as if something he'd just said was horrific. More horrific even than the whine in Adam's tone. "How many people do you know in Boston?" he asked.

"Besides you and Robin?" Adam responded. He shrugged. "No one."

"Who do you use for cell service?" Jules asked, taking out his phone and dialing.

Adam blinked. "What? Why?"

"Just fucking answer my question!"

"Globe-net," Adam said. "God."

Sam looked at Alyssa. Did she know who Jules was calling? She shook her head, no.

"Yeah, Yashi," Jules said into his phone. "I need some information and I need it right away. I got a suspect named Jim Jessop. I need to know if he works for Globe-net. As any kind of employee, but we should probably check customer service first. And find out if he's recently been on the passenger list for any airline flights from the West Coast into Boston. No, make the destination anywhere on the East Coast. I need this now. Call me right back." He stood up. "I gotta get home. To my fucking *nest*."

Sam stood, too. "You really think . . ." He followed Jules out the door.

"I think that I left Robin and Dolphina home alone, with a madman on the loose."

Adam and Alyssa were right behind them.

"I don't get it," Adam said. "You actually think Jessop works for Globe-net?"

"He knows where you are," Jules said sharply as he broke into a jog, "because he works for your cell phone company, yes, that's what I think. You always take your cell phone, you always make local calls, he has access to your records, so he always knows where you are."

Jules laughed, but it was clear to Sam that he didn't find any of this funny. "And he knows that you've been *keeping in touch* with Robin and with me. And thanks to the Internet and websites like Celebrity Stalker dot-com, he also knows exactly where we live."

"Run to your nest," Alyssa echoed the e-mail.

"You ran straight to us," Jules told Adam. He still had his phone out, and he used it now, no doubt to call Robin.

Alyssa took out her cell phone, too. "I'm calling Tom," she told Sam. "See if Troubleshooters are back from New Hampshire yet. We can set up a perimeter around the townhouse, watch for this guy."

Sam nodded. Good plan. He himself dialed Cosmo Richter, who picked up on the first ring. "Cos, it's Starrett. We need you over at Jules's place, ASAP. Got a potential situation with a stalker."

"I'm on my way."

"Covert approach," Sam said, silently thanking God for enlisted men like Chief Richter. The SEAL didn't waste time with so much as the smallest what-the-fuck. "And do me a favor, Chief, ask Jane to call all the civilians—like Jules's mom. Anyone who might drop by. We need to keep everyone away from the house for a while."

"Will do."

"Robin's not answering," Jules grimly announced.

Robin's cell phone rang, the theme from *Buffy the Vampire Slayer* wailing throughout the house.

He'd had his phone out and open, and was just about to dial Jules when it exploded in a deafening burst of electric guitar power chords.

"What is that?"

Robin held his breath and didn't move as the gunman came toward the stairs. It took every ounce of his self-control to stay still—to *not* slam his phone shut and end the music. To not push the silence button. To not answer.

Jules was on the other end. Jules, who was probably calling to tell him he was on his way home. Jules, who unless Robin warned him, was going to walk blindly into a hostage situation in his very own home—a situation in which this stranger with a gun had already shot Will Schroeder.

But if Robin didn't just let the phone ring, the gunman would know he was up here.

"Robin must've left his cell phone home when he went out," Dolphina said, thinking on her feet, remarkably composed considering that Will was bleeding from a gunshot wound. "He does that all the time."

His cell phone finally stopped ringing, and Robin quickly reset it to silent, but didn't dare to move.

"Let Dolphina go." Will was still conscious, and determined to get Dolphina to safety.

She, however, was just as adamant about not leaving him.

"I'm telling you," Will said. "She's . . . not a robot."

She's not a *what*? Holy shit.

Adam's stalker. This was fucking Adam's stalker. Somehow, when he'd come to Boston, he'd fucking brought his fucking stalker with him. *Son* of a *bitch*.

"Look, I know she's not a robot," Will persisted. "She's my girlfriend. I think I would've noticed her . . . metallic exoskeleton."

"She may have been changed since you were with her last," the stalker pointed out.

Robin's cell phone lit up as Jules called him again, and he froze as fucking Adam's fucking stalker came halfway up the stairs. He couldn't make it back into the bedroom without being seen, so he turned the speaker volume to zero and answered the phone, slipping it into his pocket, then closed his eyes and prayed.

Please God, let the dismal Boston weather that he'd complained about so often provide enough shadows for this crazy bastard not to see him standing here . . .

"You need to let me call an ambulance," Dolphina said, her voice carrying clearly up from downstairs. Robin knew she was trying to draw the gunman back down to her. "Please."

"That's not possible."

"He's going to die! He's not a robot, he's a human being and you shot him!"

"Dolph, come on," Will said. "Don't piss him off."

"No one wants collateral damages," the man said, "but it happens. It's the price of this war we're fighting."

No doubt about it, he was completely insane.

As Adam watched, Jules went bullshit.

Apparently, Robin, Dolphina and some reporter named Will were all in the house with Jim Jessop. Robin had managed to answer his phone and leave it open, so Jules could listen in. Whatever was happening in there, it wasn't good.

Adam didn't know the details, but it became clear that Jessop wasn't afraid to use his weapon. He'd already shot the reporter.

Christ, he felt sick. If Robin died, it would be Adam's fault . . .

"I need a negotiator and a SWAT team," Jules barked orders into Alyssa's phone as Alyssa used his cell to monitor the situation in the house, "and at least one ambulance. And I need them all to stay a block away, sirens off as they approach."

Robin's brother-in-law, Cosmo, was waiting for them on the corner. As Adam watched, Cowboy Sam went over to fill him in.

"Jessop's talking to Dolphina and Will," Alyssa reported. "Will is still conscious, but he doesn't sound good. Dolphina's doing her best, but . . ."

Jules looked at his watch and shook his head. “I’m not going to wait. I’ve got to go in there. I’m just going to walk in the door like I’m coming home.”

“Slow down, Cassidy,” Sam said. “There are four of us. Don’t knee-jerk. Let’s figure this out.”

Figure *what* out? This was crazy. Sure, they outnumbered the gunman, but they had no weapons. What were they going to do, rush inside and hope one of them could grab that gun before they all got shot? Talk about insane . . .

“Let me talk to him,” Adam stepped forward and volunteered. “To Jessop. Maybe if I . . . I don’t know, stand in the street and shout to him, he’ll come outside.”

“And he’ll shoot you down like a dog,” Sam pointed out. “You’re his target, Astro Boy.”

Good point. But still. If Jessop stayed inside the house, he could well shoot *Robin* down like a dog. “I’ll get behind a car,” Adam said, but they’d already dismissed his idea.

“Will and Dolphina are in the foyer, near the front door,” Cosmo reported. Apparently he’d gone over to the house to look in the windows. Adam hadn’t even realized he was gone, and he was already back. “Jessop’s on the stairs.”

“Jessop just found Robin,” Alyssa announced grimly, phone to her ear. “Jules . . .”

Oh, Christ.

“I’m going in there,” Jules said again, ready to march into hell if he had to. “*Right* now.”

“Okay,” Sam said. “Here’s what we’re going to do.”

“Who else is up here?”

And yes, that would be the robot-hunter speaking directly to Robin.

He was busted—and quite possibly dead.

"I'm the only one," Robin admitted, praying that Jules was listening in to all of this. "I was taking a nap. Dolphina didn't know I was home." Crap, he was babbling. He had to calm it down—he wasn't the crazy one here. He forced himself to smile. "I was just coming downstairs to talk to you."

"You're Robin Chadwick."

Breathe. "Yeah, but only until tomorrow. Tomorrow it's going to be Robin Cassidy. I'm getting married—taking my partner's name. I'm excited. I've, uh, never been married before and I'm crazy in love with him. Big feelings for this guy. Huge, you know?"

As an actor, it was all about the subtext, and he hoped that what he was really saying came through. *Dear Jules, if I don't survive this, please always remember how much I loved you . . .*

The man with the gun didn't react, didn't smile, didn't blink. And Robin kept his smile wide, trying his Oscar-nominated best to be charming and pleasant—and to completely ignore that totally non-ignorable gun. Maybe if he didn't stare at it as if he were a terrified antelope, or whatever it was that hunters hunted, Crazy Stalker Man wouldn't feel the urge to use it on him. "You're here about Adam, right?" Robin continued. "Because he's"—he lowered his voice—"a robot?"

The man's gun hand dropped a bit. "You know about Adam?"

"Shit, yeah," Robin said, wracking his brain. What was this guy's name? Jules had told him he'd signed all of the e-mails he'd sent . . . "I've known for a while. Dude, I'm glad you're here. I wasn't sure who I should call to report it. I mean, yeah, Jules works for the Bureau, but robots aren't exactly his department. Still, he tries to stay informed, and he heard the buzz that you were in town, chasing Adam, which is good, because, you know, uninvited robots at a wedding . . . ? Very uncool." He held out his hand, as if offering it to shake, as he moved toward Jim Jordan? Jesse Jordan? Jesse

James . . . ? And he found the bastard's name, somewhere in a cobwebby corner of his brain. "Jim Jessop, right?"

Jessop switched his gun into his left hand so he could shake Robin's hand. *Score.*

"Jules, come in now!" Robin shouted and kicked the motherfucker's gun out of his hand and down the stairs.

Jules didn't need his cell phone to hear Robin, and he shouted "Go," to both Sam and Cosmo as—God, no!—a gunshot rang out. He kicked open his front door and burst inside.

He'd been moving into position on the front porch, staying low so the gunman wouldn't see him through the window, waiting for the others to get into place, too.

The streak of blood on his stairs had brought him to a state of deadly calm, where events played out almost in slow motion. He'd been here before, and he recognized the surreal, almost-detached feeling. He would, if he was not careful, kill the man who'd shot Will. And not give a damn about it—not until later.

He also wouldn't give a damn about the fact that he was putting himself into range of the gunman's weapon. If he got shot, he knew he wouldn't feel it. It was and would be inconsequential.

As long as Robin was safe.

The door he'd kicked open hit the wall with a smash, and he heard windows shattering from the back of the house—Sam and Cosmo—coming to help him. In that long, drawn-out fraction of a second, as Jules scanned the foyer, he saw Dolphina crouched beside Will, in front of the door to the office.

He saw Robin, too, on the stairs with the gunman. It was hard to tell who'd grabbed who, but they were tumbling down together, and Jules's heart damn near stopped, because it seemed almost certain they were struggling to gain control of that gun.

The one that had just been fired, perhaps already mortally wounding Robin . . .

Jules leaped toward them, even as they bounced toward him.

"Get down," he shouted to Dolphina, afraid the weapon would discharge again, and she moved, not back, but over and across Will's prone body, as if to protect him.

Robin had Jessop around the waist, but the man was struggling to get free, and Jules grabbed him too, shouting, "Where's the gun?"

Where the fuck was it? It wasn't in Jessop's hands. The man was a freaking lunatic, flailing and fighting—it was all they could do, both Jules and Robin together, to restrain him.

Enough bullshit—Jules hit the motherfucker in the face with his fist, cleaning his clock. Jessop slumped unconscious.

"God," Robin said, as he flopped back onto the floor. "Oh, my God!"

"Are you hurt?" Now that the danger was past, the calm vanished. It was replaced by something far more frantic as he turned to his fiancé. "Were you shot?"

But there was no blood on him, nor on Jessop. Robin was just lying there to catch his breath. He shook his head, pointing up at the ceiling, where, indeed, there was a hole in the plaster. "Dolphina," he gasped.

Shit, was she hit, maybe by a ricochet?

But when Jules turned, he saw Dolphina was holding Jessop's weapon. She had it clasped in both hands, and very accurately aimed at Jessop's prone body.

Sam and Cosmo were there—Sam taking possession of Jessop. Alyssa was in the house, too. She gently took the weapon from Dolphina as Jules grabbed Robin, as Robin grabbed him back, and they both just held each other tightly, but only for a few short seconds.

"He shot Will," Robin told him, his voice breaking. "He needs an ambulance."

Jules nodded. "We've got one standing by."

Just like that, it was over.

Dolphina had let Alyssa take the gun from her numb fingers, as Cosmo knelt next to Will.

"He needs to go to the hospital," Dolphina said.

"Yes, ma'am," Cosmo replied as he looked at the makeshift tourniquet Dolphina had tied around Will's leg. "Send in the paramedics," he roared out the broken door. "We're clear in here, but we've got a man down, in need of immediate medical aid."

Then Jules was there, too, his hand reassuring and solid on Dolphina's shoulder as he smiled past her, at Will. "Hey, Schroeder. So that sucked, huh?" He looked at Cosmo, with Robin right behind him. Dolphina could see worry for Will on both of their faces. "How's he doing?"

Cosmo looked at Dolphina, then looked at Jules and Robin. "He's lost a lot of blood."

Oh, God.

"Will," Dolphina said, but his eyes were closed now and he didn't open them, as if the only reason he'd stayed conscious before was to try to protect her from the gunman. As if he now knew she was safe, so he could . . . "Don't die."

"Where are those paramedics?" Jules shouted, and then, thank God, they were there, carrying a stretcher and cases of medical equipment.

"We need space," one of them said.

"Will," Dolphina said again, as she was pushed back, away from him.

"I'm still here," he mumbled. "I wouldn't dare die. I promised . . . you . . ." He opened his eyes then. "Dolph . . . Maggie . . . She's at home . . ."

"I'll get her," Dolphina said as they wheeled him out. "Don't worry. Just . . . We'll see you at the hospital, okay?"

Alyssa was there then, with Dolphina's coat. "Come on," she said, gently helping Dolphina into it. "I'll drive you."

Sam stuck his head into the living room, where Jules was giving his statement to the detective from the Boston Police.

The FBI agent had champion-class peripheral vision, and when he looked up, Sam caught his eye.

"Excuse me," Jules interrupted himself to turn more completely to Sam.

"I wanted to let you both know," Sam said, coming farther into the room, "that Troubleshooters and Team Sixteen have arrived. They're going to be providing security here at the house tonight—at least until we have a chance to verify that when Jessop said *we* it was only because he also thinks he's the Queen of England."

Jules laughed. "Thanks."

It seemed kind of obvious that Jim Jessop was a loner, and that his use of *we* was at the most more delusion, but Sam also knew that Jules was grateful to not have to worry about that.

Sam went back into the kitchen, checking his cell for text messages from Alyssa. She and Dolphina had picked up Maggie and arrived at the hospital, where Will was in surgery, getting his leg repaired. It had been a good hour, but there was still no word.

He was starting to get antsy. The reporter had pissed him off in that clumsy episode with Jones last weekend, but dying from a gunshot wound was too severe a punishment for his crime.

Cosmo was making coffee, which was a bad idea. More caffeine. Just what Sam didn't need. He'd pulled open the fridge and was browsing, when he realized that Adam was no longer sitting at the kitchen table, eating a sandwich.

Fuck.

He swiftly went back through the living room, and into the front of the house, but the little prick wasn't in the office, where the glass was being replaced in the window Sam had gone through, feet first. And, yeah, somewhat unnecessarily. Still, neither Jules nor Robin had complained.

He checked the first floor bathroom.

Empty.

Sam looked up the staircase. Adam hadn't yet talked to the police, and there was nowhere else in the house he could have gone . . .

Sam took the stairs to the second floor, two at a time.

Robin had gone up after giving his statement to the police, announcing that he was going to take a shower, try to ease some of the muscle pulls and bruises he'd gotten when he'd used himself as a wrecking ball to knock ol' Jessop down the stairs.

Boy Wonder had some balls, that was for sure. And faith, too. He'd shouted to Jules as he'd gone for the guy, certain that Jules was right outside—as indeed he had been.

The door to the master bedroom was ajar, and Sam could hear voices. Robin and, yes, Adam. Fan-fucking-tastic.

Bracing himself, he knocked on the door even as he pushed it open and . . .

Adam and Robin stood by the door to the bathroom, and they both looked up, clearly startled as he came into the room. It wasn't quite that they sprang apart, but it was pretty damn close.

And great. Robin wore only a towel—bath sheet—around his waist.

Adam was amused by Sam's discomfit.

"I was just telling Adam he shouldn't be up here," Robin said.

"Yeah," Sam said dryly. "I couldn't help but notice how you were on the verge of kicking him down the stairs."

Robin's temper sparked. "I generally try talking first, before resorting to violence."

"This is what your life is going to be like," Adam murmured, just loudly enough for Sam to hear him, too. "Everywhere you go, Cowboy Sam here is going to be checking up on you. Won't *that* be fun?"

Now Robin turned his impatience on Adam. "Will you please just go back downstairs?"

"Adam, get the fuck away from him."

Sam turned to see Jules coming through the open doorway behind him. Oh, good. Just what this happy scenario needed. Mr. I'm-Too-Jealous-For-My-Shirt.

Robin flashed Sam a look. *Help.*

"This was my fault," Sam said, trying to slow Jules down. "I lost track of Astro Boy and he wandered off."

Adam wisely backed away from Robin. "Chill, J. It's not what it looks like."

"I think it's exactly what it looks like," Jules countered hotly. "Like you coming up here, uninvited, to hassle Robin and piss me off."

"I wanted to see the new bathroom," Adam lied obviously. "It's very nice," he added, but he wasn't looking at the renovations, he was looking at Robin.

Apparently Adam didn't realize that, with the amount of adrenaline Jules no doubt still had in his system, he was in danger of doing a quick exit from the house, via the window.

The repair would be relatively quick and easy, considering the glass replacement squad was already working downstairs.

"I can't believe this." Jules *was* about as pissed as Sam had ever seen him. "You come to Boston to ask me for help, you put Robin and all my friends in danger, Will gets *shot*—he may die!—and this is—What is this, Adam? Your sick version of *thank you?* What were you thinking?"

Adam didn't answer—he didn't need to. Jules answered for him.

"You were thinking *Let me take Robin's temperature.*" Jules was close to laying hands on the little bastard, and Sam shifted his weight, ready to keep the peace or at least play referee. "*See if he's starting to get tired of Jules.* But he's *not.* Because he loves me—a concept that you couldn't possibly understand. He's never going to cheat on me—not with you, not with anyone."

Adam laughed at that. "Yeah, but that's not going to keep you from worrying about it, is it?" He turned to Robin. He had this way of looking at him—at anyone male, really. Sam had experienced it—as if he was mentally undressing him. "Doesn't that get old? *Where were you, who were you with, why'd you get back so late . . .*" He cut himself off and changed the subject, intentionally baiting Jules. "Damn, R., whatever workout you've been doing, keep it up, baby. You are looking *fine.*"

"Knock it off, Adam," Robin said from between clenched teeth.

"You *might* want to put on a robe." Jules had had enough, but now his anger reached out and smacked Robin.

"Yeah, Robin," Adam mocked as Robin went into the bathroom to do just that. "What are you doing, walking around looking like a God, tempting all the boys, the way you do? Except, oh, wait. Word has it this new show you're in has an awful lot of nudity. Kinda seems silly to put on a robe when all anyone has to do to get an eyeful is turn on their TV." He turned to Jules. "News flash, J. You're going to have to get used to sharing. And not just figuratively, but literally, too. Man, all those love scenes he's been shooting with all those hot, young actors . . . That must be driving you mad."

Uh-oh.

Robin came out of the bathroom in a thick, dark blue bathrobe. "I asked you to leave when you first came in"—he got in Adam's face—"but now I'm *telling* you to leave, or I *will* throw you down the stairs."

"Of course, maybe you're into it," Adam told Robin, not backing down. "Watching Jules squirm when you show him the dailies and . . . Ah," he said as he correctly read Robin's surprise, "*that's* how he's handling it. He hasn't been watching the dailies. He's just been *imagining* what you've been up to, eating himself alive with jealousy."

Robin turned to look at Jules, with a giant question mark practically inscribed on his face.

"Sam," Jules said quietly.

And Sam all but picked Adam up and carried him out of the room.

It took everything he had not to make like Robin's threat and toss the bastard into the foyer, express.

"Why the hell do you do that?" Sam asked instead, but then he saw Adam's eyes. And he knew the answer. And when he spoke again, he managed to make his voice less gruff, less angry. "They're getting married tomorrow. It's time to . . . wish them both happiness and to move on."

Adam didn't want to quit, and Sam had to give him credit for that. Still, it was important he understood.

"It's time to let him go," Sam said quietly. "He doesn't want you anymore, Adam."

"He never wanted me," he said, just as quietly. "It was always Jules. Always."

"You want to give Robin a wedding gift?" Sam asked. "Write Jules a note and tell him that. And then tell them both good-bye."

Robin closed and locked the door behind Sam and Adam.

Jules had sat down on their bed, a picture of tension.

"Why didn't you say something?" Robin asked him.

Jules just shook his head.

"You know, I was starting to think you weren't interested," Robin said, and Jules looked up at him, horrified disbelief in his eyes. Still, he went on. "I was. I thought . . . maybe you didn't think *Shadowland* was a project that was going to go anywhere, that, I don't know, I was maybe wasting my time or . . ."

"No," Jules said. And now his eyes filled with tears. "God, Robin, I'm so sorry."

"Every time I talked about it, you kind of zoned out," Robin said. "I thought you just didn't want to tell me that I wasn't good enough—"

"I watched the promo you brought home," Jules interrupted him. "It was amazing. *You're* amazing. But . . . Adam was right. It was . . . really hard for me to watch. Seeing you . . . I know you're acting, but—"

"Do you?" Robin said. "Do you really understand?"

His leather bag was next to the table on his side of the bed, and he rummaged through it, looking for the DVD he'd brought home just a few days ago. He found it, opened the DVD player and turned on the TV.

"Oh, God," Jules said. "Please let's not do this now."

Robin slid the DVD drawer closed. "When *do* you want to do it, Jules?"

"Never," Jules admitted. "I want to do it never."

Jesus, watching this was going to bother him *that much*? Robin swallowed hard past the lump in his throat. "You know, if you don't trust me, maybe we shouldn't be getting married." Jules was silent, and Robin felt a flare of panic. "Do you want me to quit?" he asked. "Because I will. I'll only take roles that are—"

"No, I don't want you to quit." Jules took a deep breath, looked at him, and said, "Play the DVD. Just . . . help me understand, okay?"

And just like that, in a sudden realization, in a flash of insight that was blindingly clear, Robin realized that Adam had left out the most important part of his observation about Jules's jealousy and possessiveness. Of course it was entirely possible that Adam, who was not a particularly deep thinker, had never figured it out.

Yes, Jules was possessive, and yes, he got jealous quite easily.

But he hated himself for it.

This man, who was so okay with himself about everything else in his life, was *not* okay with this.

"Do you know what I think when you get jealous?" Robin told him now. "I think, *wow, he's a little intense, but it's okay, because there's one thing that I'll never doubt and that's how much he really loves me.*" He found the remote and sat down on the bed next to Jules. "You know what I really love?" Again, he didn't wait for Jules to answer. "When we're walking and you put your hand on my back, right here." He moved Jules's hand to the very spot, at the small of his back. "It's such a possessive move—it's subtle, but it's so clear. Just like the body language you use when you're with me. You probably don't even know you do it, but you do everything but pee in a circle around me, staking out your territory."

"Oh, God," Jules said, wincing. "I do?"

"Don't make that face," Robin chastised him. "Listen to what I'm telling you. I love it, don't you get it? I freaking *love* it."

Jules didn't look convinced, so Robin tried saying it a different way. "Please stop beating yourself up for doing something that I find incredibly attractive."

Maybe it was time for some visual aids. He pushed the play button and the DVD started, with the opening credit sequence that Art's team of editing magicians had already put to music. After a few establishing shots of Boston, the camera focused on Joe Laughlin and his friends, walking down the street.

"That's not me," Robin said. "Okay? That's Joe. I don't walk like that." He glanced at Jules, who was watching the screen. "But you do."

The scene changed to Joe in his bedroom—the shirt-ripping sequence, and Robin hit pause. "This may . . . look familiar," he said. "But again, babe, it's not me. Look at Joe's face. He doesn't really want any of these guys. He wants *you*—well, his version of you. He's got a Jules of his own. There's a character, Tommy, that Joe's in love with—and has been for years. But he can't have Tommy unless he comes out, and Joe's never coming out. And now Tommy's with someone else . . . and Joe's totally miserable."

"When you got home that night," Jules said, "after filming these scenes . . ."

"Yeah," Robin said. "I kinda brought Joe along. Sometimes I struggle to leave the character behind. I used to drink to, you know, flush my character from my system, but now I've found that it works to . . . Well, you could think of it as a reverse of Angel's curse, you know, from *Buffy*? Instead of turning into a monster from that moment of true happiness, I lose my monster. Thank God. To be honest, playing Joe is kind of hard. It's the life I didn't choose, the path I didn't take. It's a wonderful role as an actor, but, babe, there's not a day that goes by that I don't thank my higher power that Joe's life isn't *my* path."

He unpaused the DVD, and they watched it run. "That's not me," Robin just kept saying. "It's not me."

And finally Jules nodded. "Yeah, I see that."

"Are you just saying that so I'll turn off the DVD?"

He laughed. "No. It's weird. It's you, but it's not. It's . . ."

"Oddly familiar?" Robin asked, and Jules nodded again. "That's because I'm channeling you. Joe's more you than me."

Jules obviously didn't understand.

"See, Joe's really alpha," Robin explained. "Like you. Everyone's always comparing me to Joe, because the surface similarities are so obvious. Yeah, if I hadn't come out and gone into rehab, there but for the grace of God, yada yada . . . But in truth, I'm playing Joe as if *you* had decided you wanted to be an actor. If you hadn't had the parents that you had . . . Jules, Joe is a dark alter-ego of *you*. When I'm playing him and I'm in character, it's like part of you is there, inside me. And when I'm not in character, I'm thinking about you, about how you would move or react. I spend my days thinking about you constantly, and . . . I should've seen what was going on. I should've figured it out, and I'm sorry I didn't."

"I'm the idiot," Jules said. "I should have been able to admit—"

"You know what you do that really pisses me off?" Robin said. "You beat yourself up for not being perfect. Do you know how totally screwed I'd be if you were perfect? Because then I'd have to be perfect, too, and not only am I not perfect, but there's no chance that I'm ever going to achieve perfection, so . . ."

The DVD had reached its end, and Robin turned off the TV.

"If you want, I'll take you over to the studio," he told Jules, "and I'll show you exactly how we film the intimate scenes. The process is nothing like the final product. There are forty people on set, and the direction is . . . It can be pretty funny. It's hard to stay in character and not just laugh. I think if you saw the way it's done, that might help. You'd see how much the music and editing really creates the mood of the final cut."

Jules nodded. "I'd like that."

"And next time I come home in character," Robin said, "pay attention to the way I look at you. Because that's the way you look at me all the time. And yeah, it's possessive. But that's what makes it sexy as hell. Someone once told you that was a bad thing—your being so possessive—and maybe it was—for them. But babe, it *really* works for me, because I meant what I said that first night we made love. I'm yours."

Jules looked at him, and Robin could see that he finally got it. But still, he said it again, and he knew he would say it often, just to remind Jules. "I love that I'm yours."

Jules smiled. "Will you marry me?" he asked.

Robin's heart went into his throat as he smiled back into his partner's beautiful eyes. "Funny you should ask. It's at the very top of my *to do* list for tomorrow."

The call came in after Adam had given his statement to the police detective.

He was bracing himself to go out into the cold with only his lightweight jacket on. He didn't have a lot of room left on his credit card, so he was going to walk to the nearest T station and take the train out to Logan Airport.

Cowboy Sam had already helped him book a flight—he had to get going, or he was going to be late.

But he stopped when he heard the whoops from the kitchen, and with the noise came the news that Will Schroeder had come out of surgery with flying colors. He was going to be all right.

Thank God.

Adam stood in the foyer of this beautiful house that Robin shared with Jules. He couldn't stop himself from gazing up the stairs. Neither of them had come down since he'd been up there with Sam, over an hour ago.

"I'll tell 'em you said good-bye," Sam said now, still following him around.

"Thanks. I wrote that note," Adam said. "You can read it first if you want."

"I will."

And still he hesitated.

"He's really happy with Jules," Sam reminded him.

"Yeah," Adam said. "I know."

"Sure you don't want a ride to Logan?" Sam asked.

"No," Adam said. "You should be here in case Jules needs you. Best man."

"Stay away from them," Sam said, not unkindly, "or I will fuck you up."

"Yikes," Adam said. "You almost gave me a heart attack—until you added that last *up*."

Sam exhaled his disgusted exasperation. "Good-bye, Adam." He opened the door and pushed him out onto the porch.

The door closed tightly behind him, and Adam jammed his hands into his pockets and went down the stairs.

There was a group of SEALs standing on the sidewalk out front, and as he went past them, one of them said, "Hey, you're that actor, right? Shoot, I'm blanking on your name, but I loved you in *American Hero*."

"Thanks," Adam said, but he didn't stop walking, because Christ, all he needed to make the day perfect was to get hassled for being gay by some crew-cut-sporting no-necks.

But the movie-literate SEAL disengaged himself from the others, trotting slightly to catch up, and then matched his stride to Adam's. "You were amazing in *Memphis Moon*, too."

"Thanks." Adam increased his pace, but the SEAL was taller than he was, and he easily kept up.

So Adam stopped at the corner, beneath the streetlight. "Look, if you're going to—"

"I also loved *Snow Day*. I mean, yeah, it was light, but you were incredible." He was really just a kid, early twenties, nice smile, good-looking in a born-and-raised-in-Kansas kind of way.

Adam looked at him, and the kid held his gaze. And held his

gaze. He had blue eyes. Very, *very* blue eyes. But, shit, he was young.

"I'm Tony," he said.

"Yeah, well, I'm trouble," Adam told him.

Tony laughed at that. He actually had dimples. "I'm a SEAL," he said to Adam with a shrug. "I like trouble."

Hey now, as Robin would've said.

"It's Adam, right?" Tony remembered his name. "Wyndham."

Adam nodded. "I'm kind of . . . nursing a broken heart," he admitted.

Tony nodded. But he took a pen out of his pocket, took Adam's hand, and actually wrote his phone number on it, right on the palm. "Give me a call if it mends." He pocketed his pen, flashing another of those killer smiles. "And in case you had any doubt just how much I like trouble, I'm pretty sure I just came out to my teammates."

He walked backward, moving toward those very teammates, facing Adam and smiling all the while.

It was hard not to smile back, and as Adam finally headed for the T station, he even managed to laugh.

What was it Cowboy Sam had said? Time to move on.

Yeah. If he put his mind to it, he could maybe imagine doing just that.

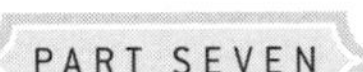

PART SEVEN

joyful noise

Saturday, December 15
Boston, Massachusetts

Robin was feeling a little lightheaded.

He and Jules had gotten up early enough to eat breakfast, but he'd had only a few bites of his English muffin. All he'd wanted to do was to fast-forward to eleven o'clock, to that moment when they would stand at the altar of the church and say their vows.

He probably should have had more to eat.

"You okay?" Jules asked as they rode to the church in the limousine, his hand warm as he interlaced Robin's fingers with his.

"Yeah," Robin said. "I'm just . . . marveling at the fact that it's finally today, you know?"

Jules smiled. "Yeah. This is it."

"Do you . . ." *have any doubts?* Robin was about to ask but, crap, Jules's cell phone began to ring.

Jules looked at him, waiting to answer it, but Robin shook his head. "You better . . ."

They were way wicked early, but Jules had wanted to make sure he was on hand to talk to the head of the Secret Service. And sure enough there was a potential problem with the President and Mrs. Bryant's seating.

"We've just pulled up at the church," Jules said into his phone. "I'll be inside in thirty seconds."

"You *are* going to turn that off during the ceremony," Robin said. "Please say yes."

"Oh, yeah." Jules laughed. "It'll not just be off, but it will be off my person. I don't want Mario tackling me on my way down the aisle."

Art Urban's costume designer had gifted them with hand-tailored tuxedos. Robin had never worn a tux that fit as well or looked as sinfully good. But, "No wallets, no cell phones," Mario had sternly ordered them before going off on a rant about how American men loaded their pockets and then were surprised when their suits didn't have clean lines.

"You can put it in my bag." Robin had already put his own phone in his bag, since he needed to bring it anyway, to carry the . . . "Crap."

"What?" Jules asked.

"Nothing. It's okay." He couldn't believe it. He'd left part of his present for Jules at home. But then he *could* believe it, because he always forgot things when he skipped breakfast.

"I've got to run in," Jules told him, giving him a swift kiss.

Robin caught him by the arm, and kissed him more thoroughly because once they got inside, Sam and Alyssa were going to grab Jules, and Janey and Cos were going to grab Robin. They'd drag them into separate rooms to wait, out of sight, for the guests to arrive.

Robin wasn't going to see Jules again until they met at the back of the church, to walk Jules's mom down the aisle.

But then he had to smile, because it was really just a matter of minutes now. Less than an hour until the majestic organ music began to play.

He'd once gone two years without seeing Jules, because of his own foolishness and fear. In hindsight, it didn't seem possible that he'd survived two, long, dreary, Jules-less years . . . Especially when, these days, too many hours apart from Jules made him antsy.

Robin kissed him again, and Jules smiled back at him, his heart in his eyes.

"Go," Robin told his partner. "I'll be right behind you."

He watched Jules dash up the steps into the church, and then he pressed the intercom button that allowed him to speak to the driver.

"Hey, Pete, do you need to pick up anyone else?" Robin asked.

He could hear the sound of paper—pages being turned—as the driver checked his schedule. "No, sir," he reported. "I'm supposed to be on hand for emergencies, but other than that, I'm to sit and wait until you and Mr. Cassidy come out of the church, after the ceremony."

Robin looked at his watch. It was two minutes after ten. "I left something at home," he said. "How long do you think a round trip, there and back, would take?"

"This time a day? Twelve minutes," Pete said. "Fifteen, tops."

"Let's do it," Robin decided. He'd be back before anyone even knew he was gone.

Maggie didn't want to go to the wedding.

Will had spoken to her on the phone, and she was adamant about coming to the hospital and staying with him, instead.

Dolphina, who'd sat with him for the entire night, holding his hand, was dropping her off.

Dolphina, who'd cried—or so the nurses said—when she was finally allowed to see him, after surgery . . .

Christ, he was nervous about seeing her. Last night, he'd been too out of it to talk, and when he woke up this morning, she'd been asleep, curled up in the chair beside his bed. He'd fallen back into a kind of crazy, drug-dream state, and when he woke up again, less cloudy-headed, she was getting ready to leave.

"I'll be back later," she said, and after checking with the nurse, to be sure that he truly *was* improving, she went out the door.

Now, as he waited for her to return with Maggie, Will used the remote to flip on the TV and channel surf, stopping on a news program that was doing a celebrity news feature on Robin and Jules's wedding.

They played the famous footage called "the kiss heard 'round the world"—taken from a newscopter after the movie star had helped Jules thwart a terrorist plot down in Sarasota, Florida. As far as coming out went, that kiss pretty much blew the doors off Robin's closet. It was clear, too, that both Robin and Jules knew the copter was filming them. Robin grinned at the camera, signaled a thumbs-up, and then kissed Jules again.

They showed the other famous footage, too: Robin's interview outside of the rehab facility where he was checking himself in. The YouTube clip, taken before Robin's twenty-eight-day program, in which, blind drunk, he did a balance-beam routine on the rail of an open balcony, twelve stories above the ground . . .

Dolphina came in while that classic was playing. Will turned the TV off, but not before she looked up, saw it, and winced.

"They're showing it again, huh?" she asked.

"Oh, yeah," he said. She was dressed for the wedding, and with her hair up off her graceful neck, she looked like some kind of fairy-tale princess. A very tired princess. "How *are* you?"

"How are *you*?" she countered.

"Rumor has it I'm going to live," Will said. "But the doctor won't let me leave until tomorrow. I've got a team from the *Globe* setting up a webcam so I can watch the wedding from here. Did Maggie bring my laptop?" Where *was* Mags?

"She did," Dolphina told him. "She, uh . . . I asked her to hang back at the nurses' station so I could tell you . . ." She stopped. Cleared her throat.

Here it came. The happy ending he'd been praying for. Getting shot had hurt like hell, but if it meant that he now would get a second chance with this incredible woman, then hallelujah and thank you, Jim Jessop.

"I'm so relieved that you're all right," Dolphina said, tearing up. "I thought you were going to bleed to death, right there, and I wasn't going to be able to help you—"

"Hey," Will said. She was standing too far from his bed for him to reach for her, so he kind of flapped his arm ineffectually. But she didn't move any closer, so he stopped flapping. "I'm okay. And you did help. Just knowing you were there with me was huge."

"I just wanted to make sure you understood," Dolphina told him, as a tear escaped and rolled down her face, "that as glad as I am that you're all right? This doesn't change anything between us."

What?

Will turned and looked out the window, because he was so surprised. And disappointed. And, frankly, stunned.

"Oh," he said, because someone had to say something. And saying, *No fair. This isn't the way it happens in the movies—when I almost die, you're supposed to realize how much you love me*, no doubt would not go over well.

"I'm sorry," she said quietly.

"Yeah," he said. "Me, too."

"We're too different," she told him.

"I disagree. I think—"

She cut him off, finishing for him. "That I'm scared. Yes. I am. You're right. I'll admit it. I gave my heart away once, and . . . I'm not going to let myself get hurt like that again. I can't do it."

"So . . . you just sit up all night, in the hospital, with people you don't particularly give a damn about?" Will asked.

Dolphina had no response to that. She just turned away. "I have to go."

Great. Run away.

He watched as she went to the door, calling for Maggie. "Oh. You're right here. Thank you for . . . You can go in now."

"Congratulate Robin and Jules for me," Will said, and Dolphina turned to look at him. She had the strangest expression on her face, as if she hadn't understood him.

He tried again. "Tell Robin and Jules—"

"Right," she said. "I will."

Will couldn't bring himself to look at Maggie, as Dolphina vanished into the hall.

His niece was uncharacteristically silent for several long moments, but then she said, "Do you want me to, like, leave so you can cry?"

Will forced a laugh. "You heard that, huh?"

She nodded, her eyes sympathetic. "I'm sorry. She was nice."

"Yeah," Will said. "She was."

Maggie kissed him on the top of his head as she moved the little box of tissues onto his tray.

"I'm not going to cry," he told her, and yet there he was, looking out the window, having to blink a lot.

"Okay." She pretended to believe him as she headed for the door. "I'll just . . . go get us a snack from the vending machine."

"Thanks, kid," Will said.

She stopped and looked back at him from the doorway, and in that moment, she looked exactly like his sister, back when Arlene was Maggie's age. "Mom says it's okay to cry," she told him. "But if you really want something, then you need to blow your nose and pick yourself back up and be ready to work for it—you've got to want it, and you've got to earn it."

She disappeared down the hall and Will looked at the tissues she'd left for him.

He could sit here, crying.

Or he could get to work.

He blew his nose, then pulled back his covers and swung his legs out of bed.

Jules first became aware that there was a problem when he came out of the men's room to find that Cosmo had pulled Sam aside.

The two men were talking quietly, and while they weren't exactly frowning, they weren't smiling, either.

"What's up?" Jules asked.

"I'm sure Robin's here somewhere," Cosmo said. "We're just . . . having a little trouble locating him."

"He came with me," Jules told them. "In the limo." He took out his phone and speed-dialed Robin, even as he looked at his watch. "We got here thirty minutes ago."

"He's not picking up," Sam already had his own phone to his ear. "Let's get more people looking for him, try to find out who saw him last. But discreetly," he ordered Cosmo, who nodded and headed down the hall to the church.

Jules, meanwhile, was bumped to Robin's voicemail. "Robin, where are you? Call me."

He looked at Sam, who was looking back at him.

"Don't think that," Jules chastised him.

"I'm not thinking anything," Sam protested.

"We talked," Jules said. "Robin and me. About . . . everything." Adam's presence, although unpleasant, had finally sparked the conversation Jules and Robin had needed to have. And Jules had slept better last night than he had in weeks.

"Adam made it onto the flight to L.A.," Sam reported. "I checked."

"I'm not going to respond to that," Jules said tightly, "because the implication—"

"I'm just saying," Sam told him.

"Well, you didn't need to."

"So Robin's AWOL, and I should just stand here and not tell you what I *do* know?" Sam countered.

Jules took a deep breath. "Sorry," he said. "You're right. Will you please . . . just find Alyssa and help me find Robin?" He speed-dialed Robin's number again.

Robin's cell phone rang.

And then it rang again.

And again.

Sam's ring—the theme from *SpongeBob Square Pants.* Cosmo's ring—the theme from *Gilligan's Island.* Jules's ring—the theme from *Buffy.*

Robin went through the cabinets in his perfect, newly renovated master bathroom, searching for a screwdriver, as his cell phone rang from the depths of his bag, which was in the other room, on the bed.

Buffy again. More *Buffy.*

He'd gotten back to the house in mere minutes—only to find Jules and Cosmo's moms über-decorating the place with wreaths and garlands and fields of gorgeous poinsettias. Rich, deep red Christmas bows hung down from the staircase and were tied to the balusters.

It was so beautiful—and so obviously meant to be a surprise. They were just finishing up in the kitchen, so Robin dashed up the front stairs to the bedroom, hoping he could grab what he'd forgotten—his wedding present for Jules—without letting them know he'd ever been here.

But when he pushed open the bedroom door, he discovered that they'd been in there, too. Their bedding had been replaced with a gorgeous, snow white comforter and sheets that must've had a thread-count of four million.

There were bloodred roses everywhere, and candles everywhere else. They'd even put out one of those boxes of extra long matches to make it easier to light them.

There was mistletoe—as if they'd need it—hanging from the end of the ceiling fan pull.

It was so beautiful, and so sweetly romantic, Robin couldn't help it. He started to cry. All that care and effort spoke volumes about Jules's mother's love and acceptance of her son—not to mention Cosmo's mom's generosity. He was struck by Lois Richter's willingness to help out in this way, enthusiastically taking on the role of the loving parent Robin had never had.

His tears were his downfall. He grabbed the CD case that he'd hidden in his bedside table, sticking it into his bag.

And then he'd gone into the bathroom, to carefully splash cool water onto his face and search for his Visine, so that he didn't show up at the church with red eyes.

He'd closed the door behind him so that the two moms wouldn't hear him. He took a leak while he was in there, waiting for the Visine to kick in.

He'd washed his hands, checked himself in the mirror, went to the door, grabbed and pulled . . . and the knob came off in his hand.

Thunk.

The doorknob on the other side fell onto the bedroom floor, taking the mechanism with it.

No. Oh, no. No, no.

But yes. Robin was, without a doubt, locked in his bathroom.

He'd shouted, but it was too late. He heard the alarm system go on, and he rushed to the bathroom window and opened it, but—crap—since it was on the second floor, it wasn't wired into the system.

Robin could see the driveway, see the limo idling there.

But Pete, the driver, had backed in. He was facing the street, and wouldn't be able to see Robin, even in his rearview mirror. But then . . .

"Hey!" Robin shouted as the two women hurried to the waiting car. "Lois! Linda!"

But they didn't hear him. He kept shouting, but they didn't look up. They just got in and closed the doors.

Okay. Come on, Pete. Ask the question. *Where's Robin?*

Sure enough, the limo didn't move.

Come *on*, Pete. Come on, come on . . .

But as Robin watched in dismay, the limo pulled out of the driveway. And he knew exactly how that conversation had gone down.

Pete: *Where's Robin?*

The moms: *Oh, he went to the church in a different limo.*

Pete: *He did? Are you sure?*

The moms: *Very. We need to get to the church right away—we're running a little late.*

Pete (pulling away): *Okay . . .*

Robin (watching from the window): *I'm so totally fucked.*

It was obvious to Dolphina that Jules was starting to get really worried.

"Can I get you anything?" she asked him, and he forced a smile.

"If you could bring me Robin, that would be really nice," he told her.

She smiled, too, trying to be reassuring. "I'm sure he's just . . . found someplace quiet to take a deep breath."

Jules had been on the phone for quite some time, talking to the detectives in charge of the Jim Jessop investigation. All evidence they'd found supported the theory that Jessop was not part of some kind of conspiracy. He was merely a very lonely, mentally-unhinged man, whose mother had recently died and who had gone off his medication. He didn't have a girlfriend or an equally unbalanced brother. He didn't have any friends, and he'd apparently kept entirely to himself at work.

Still, it was clear that Robin's vanishing act was freaking Jules out. He was also kicking himself for not maintaining a higher level of security, for not waiting for Robin to go with him into the church. Dolphina knew that Jules was a heartbeat from calling for massive search and rescue teams, to canvas the area.

Sam and Cosmo, however, were doing a little canvassing of their own. They'd quietly sent the men of SEAL Team Sixteen, looking resplendent in their Navy uniforms, to check all the bars in a several block radius.

It was the SEAL named Izzy Zanella who blew the covert status of that little op. He was coordinating the search with a Popout map of Boston and his cell phone, and he stuck his head in the room where Jules was impatiently waiting. Cosmo and Sam had just come in to try to figure out where to look next.

"He's not at the Ritz," Izzy reported to Sam, and Jules, of course, overheard him.

"Why would Robin be at the Ritz?" Jules asked, and Sam didn't answer immediately. He was clearly trying to find the right words.

"At the *bar* at the Ritz." Jules put it together without Sam's help and he was furious. "Fuck you!" He looked at Cosmo. "And you, too. Don't you have *any* faith in him?"

The two men exchanged a look, and Dolphina knew what they were thinking, because she was thinking it, too. There was faith, but there was also common sense. She could still remember the pre-rehab Robin, and she knew Jules could remember, too. It was hard not to with that YouTube clip playing on the news every time anyone turned around.

"If you were running this search, you would've given the order to check the bars, too," Sam told him quietly.

But Jules shook his head. "No," he said, absolutely. "No." It was clear to Dolphina that he had enough faith in Robin for all of them.

But dear God, what a risk he was taking by being in this relationship. The enormity of it all caught Dolphina off-guard, and she had to sit down. Everyone—*everyone*—who was helping to look for Robin harbored a fear that the movie star may have stumbled under the intense pressure of the day. It was natural to think, *Oh, Robin's slipped. He must be drinking again.*

But somehow Jules had gotten past that. He *did* have faith in Robin. He trusted him completely. Which meant that if Robin *did* fall, Jules would be crushed. But despite that risk, Jules loved him with all of his heart.

And Robin—he loved Jules, too. Despite knowing the dangers of Jules's job. Despite the reality that he could lose Jules, at any day, at any given hour.

And here Dolphina sat, too frightened to even *consider* taking a chance with a man whom she believed really did love her. A man who had admitted that he'd made mistakes, who took responsibility for his wrongdoing, who'd apologized—sincerely. A man who was brave enough to take another chance after being badly hurt.

A man who wanted to learn to be a team player again . . .

No doubt about it, she was a wimp.

"I've been trying to replay the conversation we had in the limo," Jules was telling Sam. "There was something that he . . . said or did, and I just can't remember."

"Try running it backward," Cosmo suggested. "You went into the church. You walked to the church—"

"I kind of ran," Jules said. "Up the stairs."

"You got out of the limo," Cosmo prompted.

Jules nodded. "He kissed me, I told him I loved him, he said he'd be right behind me . . . I got a phone call about the President, I had to take the call and he wasn't all that happy about the fact I had my cell phone, but he was joking about it. He told me I could put it in his bag, and then . . ." Jules laughed. "He said *crap*."

Jules went out of the room, as if what he'd just said—Robin said *crap*—actually meant something important. Cosmo and Sam were right behind him, clearly bemused, as Dolphina followed, too.

"Where are you going?" she asked.

"Home," he told her. "Robin went home to get something that he forgot."

"What?"

"Tell the violin trio to keep playing," Jules ordered. "Tell them to stall." He took the quickest route to the front of the building, where the limos were waiting—right down the center aisle of the crowded church. He was creating a stir, but he clearly didn't give a damn. "I'll be right back!"

"I'm going with him," Sam said to Cosmo and Dolphina, then took off after him.

After living for months with a full tool kit—including a drill and a sander—in the master bathroom, how could there not have been at least a *small* screwdriver left behind?

But apparently, it had happened. Robin was locked in his bathroom without the tools he needed to set himself free.

The linen closet held what looked like a year's supply of toilet paper. Dolphina had recently discovered Costco, and no longer bought anything in quantities of less than four dozen.

Of course, Robin should talk. He'd just bought twenty new bath sheets. But he hadn't washed them yet—they were all down in the laundry room. He had, however, cleared space for them in this closet, which meant that most of the shelves were empty.

As Robin moved the TP to see if there was a screwdriver hidden in the back of the closet, he realized that he should have opened the window screen and thrown rolls at the waiting limo—caught their attention that way. Instead, he hadn't been thinking quickly enough, and now—he looked at his watch, it was twenty-five minutes to eleven—if he didn't act fast, he was going to be late to his own wedding.

God only knew what Jules was thinking.

His phone rang again, with Jules's familiar ring tone, from out in the bedroom.

"Shit," Robin shouted. "Shit! *Shit!*"

That was kind of stupid, because when he stopped shouting, nothing had changed. He was still locked in his bathroom.

The hinges of the door were inside the room with him, but the pins probably hadn't been removed since 1865. Still, he looked at them more closely. Yeah, those weren't coming out—not without a screwdriver and a hammer.

And the door was solid mahogany—no way would he be able to kick his way through it.

Robin looked at the window again, opened the screen, stuck his head out and looked down. It was a straight drop to the ground below, with no toe- or handholds to help him climb either down or up to the roof. And since the house had eleven-foot ceilings, the drop to the ground was daunting. The bonus was the cast-iron fence that was almost directly beneath the window, providing an alternative to death by broken neck—death by impalement.

If he'd had his new bath sheets, he could have cut them into strips and tied them together to make a rope. After anchoring it around the toilet, he could have climbed out the window.

Which Robin now closed and locked. He was a little afraid he would be tempted to try getting out that way even without the bath sheet rope. He went back to the cabinets beneath the sink, taking inventory again. He opened the medicine cabinets, too, and all the drawers.

Along with all that toilet paper, he had a blow dryer, a pack of extra toothbrushes, cotton balls, razor blades, makeup remover, shaving cream, hair care products and skin moisturizers of an embarrassing quantity and variety, alcohol-free cold medicine, antiseptic hand gel, deodorant—mmm, that smelled like Jules—sunblock, Band-Aids, a nose-hair clipper, scissors . . .

If he were an astronaut aboard Apollo Thirteen, he could no doubt use these items to build a booster rocket and fly down to the ground. He'd wanted to go to Space Camp when he was a kid, but his father had told him that nobody who got only a B in science would ever be welcome at NASA.

So he was stuck with finding a more traditional route out of here.

Robin looked at the scissors. They were long and sharp—of the haircutting variety.

Maybe . . .

He looked at the scissors and the razor blades and then at the pristine perfectness of the recently patched and painted wall between the door and the toilet.

Robin took off his tux jacket. On second thought, he took off his pants and shirt, too. And he got to work.

It was possible Jules was on to something.

As they raced back to the house, Sam had Alyssa on the phone. "She spoke to all the drivers," he told Jules. "Guy named Pete reports that yeah, he drove you and Robin to the church, and yeah, he took Robin back to the house to pick up something—he didn't know what."

Jules just nodded. As they pulled up to a red light, it was clear that he was restraining himself from jumping out and running the rest of the way.

Sam put Alyssa on speaker so Jules could hear her himself.

"Pete told me Robin went inside the house, but then, a few minutes later, your mother and Lois Richter came out," she said. "They insisted Robin was already at the church. Pete says he assumed Robin went out the back door, caught another ride . . . Apparently, Lois and your mom were worried they'd be late and Pete bowed to the pressure and took the path of least resistance. Meanwhile, the limo that was assigned to pick them up—the moms—still hasn't returned."

Sure enough, as they approached the house, the limo was there, idling out front.

"We're here, I'll call you back," Sam told his wife.

Jules was out of the car before it stopped, running to the front door. The alarm beeped as they went inside, and Jules disabled it. "Robin!" he shouted into the silence of the empty house.

But it wasn't empty, because Robin shouted back.

"Jules!" His voice was distant, but definitely coming from the second floor.

Jules took the stairs two at a time, Sam on his heels.

"Oh, my God," Jules said as he went into the bedroom.

Sam stopped short. That wasn't an *oh, my God* there on the floor in front of them. It was a full scale *holy fuck*.

Robin had apparently gotten locked in the bathroom. He'd somehow managed to cut a hole in the wall—both the drywall in the bathroom and the plaster on the bedroom side. He was in the process of emerging from it, seemingly naked—at least from the waist up. But he hadn't quite made it large enough and he'd gotten stuck.

And yet his first words to Jules were an apology. "God, babe, I'm so sorry," Robin said as Sam took out his phone and dialed Alyssa.

"Got him," he reported. "Keep stalling, we'll be there as soon as we can."

"Are you all right?" Jules asked Robin, his relief making him laugh as he . . . started to take his clothes off . . . ?

"These fucking doors." Robin laughed, too, but then he started to cry, which, to Sam's surprise, seemed to mortify him. "Oh, Jules, I was so afraid you'd think—"

"Shh," Jules said, as he quickly took off his pants and went over to Robin. He knelt on the floor and kissed him, and Robin clung to him. "Sweetie, no. I was worried that something bad had happened, yeah, but I *never* thought . . ." He kissed him again, longer this time. Deeper.

Yikes. "Uh, guys?" Sam said. "I'm kind of here in the room?"

"The President's already at the church, Starrett," Jules told him, heavy on the sarcasm. "And Robin's doing a Winnie-the-Pooh-in-the-honey-tree in the wall. So yeah, we thought we'd have sex. Jesus. If you're going to help, you better get your own tux off."

And Sam realized that Robin was coated with fine, white plaster dust. It was everywhere—in his hair, on his arms and shoulders. It was also all over the floor.

"Can you push yourself back into the bathroom?" Jules asked Robin.

"I think so," he said, wiping his eyes, smearing his face with dirt as well as the plaster dust.

"Don't hurt yourself," Jules warned him, but then caught sight of Robin's hands. He'd torn them up pretty good making that hole. "Oh, sweetie . . ."

"Yeah," Robin said, "I kind of fucked up my manicure. If you could . . . maybe push my shoulder . . ."

"Here." Sam came over, stripped down to his boxers. "Hunch forward and put your head down."

Robin looked at him. "My safe word is *monkey*."

"Ha ha," Sam said. "You're a fucking comedian. You want me to help or not?" He didn't wait for Robin to respond. "Hunch forward and put your head down."

Robin did, inching his way as Jules and Sam helped push him back into the bathroom.

"At first I made a hole just big enough to reach through," Robin told them, because he could not remain silent for more than a few seconds at a time. Sam had always considered Jules to be talkative, but Robin could make him seem taciturn.

"I thought if I could grab the other doorknob and the, you know, rod-thingy that works the mechanism," Robin continued to narrate, "I'd be able to open the door. But it didn't work. Ow!"

It was like birth in reverse, and Robin was finally back in the bathroom.

He stuck a battered hand out of the hole, presenting them with the knob and rod. Jules took it and put it into the door. From the bathroom, Robin attached the other end of the knob and . . .

The latch clicked and the door swung open.

Jules just looked at Robin, who looked as if he might start to cry again.

"Thank you," Robin said, and he wasn't just talking about being rescued.

Jules hugged him, plaster dust and all. "I love you," he said. "Come on, let's go get married."

Robin turned to where his tux was hanging from a towel rack, but Jules grabbed him by the waistband of his boxers, and pantsed him, in a move that was clearly practiced. It made Sam hyper-aware of the fact that he was wearing only his boxers in the bedroom of his two gay friends—one of whom was now buck-naked.

"Shower," Jules ordered Robin. He turned to Sam. "Vacuum's in the front hall closet. Will you grab it and—"

"Yeah," Sam said. He dashed down the stairs and was back in record time. It was five minutes to eleven, but if Jules wanted him to vacuum, vacuum he would. Although this was definitely turning out to be the weirdest best-man gig in the history of the world.

Robin got out of the shower as Jules took his tux into the bedroom, shaking off any dust that might've gotten onto it. He grabbed Robin a clean pair of shorts and some socks from a dresser drawer, laying it all out on the bed.

Jules himself didn't shower—he just used a towel to dust himself off.

"Did you do this to the room?" he asked Robin, and Sam, too, realized that there were flowers and unlit candles everywhere. The place reeked of romance—no doubt about it, someone was getting laid tonight.

"It was your mom," Robin told him as he quickly fixed his hair.

"My contribution was putting a hole in the wall." He started to laugh. "Two months of construction, it's finally done and—"

Jules shut him up with a kiss. "Ask me if I care."

He'd already gotten dressed, and he helped Robin on with his tuxedo, buttoning his shirt and fastening his pants for him, since Robin's fingers were obviously hurting him.

And then, finally, they were ready. It was eleven hundred hours on the dot, and they were hurrying down the stairs.

But then "Crap," Robin said, and he dashed back up to get his bag.

The wedding was beautiful, even if it started a few minutes late.

The flower children started the procession. They danced down the aisle, spreading rose petals. There were five of them: Hope Jones, Emma Bhagat, Billy Richter and Charlie Paoletti were led by six-year-old Haley Starrett—Sam's daughter from his first marriage. As the oldest, she was clearly in charge—and no doubt about it, she was her father's daughter.

She kept everyone moving, and when they got to the altar, she reminded them first to greet the President and shake his and Mrs. Bryant's hand, and then to run and sit with their parents.

Cosmo and Jane went down the aisle next, followed by Sam and Alyssa.

And then came a last minute change in their plans. Robin and Jules had originally intended to walk Jules's mom down the aisle together, one on either side of her.

But Robin had called Dolphina as he and Jules and Sam were rushing to the church, and he'd asked to see if Cosmo's mom wouldn't meet him for a moment, over by the front doors.

Dolphina hadn't heard what he'd said to her when they'd met there, but Lois Richter had hugged him and nodded.

And now he was escorting her down the aisle amidst a flurry of flashbulbs, stopping to seat her in a place of honor in front of the President—a place usually reserved for the mother of the groom. She kissed him and hugged him again. And Yashi's dad, who was already seated there, stood up and, with a big smile, he hugged Robin, too.

Robin laughed his surprise, but then hugged Yashi's dad back.

Jules, who was watching Robin from the back with his mother, had an expression on his face that was beautiful—happiness and love mixed with something bittersweet. And Dolphina knew that he was thinking about Robin's father—who had chosen not to be here today.

Jules looked at his mother and smiled. "God, I'm lucky."

"Back at you, kiddo," Linda Cassidy said. "Shall we do this thing?"

"I'm ready." He offered her his arm and they went down the aisle.

Again, flashbulbs went off. Jules seated his mother next to Cosmo's mom, then joined Robin at the altar with a smile—holding out his hand.

Robin took it and they stood there for a moment, just gazing into each other's eyes.

The guests in the church sat down, and Dolphina sat, too, right there in the second to last row—just in case there were any last minute problems to deal with.

More last minute, that is, than Robin getting locked in the bathroom.

Jules had been right to have faith.

Although Dolphina knew that had Robin been found in the bar at the Ritz, Jules would still be standing beside him.

For richer, for poorer, for better, for worse.

They'd purposely chosen to use fairly traditional vows, adjusting the words only slightly.

"Do you, Jules, take Robin, to be your partner for life? Do you promise to love and comfort him, honor and keep him in sickness and in health, for richer and for poorer, for better or for worse, to be faithful and true to him, as long as you both shall live?"

"I do."

They both spoke loudly—their voices ringing clearly in the beautiful church.

"With this ring, I thee wed."

"I now pronounce you partners for life. What God has joined together let no man put asunder. May the love in your hearts give you joy. May the greatness of life bring you peace. And may your days be good and your lives be long upon the earth. You may greet each other now with a kiss."

Back at the bachelor party, Jules had told Robin that he was intending to kiss the shit out of him at their wedding, but apparently he'd lied.

As Dolphina and the other guests watched, Jules and Robin shared the sweetest, most tender kiss she'd ever witnessed—a true greeting and celebration of this wonderful new phase of their life together. And then they stood there again, just smiling into each other's eyes, a picture of pure happiness, joy and love.

Married.

The organ began to play, and everyone stood up and applauded, and Dolphina wiped her eyes and put on her coat—to make sure the limos were ready and waiting outside. And of course Robin and Jules had to officially greet the President and Mrs. Bryant and . . .

Whoa.

Will and Maggie were directly behind her.

Maggie was standing, applauding, but Will was just sitting there, looking at Dolphina. He managed a smile. "Hey."

"What are you doing here?" she asked, sliding into the pew so that she was next to him.

"I didn't want to miss it," he told her. He was so pale he was practically gray and it was obvious he was in pain. Clearly he should not have gotten out of bed. "It was . . . lovely."

Dolphina looked at Maggie. "I thought he wasn't supposed to leave the hospital."

The girl shrugged. "He wasn't. In fact, the first thing he did when he got out of bed was fall on his face."

"It wasn't that bad," Will protested.

It was that bad, Maggie mouthed to Dolphina.

"I had to talk to you," Will admitted. "Look, I know you're busy."

"Very," Dolphina said. There were photos to be taken, then she had to get over to the restaurant where the reception was being held, to make sure everything was ready. They were holding the receiving line there—a slight change in plans—because it was so cold outside today.

"I just wanted to say," he started.

She cut him off. "I was going to come to the hospital tonight, after the reception."

Hope flared in his eyes. "Really?"

"Yeah, but I'm not anymore, because it's one thing to have a boyfriend who makes a mistake and apologizes, but it's another thing entirely to date a Darwin Award recipient, who's too intellectually underdeveloped to know when to stay in the hospital."

Will nodded, trying to hide his smile. "And if I apologize for this mistake, too . . . ?"

"It'll probably work," she admitted.

He touched her face, pushing her hair back behind her ear. "Problem is, I'd be lying if I said I was sorry. And I told you I'd never lie to you again."

"Please go back to the hospital," she said.

"I love you," Will told her. "That's what I came here to say. And that I *am* sorry. And if leaving the hospital early means I get a Darwin Award, so be it. I didn't think you were going to come back. And truth is, I don't want to propagate the species with anyone but you."

She laughed at that. "Dear God, I'm an idiot, but I think I might love you, too."

"Think," he repeated.

"I . . . love you," she said, "but I'm still too afraid to, um, admit it, so I'm saying *think* right now. Is that a problem for you?"

Her voice came out sounding a tad too sharp, but Will just smiled. "No, it's not." The hope in his eyes had turned into something else. Something warm and soft and tender. He was looking at her now with such love, she almost started to cry again.

Instead, she leaned over and kissed him. She'd surprised him by doing that, right here in the church, but it didn't take him long to wrap his arms around her.

"Oh, God," he said. "Dolphina."

He kissed her again, and it was *way* not the kind of kiss for a church—even the back of a church during a wedding. But this was a fact that Dolphina didn't consider until she heard Maggie say, admiration in her voice, "Go, Uncle Will."

She pulled back, and it was entirely possible that he had tears in his eyes, too, as she touched his face. "Go back to the hospital," she told him again. "I'll see you later. I've got to go make sure Robin and Jules have a perfect day."

Will smiled at her, taking her hand and kissing her palm. "It can't be more perfect than mine."

"Said the man with the bullet wound in his leg," Maggie pointed out, in case the thought hadn't occurred to Dolphina.

Dolphina smiled at them both, because the thought definitely had.

The President wasn't staying for the reception—but not because he didn't want to. He made that more than clear as he shook both Jules and Robin's hands. It was obvious, too, that he wasn't here simply as a good PR move. He was genuinely fond of Jules.

Sam stood off to the side, watching as the photographer snapped a few pictures, and then President and Mrs. Bryant were led out to their waiting motorcade.

And everyone inside the church sighed with relief. Including Davis Jones, who no longer had to restrict his movements.

He came up to Sam now, and they shook hands.

"That was nice," Jones said. "The ceremony."

"Yeah," Sam agreed as the photographer took a series of shots of Jules and Robin, hand in hand at the front of the church.

"I used to . . . get freaked out by . . ." Jones shook his head.

"Live and learn," Sam said and Jones nodded.

As they watched, the two grooms now got their picture taken with their collective families. For Robin that meant just Jane, Cosmo, Billy and Cos's mom. But all of Jules's cousins were there—he had seventeen of them, most much older, with families of their own. Jules had told Sam once that he wasn't particularly close to most of his cousins, due to the age differences, but that they'd rallied around and supported him completely when he'd first come out. They'd also all gone to great efforts to attend this wedding, and their love for their little cousin was evident in the multitude of wide smiles.

"Jules wants to do a group shot, so don't go anywhere." Sam turned at the sound of Alyssa's voice.

She was smiling a greeting at Jones. "Thank you for not assassinating anyone during the ceremony."

The man laughed aloud. "It was hard," he teased back, "but I managed to control myself."

"I'm rounding up everyone from Troubleshooters Inc., and Team Sixteen, too," Alyssa continued. "But Jules wanted to make sure you knew that he wouldn't take it personally if you don't want to be in the picture. He said to tell you that Jim Nash doesn't do photos either, so . . . The words he used were *Tell Jones it's no biggie.*"

Jones nodded. "Typical of Cassidy," he said. "Always watching out for his friends." He straightened up from where he'd been leaning against one of the old-fashioned boxed pews. "I'll go give the rest of the Florida contingent the heads-up."

"Thanks," Alyssa said, and then her smile was all for Sam.

He put his arm around her, unable to resist touching the swell of her belly where their baby was growing. And there they both stood for a moment, watching as the photographer set up the next shot, as Jules burst out laughing from something Robin had whispered into his ear.

Max and Gina were nearby—Max holding little Emma in his arms. They laughed, too, as did Cosmo and Jane, who were holding Billy's hands.

The rest of the Troubleshooters team were gathering, as well as all the SEALs, and the joy in the church was a palpable thing.

"May the greatness of life bring you peace," Alyssa quietly repeated the words that the pastor had spoken. "And may your days be good and your lives be long upon this earth." She turned to look up at Sam with a smile that was pure love. "In case you were wondering? My days are very, very good."

Sam greeted his wife with a kiss. "Mine are freakin' great," he told her, past a sudden huskiness in his throat.

Laughing, Alyssa pulled him toward the front of the church, where their friends were waiting.

"Do you miss having champagne at times like these?" Robin asked as the limo pulled away from the church.

"Nope." Jules didn't hesitate as he brought Robin's poor, battered hand to his lips and kissed him.

"I'm glad," Robin said. "Jeez, it looks like you married a boxer."

There had been a moment, during the ceremony, where Jules had worried that Robin wasn't going to be able to get the wedding ring past his swollen knuckle. He'd pushed it on, and it must've hurt like hell, but he didn't flinch—he just smiled.

"Maybe you should take the ring off now," Jules suggested, but Robin looked at him as if he were crazy. He laughed. "Or not."

Robin tugged him close and kissed him. Mmm. But then he reached out and brushed something from Jules's hair.

"Bird seed?" Jules asked, smiling up into Robin's incredible eyes.

"Yeah, mixed in with the *plaster*," Robin said. "Jesus."

Jules laughed.

"I am so sorry about that," Robin said. "*So, what'd you guys do on your honeymoon? Well, we patched and painted the master bath* and *bedroom.*"

"So what exactly was it," Jules asked, "that you went back to the house to get?"

Robin rolled his eyes. "It seems kind of stupid right now. Especially since . . . I feel like I need to take lessons in being romantic from your mother."

Jules gazed at him, just waiting.

"That didn't make sense, huh?" Robin asked.

"Not much," Jules agreed.

"Your mother put all those candles and flowers in our room," Robin reminded him. "It was . . . really beautiful. And romantic."

"And how that relates to whatever it was that you went back to get is . . . ?" Jules let his voice trail off.

"I was trying to be romantic," Robin confessed. "So . . ." He dug in his bag and pulled out . . .

He handed it to Jules—it was a CD case. He opened it. "A mix CD?"

Robin went back to the house and got locked in the bathroom because he'd forgotten a *mix* CD?

Robin obviously saw that Jules was struggling to comprehend, so he said, "The photos didn't take half as long as we thought, and . . . it occurred to me that maybe we could, um, decompress here in the limo."

They'd purposely put some extra time between the ceremony and the start of the reception, in case the wedding photos took longer than they'd anticipated. They'd also thought it would be nice to have a little extra time to arrive at the restaurant before the crowd, so that they could . . . and yes, the word Jules had used was *decompress.*

As he looked at that CD, he suspected Robin's definition of *decompress* might be slightly different than his. Still, he took it out of the jewel case and put it into the CD player and . . .

Jules laughed, because sure enough, "Hooked on a Feeling" was the first cut. That was the song that had been playing on the radio the first time he and Robin had made love. They'd been in a limo, just like this one.

But only a dozen bars of the song played before it faded out, and another song started. It was "All Through the Night"—the old Cole Porter song with the haunting melody and even more haunting lyrics.

All through the night I delight in your love . . .

It was one of Jules's favorite songs. He looked at Robin again, this time questioningly.

"I figured, unless we did something about it, we would still be dancing to "Hooked on a Feeling" at our fiftieth wedding anniversary," Robin told him quietly. "And maybe we will anyway, but . . . I thought, maybe, our first time making love now that we're married . . . you might prefer a different soundtrack. So I made a mix CD of your favorite songs."

"You definitely don't need lessons in being romantic," Jules said, past his heart, which was wedged tightly in his throat.

Robin wasn't so sure. "Flowers, candles, the softest sheets in the universe, versus a mix CD to play while I jump you in the limo . . . ?"

"After promising to love me forever," Jules reminded him. He kissed Robin—his lover, his best friend. His spouse. "Works for me."

Author's Note

I created the character of Jules Cassidy long before my son Jason came out, long before he was old enough to identify as gay, back when he was still just a little boy.

But all those years ago, I suspected that Jason was gay (I had a few clues!), and as I looked around at the world, I could see that attitudes were changing in terms of acceptance and tolerance. But things weren't changing fast enough for me.

So I brought Jules Cassidy into the world of my Troubleshooters series, because not only do I believe that diversity is what makes America great, I wanted my readers to meet a gay man who was out and okay with himself—and a damn fine FBI agent, to boot.

Jules's first appearance in the series was in the second installment, *The Defiant Hero*. After that, he played a part—usually a major one—in nine of my eleven Troubleshooters books. And as the series grew, Jules grew, too.

In the early books, Jules was in a serious relationship, but his partner, Adam, was only mentioned in passing. And then the terminally unfaithful Adam left Jules to go to Hollywood to try his luck at becoming a serious film actor.

For the next several books, Jules nursed his broken heart, but finally, in *Hot Target,* he was forced to confront Adam again. He also met Robin Chadwick in that book—although at the time Robin was so deep in the closet he didn't even know he was there. In *Hot Target,* Jules, entangled with both Adam and Robin, graduated from his role as witty gay sidekick and finally got his own romantic subplot, including a steamy kiss or two.

And the world didn't end.

In fact, *Hot Target* not only hit the *New York Times* hardcover bestseller list, but was given the Borders Group award for Bestselling Hardcover Romance of the year.

Late in 2006, I wrote this past summer's release, *Force of Nature,* which featured Jules and Robin. This book was supposed to be the next installment in their ongoing story arc, but Robin surprised me. He mutinied and demanded his happy ending right away.

I've dealt with unruly characters in the past, but this time (and it was the first time in forty-five books that this has happened to me!), no matter how much I threatened or cajoled, Robin would not compromise. I told him that I'd planned, in a few years, to write a romantic suspense where he and Jules were the two main characters. It would be one of the first mainstream romance novels where there was a hero and a hero instead of a hero and a heroine. It was, I told Robin (I often converse with my fictional characters), going to be an Important Book.

But he just shook his head. He wanted to spend the rest of his life with Jules, and he wanted that rest of his life to start immediately.

In the end, I was the one who compromised. I let *Force of Nature* end the way Robin wanted it to end.

Which brings us to January 2007.

As a mother of a gay son, and as a Massachusetts resident, I've spent years supporting groups such as the Human Rights Campaign, the Freedom to Marry Coalition, and MassEquality. I've donated both money and time. I've stood, one of thousands, shoulder to shoulder with my son, in candlelight vigils. I've fought against prejudice and ignorance, trying to open eyes and minds. And I've celebrated the milestones and victories, toasting the happiness of gay friends who, after decades of devotion and commitment, could finally be legally married.

By the end of 2006, we thought we'd had the battle won. We thought that hope, tolerance, freedom, diversity and love, sweet love, had triumphed over ignorance, fear and hatred. But in January 2007, we found out that, like Frankenstein's monster, the attempt to take away equal marriage rights had been brought raging back to life.

And that's when I got really angry.

This is *my* son's future we're talking about. There are people out there who want to take away *my* son's right to someday marry the person he loves, the right to have the kind of solid, legally recognized relationship that I've shared with my husband of twenty-four years. (One of these days I'll write a blog about my idea of a truly invincible army made up of perimenopausal PFLAG moms. Don't piss us off. We *will* kick your ass. Have a nice day.)

So in January 2007, I decided to do something that my publisher had been urging me to do—write a holiday novella. I did it in somewhat record time, in order to have it ready for release this year. And I decided to continue Jules and Robin's story and do what I'd originally intended—make them the hero and hero of a mainstream romance novel. I also decided to turn the concept of the holiday romance novella onto its ear by writing a story centered around Jules and Robin's wedding, set in Boston.

And I decided that every single penny I earned from this book, from now until the end of time—all advances, royalties, subrights, the whole enchilada—was going directly to MassEquality, an organization whose sole purpose is to preserve equal marriage rights in Massachusetts. Because *enough is enough.*

I hope, with all my heart, that by the time you read these words, the battle will have been won, and the citizens of Massachusetts won't be facing a ballot vote in which the majority gets to decide whether or not to *take away* the marriage rights of a minority group. (Could that really be possible in America . . . ?) I fervently hope by the time you read this that my son's right to marry will have been preserved.

But if not, then I have this to say to the people who are rapidly becoming a minority themselves, people who don't think that gay Americans should have the same rights as the rest of us—

What part of *love* don't you understand?

To everyone else, to all the friends of Jules—past, present, and future—thank you for believing, and for helping to change the world.

Happy Holidays,
Suz Brockmann

ABOUT THE AUTHOR

Since her explosion onto the publishing scene more than ten years ago, SUZANNE BROCKMANN has written more than forty books, and is now widely recognized as one of the leading voices in romantic suspense. Her work has earned her repeated appearances on the *USA Today* and *New York Times* bestseller lists, as well as numerous awards, including Romance Writers of America's #1 Favorite Book of the Year—three years running in 2000, 2001, and 2002—two RITA awards, and many *Romantic Times* Reviewer's Choice Awards. Suzanne Brockmann lives west of Boston with her husband, author Ed Gaffney. Visit her website at www.suzannebrockmann.com.